The Warlow Experiment

for N with love

'It is human nature to hate the man you have hurt'

Tacitus, *Agricola*, 42

A Reward of £50 a year for life is offered to any man who will undertake to live for 7 years underground without seeing a human face: to let his toe and fingernails grow during the whole of his confinement, together with his beard. Commodious apartments are provided with cold bath, chamber organ, as many books as the occupier shall desire. Provisions will be served from Mr Powyss's table. Every convenience desired will be provided.

– Herbert Powyss, Moreham House, Herefordshire
January, 1793

Part I

Chapter 1

DOWN AND DOWN. He sniffs dank air, listens to the man. Powyss.

'I'm providing plenty of fuel and kindling, Warlow. You'll have four baskets of wood a day and a scuttle of sea coal. They'll come down in the morning. There's a tinderbox, oil lamps, boxes of candles in that cupboard over there. The jar of lamp oil will be refilled each week, but that'll depend on your use of it. Send a note if you need more.

'I've tried out everything myself and it all works perfectly. Samuel, get a fire going for Warlow.'

'I makes my own *fire!*'

'Yes, of course, of course. But let's warm the place while I'm showing you round.'

White cloth. Fork, spoon. Them's silver. Wine glass! Chair legs like bent knees; never sat on one of them. Look at it! Candlesticks all shone up. Brass. Pictures.

Who's that in the mirror? Me is it? Him?

'Three meals a day, as I said. When Jenkins carves at table he'll dole out a serving for you and send it down by lift. I'm rather pleased with this. Over here. Look: you open it up

3

and inside are two shelves. It's just a dumb waiter table but without legs and fixed to a pulley. Like hauling sacks up into the barn.

'Don't look dumbfounded, Warlow! It's quite big enough for trays, strong enough for the fuel box. Has to come a long way down but with covers the food should remain hot. Pull the cord to send back empty dishes. Ring the bell first to alert them in the kitchen.'

Powyss moves to the other side of the room. He follows, doglike.

'Here's the organ.'

Organ?

Powyss opens the doors of a cupboard.

Not a cupboard. Metal pipes stand in order. Big ones, little ones.

Powyss lifts the lid on the keys. His fingers are thin, very clean.

What's him want me to do now?

'The case of this chamber organ is walnut. Beautifully made. I hope it will amuse you, Warlow. It's a good one; I tried several and this was certainly the best. While you play you pump with your feet to keep the air going through the pipes. Not too heavily. You don't want to crack the underboard.'

He sits. Feet up and down, treading. It wheezes like an old woman.

'See?' He plays a tune, humming with it. 'The conquering hero! That'll keep you in the right mood.'

'Couldn't never do that.'

'Mm. Well, you can sing, can't you? You could pick out the notes of a tune with one finger.' *I sings in the Dog. The others'd laugh at this!* Looks away, sheepish.

'Of course I didn't know who would take up the offer. There's a whole folder of music: more Handel, hymns, J.C. Bach. But no matter.

'Now, come this way. This little room's the bathroom. Water comes into the bath from the cistern. Turn the tap.'

'Bath? Sir?'

'I know there'll be no one to see you, but you'll want to wash yourself. Even without grime from fields and horses and so on. Your beard and hair will grow long. Remember? No cutting. There are no scissors, no knives. You couldn't cut your own hair anyway, could you?' *Gabble, gabble. Him's gabblin like a goose can't stop. Not drunk though. Don't get drunk not him.*

Powyss looks him up and down. 'Hmm. You may find the bathtub a tight fit, Warlow. But look, here's the soap, Military Cake, nothing too perfumed. Toothbrush, powder. When you need replenishments you must ask. Do that by writing a note, then ring the bell and send it up. The water's cold of course. At one time that was thought to be very good for the health, but the bath's not *so* far from the fire. The cistern's over there to one side. Keep an eye on it, please.'

They wander back. Fire's blazing merrily.

'Send up your dirty linen. Send up your pot from the close-stool.'

Pot! Close-stool! He looks down. Sees his feet, his great clogs. Powyss's leather shoes. Small for a man.

'What work'll I do, sir?'

'Living here will be your work. Living here for seven years. For the sake of knowledge, of science: to see how you fare without human society. Your name will become known, Warlow! You'll become famous.

'Think of hermits who choose to live on their own for the rest of their lives, let alone seven years. Still, hermits spend their days in prayer and I'm not employing you to do that.' He breaks off.

'Do you believe in God, Warlow?'

'I goes to church Christmastide.'

'Well, never mind, I'm not quizzing you. Rarely go myself.

I've put a Bible here among the books, though. That could occupy you for seven years at least!' He laughs, uneasy-like. *Wish him'd go, let me get on with it.*

'Keep the place tidy and swept, won't you. There are brooms, everything you need of that nature. Wind the clock every eighth day and note the date or you'll lose track of time. This is the date hand. See, it shows which day of the month it is. If the chimes get on your nerves stop winding that side.' *Can't remember all that.*

'Read the books and ask for any others you fancy. I've chosen them carefully. But I have a large library; you can ask for anything you like.'

'Never read a book.'

'*Blessed is he that readeth!* And now you'll have the time to do it. You *can* read, can't you? You said you could. And write? Of course you can, you signed the contract. There are pens, ink, paper and a journal. See, here's the first, 1793. Please keep the journal. I'll send a new one each year. Keeping it will help you and be crucial for me when I write everything up to send to the Royal Society.'

'Journal, what *is* that, Mr Powyss, sir?'

'You write in it what you do each day. First you write the date, then what has happened that day or you write what you're thinking. Nothing very difficult. It's a good thing you had *some* schooling.'

'It were long years afore.'

'It'll all come back to you, I'm sure.'

Powyss shakes his hand. *Him's had enough too.*

'Good luck, Warlow! Don't forget, your wife and children are taken care of. You'll do it! We meet again in 1800.'

He smiles. Goes off in his fine black velvet breeches and coat. Locks the door. Instructs the footman Samuel on the other side.

Planks nailed across. Four of them. Hammering. The sound of metal sinking into the frame.

Herbert Powyss walked straight out of the house into the orchard. He was elated. He hadn't spoken so much in such a short time for years, being normally silent; solipsism a tendency from his youth. Now, having showered the man with instructions, he couldn't keep still; paced between young trees, touching them with careful fingers as if in greeting. He felt propelled from the small of his back. Light wind pelted him with plum blossom.

At last he would contribute something important to the sphere he so admired: natural philosophy, science. He'd spent too long treading the margins. Reading, always reading, travelling when younger, attending to his small estate in middle age. Soon he would be forty-five, his hair, when he cared to look at it, was turning grey. He was pleased with the improvements made to the house, successful cultivation of flowers, trees, fruit. He bought wisely on trips to nurseries in Turnham Green, Shepherd's Bush or Loddiges in Hackney, seed shops in Fenchurch Street. Filled books of notes. He'd built a hothouse, his own design but based on those he'd seen in Chelsea and elsewhere. Nine foot wide, sixty foot long, it was heated by a boiler that ran on sea coal, lit in November, extinguished when all danger of frost had passed. Sea coal burned with little smoke, wouldn't choke tender seedlings.

Over the years he'd tested seeds, especially the newest imports from South America and the Antipodes, experimented with the grafting of pear stock. He'd sent several short papers to the Royal Society. A favourite was his recent *Investigation into the Effectiveness of Chevalier de Bienenberg's Method of Preserving Blossoming Fruit Trees from Spring Frosts, in the County of Herefordshire.* His were minor papers, it's true, but contributions all the same. Yet Benjamin Fox had asked a question some years ago, a question that pulled him up, that he couldn't quite forget. *Who is it all for?*

Well, he'd replied, a few plantsmen might read my papers on the Chinese Lily Tree or on the nervous Cape Horn Pea. A few of the Fellows might remember my name. But Powyss had no children, not even a wife, no siblings, no family at all. Everything he did was for his own satisfaction.

He both enjoyed and resented the dialogue with Fox, conducted entirely by letter. It had become a habit. They'd attended the same school, where they'd disliked each other. But an epistolary relationship that required no physical presence suited both, grew after they'd left school. It was a diversion for the intellect. Powyss entertained Fox with botanical and architectural details, Fox wagged his Unitarian finger. They quoted morsels of their latest reading and Latin tags dragged up from their schooling, exchanged political opinions, Powyss tentatively, since he wasn't really interested, Fox with vigour. Fox would insist on comparing the condition of the poor in London with the poor in the Marches, though Powyss saw little enough, ensconced as he was most of the time in his house and garden. Even when Fox walked on the Heath he encountered tinkers and gypsies. Powyss could walk for miles and meet nothing but sheep.

Only once had Powyss, on a seed-and-plant-buying excursion to London, visited Fox at his house in Hampstead. It had been a mistake.

The house was a pleasant modern design, though almost too small for Fox's large person and ebullient personality. He showed Powyss into his study.

'This is where I write my epistles to wild Herefordshire! The desk was my father's. Vicar of St Mary at Finchley. Fortunately he died before I abandoned the Trinity, else he might have cut me out.'

Comfortably if randomly furnished, the centre of the house was the dining room, in which a large oblong table apparently seated a good crowd of Fox's friends.

'Yes, here and at each other's houses, turn and turn about,

we feast on ideas. And feed ourselves too, you can be sure of *that*. How we chew on the constitution, Powyss! How we dice up the monarchy into a ragout, chop the government into a salmagundi! Of course the best gatherings are John Tooke's in Wimbledon, for which, however, the distance obliges me to rise much earlier than I should like.

'But you say you do not ever entertain, Powyss?'

'Never.'

'*And* you persist in your agnosticism? Think it's all flam.'

'Yes.'

'Then I insist that you accompany me to Newington Green one Sunday, for, you know, we Unitarians have the only rational religion in existence. It ought to suit you.'

Fox was overbearing, his sociability, his certainty oppressive. At any moment Powyss felt he'd be tripped up by a verbal foot, gouty though Fox's actual feet undoubtedly were. There appeared to be no common ground between them. In letter form it mattered not, but facing the man was intolerable. Behind Fox's fat back, Powyss strongly desired to slip away.

But now, at last, he had an excellent answer to Fox's question and a firm counter to the implicit criticism of his way of life. His experiment was *not* just for himself. It was for science, for mankind. For all who would learn how it might be possible for a human being to live without the company of others, without seeing another human face. For all who were curious about the resilience of the human mind. What could be more important than that?

He stopped to inspect a group of trees. New gages. If the spring weather remained clement and the bees continued their work there might be a small harvest of fruit even in their first year.

*

He stands unmoving. Hears Samuel's boots ascend the stone steps. Then nothing.

Well! Well, John, well! These 'apartments' be mine. *All for me. Everythin here be for me. And soon there be food comin. Well!*

He pulls the chair out from the table, presses its upholstered seat with his palms, smoothes it. Sits down, hands on knees. Wipes his cuff over his forehead. Wet with anxious sweat.

What to do? What to do first. How to begin it. What to *do*?

Just have to live, Powyss said. *Live.* That means eat. Sleep. Not cut his hair. Wind clock. *What else him want me to do?* Write journal, but he'll not do that *yet*. And the reward! Hannah, childer 'taken care of'. Shan't trouble about *them*. Then soon as he's out, fifty pound for the rest of his life. Fifty pound *every year. Very good!*

He takes Powyss's lamp by its ring to survey the place. Useful thing. Flame inside the glass chimney; won't set fire. Better than rushes. Better than tallow.

Sets off down a short corridor: bedroom. Look at that! Brass bed all shone up. Pats it like a horse's flank. Touches everything in turn: chest, mirror, press, carved-leg chair, more pictures on the wall. Covered wooden box in the corner. Lifts the lid: pisspot. What *him* calls *close-stool. Got to carry my own pot of piss from here to the waiter thing!* He tries to piss in it but nothing comes.

He sits on the bed, jumps up as if stung on the arse. *I've dirtied it. But no: it's mine!* Sits again, fingers the pillows, three and a bolster. Prods them gently: *feathers* not straw. Soft. Pushes his great face into them. Can hardly wait to sleep.

But not yet. Back again to the big room, then the small room. *Bath.* Wood round it painted green. Chair, painted cupboard. What's inside? Soap. Holds it to his nose. Ooph! Box of, what's it say? *Tooth   Pow   der.* Pats the iron cistern. Keep an eye on it, he said. What'd he mean?

Turkey carpet covers the flags in the big room, muffles the

clumping of his clogs. He puts the lamp on the table. Lights up the place set for his meal.

He sits. Look: lamp be reflected in the glass bookcase. He grips the silver spoon and fork one in each hand. Waits for a dish to appear like magic. What will it be? Huge meat pie on a golden plate. Steaming. Meaty. He salivates.

But there's no dish, no pie.

He stands. Blinking. Listening. Waiting. The clock strikes but he forgets to count.

What to do. Fire's dying down. He puts on more coal, banks it up. Picks up the irons one at a time, replaces them carefully as if not to disturb. Straightens up, notices a picture hanging above the mantle shelf. Bearded man in hat and jacket of animal skin from the looks of it, tying something. Sewing? No! Can't tell. Looks at another picture. Flowers. Old leaves. Apple going bad. Another, bigger. Men forking hay in a field. Seen *that* enough times. Children at the edge of the field in torn skirts.

He feels dizzy from peering. From strangeness. Sits in the chair by the fire, high-backed, more comfortable than any he's ever sat in in his life. Stares into the fire. Wide-eyed, rigid.

*

In fact the last thing Powyss had in mind when the experiment took root was hermits. Hermits were men who chose to live away from others for a spiritual purpose, often with extreme privations. From a sense of such sinfulness that mortification of the flesh became the only path.

Powyss had long stopped believing in God. His boyhood prayers were never answered. He knew that events happened in the world, in Moreham, in his garden, in the hothouse, that had nothing to do with any deity. And he didn't see this view as a lack; didn't *think* about it except when pushed into argument by Fox, when he usually took an agnostic position, though occasionally, for the sake of the fight, an atheist one. But he was not intolerant. If someone chose an emaciated life of repentance then let him. He wouldn't spend any time thinking about it.

No, this experiment of his had nothing to do with the spirit. Nor was there anything ornamental about it. He'd heard of estates with hermit's caves, others where the owner had huts built specially out of tree trunks, even roots, to some poetic design. Of pebble floors, walls craftily half ruined. Of bearded old men employed to mutter and scurry away from grinning visitors. He loathed the Gothic manner, its darkness of thought, its tedious novels stuffed with castles, monks, madmen, passions. There were no false battlements, minstrel galleries, sham ruined chapels at Moreham House. No castellated follies clad in ivy.

There was a real and fascinating thesis to test: that a man could survive alone, without others.

The trigger had been a brief newspaper report of a man released from confinement alone in Dorchester Castle. No information was given about why he'd been imprisoned in a cell on his own for four years, but what had delighted Powyss was the moment of the man's release. After all that time without company he'd turned to the gaoler and spouted Virgil. (Annoying that the report hadn't given the actual words: perhaps they'd been *Non equidem invideo*, if he truly bore his gaoler no grudge. On the other hand *Nunc frondent silvae, nunc formosissimus annus* would be *my* choice, he thought, assuming it was spring and trees blossoming.) But the point was that the man had retained a sprightly mind despite removal from the world.

Of course Powyss had read about Alexander Selkirk, the model for Defoe's Robinson Crusoe. It was an irresistible story, as was *Crusoe* itself. Selkirk's story was true, Crusoe's fiction. Their trials were great: thrust onto unknown lands, they had to construct shelters, make clothes, shoes, hunt for food. The details fascinated him as they did all readers who lived in houses with fires laid and lit for them and regular meals cooked by others. But as one who shunned his fellows, had avoided them even from earliest childhood, Powyss saw in Robinson Crusoe the supreme solitary. The book had haunted him all his life.

How could such resilience be tested? Selkirk had been abandoned, Crusoe survived shipwreck. What if physical danger were removed? What if there were none of the self-imposed privations of the ascetic, none of the guilt or remorse of the prisoner? What if all emotional burdens were removed, no spiritual regimes of prayer and penitence demanded? The human mind was capable of infinite journeying within itself. It needed a body in which to live, a body in health. But what need had it of other minds? How long could it survive *solus*, in solitude, feeding on its own riches? One year? Seven years? A lifetime? Could a man survive *in comfort* with the company of himself alone?

*

Waits. Waits.

Nothing happens.

What will I . . . ? Him said. Him said what?

He stands up. Walks round the table. Twice. Round the other way, slowly. Hands hang down, heavy like sacks.

Not goin in them other rooms.

He sits. Stares at the flames. Closes his eyes but there's yellow dots from the flames.

He listens to his breaths.

Tries breathing faster. Tries stopping. Gasps for air. Yawns till his jaw seems to crack.

No sound. Nothing. Nobody.

John! He's glad to hear his own voice. *John Warlow. I be here. Down here.*

What else can he say?

He thumps the table, bang, a good sound. And whack again with both hands. Whack, whack.

Quiet, terrible quiet.

He strains to hear. *Somethin. Must be somebody.*

Them be gone home then.

No! Them's sittin outside waitin to hear me move about! That's it!

He clears his throat heavily. To let them know. Spits the gob from his throat into the fire with a good fizzle.

No sound. *Them's not hearin.* Moves over to the door, stands next to it. Gives it a push. What if it be open all the time!

Coughs loudly, very loudly.

Nothing. Nothing except ticks, damned clock. *Do I wind im? Niver did have a clock.*

What will I . . . ?

Quiet. Like a weight on his head, back of his neck.

Day must be gone. Be night then. Must be. Why there's nothing to do. He turns out the lamp, snuffs the candles to see if it's night.

Dark!

But it weren't nearly night afore, when I come down. Or were it?

His heart begins to thump. *Be it night? Were it?* He doesn't know, can't remember. His mind buzzes like flies on a dead dog.

Lights a candle at the fire and it's day again.

Sits in the armchair once more. Thumping slows.

Silence pounds in his ears instead.

He pulls at his fingers, kneads swollen knuckles.

Pokes up flames. Stares till the yellow dots.

*

Powyss's experiment would be entitled *Investigation into the Resilience of the Human Mind Without Society*. Of course it was strictly limited: there was neither classification nor system-making. He'd not be remembered among the greatest natural philosophers.

In his run of Royal Society *Transactions* from 1768 he'd absorbed accounts of numerous experiments and minutely reported observations. On his shelves were various more recent, important books such as Joseph Priestley's *Experiments and Observations on Different Kinds of Air*. This he'd read and enjoyed despite the man's political tendency, and so he was familiar with Priestley's 'dephlogisticated air', now unfortunately overtaken and renamed 'oxygen' by Lavoisier. He owned the second, admirably full edition of Keir's translation of Macquer's *Dictionnaire de Chymie*. Was still undecided about Buffon's and Erasmus Darwin's opposition to Linnaeus's classification system, even though as a horticulturalist he really ought to make up his mind. As to the constant public demonstrations of electricity, it was enough to read about Galvani's dead frog twitching and jerking its legs to decide against watching anybody else's experiments with a portable electricity machine.

So, while he'd not wanted actually to mess with metals, mercury, vitriol or inflammable air, let alone the multitudes of mice employed by Dr Priestley, the rigour of testing, the disinterest, the neutrality in all these experiments drew him passionately. Here was reason, here were the actions of rational men that caused science to grow like a colossal tree.

Inspired, Powyss evolved the details of his investigation. The subject would live with all his needs answered: clean clothes, good food, mind nourished by music and books – *bona librorum et frugis copia*. But on his own; without even the sight of another human face. What effect would seven years of such existence have upon him?

(*Why seven?* Fox quizzed him. *How biblical you are, Powyss, despite your lack of religion!*

Neither too long, nor too short, Powyss replied. *Besides, it takes me neatly into the new century.*)

He contemplated it without difficulty. Thought of his own life. He was not sociable, never entertained, had no family, his one friendship conducted on paper. It was true that whenever he bought plants in London he would also visit a certain house in Jermyn Street. He accepted that this was necessary for the maintenance of good health in the human male, but believed that he could stop if he wanted to. Here in the Marches, he refused to serve on worthy local committees, abhorred balls, plays, hunting, never went near the races. He paid dues to the Hereford Philosophical Society without attending a single meeting. Weeks passed when he spoke to no one except the butler, Jenkins, then only to issue orders. Or he had a word or two with Price, the master gardener. He felt closer to his newly arrived, carmine-flowered *Penstemon barbatus*, whose growth he was recording in his firm hand, whose seeds he would collect himself, than to any person he knew. With books, music, pictures to contemplate, resources of the mind, one could certainly exist alone. Perhaps, he accused himself, the experiment was about himself? That it was the first he'd ever conducted on a human being rather than a plant or tree, excited him immensely. His ambition rose like a sudden change on the barometer.

Once he'd articulated the thesis, he worked out the conditions and how evidence would be collected. It would need to take place underground in order to ensure no human contact. At the centre would be someone who freely decided to take part, who would keep a diary of his actions, which Powyss would collate with information he himself recorded. After seven years a full interview would be conducted. He was certain it would end as a tribute to the human mind. And for himself he was sure it would answer Fox's questioning of his life, rebuff his sociable friend's implicit criticism of his solitude.

He set about preparing the 'apartments'. Moreham House was much older than it looked. In the thirteenth century it had been moated, probably as defence against marauding Welsh, though perhaps also as a demonstration of status. Five centuries later, Powyss's father, a successful man of mercantile origins, elevated himself into the gentry through purchase of the house and expensive architects. Changes were begun, but it was the son who'd really imposed reason: the façade of symmetry, raised ceilings, great swathes of light. Windows were crucial to the task of enlightening: small casements were enlarged, equalled in size and shape on each floor. Doorways were increased in height and width as though rational plans would perforce create larger men to walk through them. And windows framed external order: foreground of carefully arranged gardens, middle ground of cow-browsed meadows, distant haze of hills. Nor did he neglect the unseen region: kitchen and pantries below ground were modernised and equipped with the latest devices.

But beneath *them* a second set of cellars remained much as before: thick stone walls built into a hollow space gouged out of the undermost earth, even lower than the moat, from which dampness continued to seep despite its draining. Their purpose was yet a mystery: had the owners hidden there during the Welsh rebellions of the fifteenth century? Used them to imprison their enemies? Hoarded stores of some rare commodity illegally obtained? Powyss's father kept them locked, preferring to forget their existence.

The cellars extended beneath the ballroom, which was shuttered, untouched since his father had had it decorated with overmuch gold leaf, to just below the far end of Powyss's library. There were several unused rooms and Powyss had them thoroughly cleaned out, some of the walls brick-lined and plastered, some even papered. How pleasing to bring order to these last, most remote parts of the house! He bought all the furniture he could imagine needing were he to live there himself, chose pieces that pleased him, bought the chamber organ after a delightful morning at Longman & Broderip in Cheapside, trying out one after another. He picked engravings, mezzotints of classical scenes, a couple of

English landscapes, a small Dutch still life, a newly painted seascape; took some harmless biblical illustrations from his mother's bedroom. It was his own chalk-and-pencil sketch of Crusoe that hung over the fireplace.

He spent days thinking about books – *bona librorum*. Picked his favourite Voltaire and Defoe; thought *King Lear* not suitable; held back *Paradise Lost* until asked for. Apart from the Bible and *Annual Register* for 1789, he chose *Candide, Robinson Crusoe, A Journal of the Plague Year, The Tempest,* Thomson's *Seasons* and Ferguson's *Astronomy Explained upon Sir Isaac Newton's Principles and made easy to those who have not studied Mathematics.*

Once he knew Warlow was to be the occupier he thoughtfully reduced the number of volumes so as not to intimidate him, though the man had said he could read. At the last moment, he added his new copy of Bewick's *A General History of Quadrupeds.* There, surely, was a book suitable for someone with only elementary education.

As to long hair and nails, he wasn't being fanciful. Nobody would see Warlow. He wasn't showing off a paid hermit, didn't need him to look unkempt. But he wouldn't risk leaving scissors or knives should Warlow become melancholic as Crusoe and Selkirk had; he didn't want blood on his conscience and the experiment must run smoothly. A degree of melancholia was possible, he supposed, and could be tolerated. Yet the man's life would be considerably eased without the heavy toil he'd been used to for years; the drudgery, cold and squalor. Of course, despite what Warlow had assured him, he might grow to miss his wife and companions. But with books he could surely find consolation. He resolved to send down further volumes in due course. With so much time on his hands the man would *have* to read.

Shortly before Warlow was due, Powyss spent a week in the apartments, amused by the lift, charmed by his choice of furnishings. Pleased once more with the quality of the

Oldovini organ. Delighted with the concentration brought about by lack of outside diversion. By the wonderful silence.

*

Something breaks the stupor. Has he slept? *Is* it night? Was it? Creaking. Coming nearer. Behind the door in the wall: smell of meat.

Fully awake. Hungry, yes, he opens the door, expects to see the footman, Samuel, standing there with a pie oozing gravy. Finds a tray of heavy silver domes. Carries it to the table. Covers are too hot to take off! He hoists up his arm within its sleeve to use the cuff. Sees a neatly folded cloth for the purpose.

Three big pieces of boiled mutton, plate of potatoes, plate of green vegetables. Another dish with something white hidden under sauce. He sniffs it. Fish. *Ach!* Must he eat it? Must he eat all together? No. Which first? Begins with mutton *but there's no knife!* Only spoons and forks. He digs at the meat with the spoon, looks about him, grabs it with his hands, bites heartily. Can he leave the fish? Better not. Scoops it up. *Pap.* Fishy pap. Swallows it down with porter from a jug. Porter's good, very good.

Full, he wipes his mouth with his hand. Sits back, stretches his legs.

Tries to imagine Powyss at his table eating the same food. With a jug of porter? Doubt it. Wine more like. Is *him* thinkin of *me*?

Replaces the dishes, rings the bell, hauls on the cord. Up it goes! Distant door bangs.

He sits again at the fire, pokes it, pulls over a chair on which to rest his feet. He needs a pipe now. The others'll have their pipes. He thinks of them toasting John Warlow. Puffing, staring into the flames.

What he could tell them in the Dog! About all this.

The creaking again! This time he hears it at the start. Way up it is. Slowly, slowly descending. Stops. Judders. He opens the door, takes a new tray to the table. A sweet tart, bowl of orange jelly, dish of walnuts and raisins. Piece of cheese and roll of bread. Doesn't want it now. Full of meat. Later. But them'll expect the plates, sure to. Heaps the food onto the table. Eats the jelly with increasing queasiness. Hauls up a tray of empty dishes.

He needs a pipe. *Needs a pipe.*

*

Each entry had to be carefully noted with date and time. Already there was a full description of the apartments with neatly drawn plans of both rooms and the listening tube, and an inventory that omitted nothing. There were full details of Warlow himself of course: his appearance, height, weight, age, occupation, family circumstances. Powyss intended to record each meal sent down, the state of the dishes returned: what was eaten, what rejected. It was Jenkins who'd suggested Warlow might prefer beer to wine. He would record each consignment of fuel, kindling, lamp oil, each batch of new linen, and in due course he'd note every request, though there were none as yet. Eventually this information would be matched to Warlow's daily journal entries.

He'd written down his very first conversation with Warlow, when he answered the advertisement, as he had his last when he took him below. At the end of seven years, upon emerging, his answers to questions would be compared with these. Not that the man had said much. Reflecting on it later, he'd been annoyed at Warlow's gloomy reaction to the chamber organ, the books, the journal. If only the man had had more education. What a fascinating account some other candidate might have produced! But there'd been no choice: no one else had come forward.

Of great importance, he thought, was what he could learn *directly* of Warlow's solitary life, without it being reported by Warlow himself, who in any case didn't have the vocabulary to express much. What he might *say* he did or thought for Powyss's benefit would very likely be different from what he actually did or thought. Powyss had puzzled at length over how to know what took place down there. If only there were a way to observe; but short of placing an observation window in impossibly thick walls, there was no hope of doing it.

However, he might listen. Hear whereabouts Warlow was in the apartments, possibly even hear him speak. People much on their own did speak to themselves; he himself did it occasionally, it wasn't madness. So, using the room plans that he'd sketched when he'd begun the project, he took measurements, had Samuel drill three-inch holes in the floorboard at the far end of his library and at a parallel place in the ceiling of the main room of the underground apartments. It had already been quite a task constructing the mechanical lift to rise up from the cellar to the kitchen. Finding space without stone wall between himself and the cellar that would also *not* go through the kitchen was difficult. For he didn't want the servants to know about this part of the experiment. He'd paid Samuel well for his work and sworn him to secrecy. He was a handy young man whom Powyss had agreed to employ a while back as a favour to his neighbour, Valentine Tharpe. Loyal, willing, Samuel was more trustworthy than Jenkins, even though only a footman.

Fortunately, there were many unexplained spaces within both cellar levels: the house's medieval roots. Between the holes bored in the floor at the end of the library and the ceiling of Warlow's cellar two floors down, Powyss inserted a copper tube, of thirteen feet and four inches in length, made to his precise specifications in Birmingham. It ran through a dark space behind a pantry wall and was not likely to be seen by anyone. Each end was secured by a cork collar and furnished with a discreet funnel as an acoustic aid. Around the funnel in Warlow's ceiling were decorative plaster fruits and leaves, the better to distract attention from it. In Powyss's library, the end was similarly fixed with cork into a broad floorboard. Over it he placed a pile of papers which he could easily shift aside. When he wanted to listen he knelt in comfort on his favourite Ottoman prayer rug.

*

Warm. Bed is soft and warm. No crackling straw in the mattress, no sacking. No twigs sticking into your back. He's never slept in a bed like this. He squirms his body down into it. Head sinks into feathers. Down into down. He could stay in it forever. Could stay in it all day. *Is* it day? Clock strikes. Again he forgets to count. Utter darkness. Blinks. Black. Blinks. Still black.

Could be day. It'll always be dark here unless I makes it light. He feels for the tinderbox by the bed, lights a candle. Sticks out his feet and it's cold though he's still wearing his clothes. Only took off his coat when he got into bed. Puts on his clogs, pulls a blanket round him.

Must be daylight *some*where. How else tell the time of day? Clocks are useless.

Fire is out. No daylight anywhere. Oil lamp went out. Fiddle with that later.

Got to be daylight somewhere. He knows there isn't. Can't be. Two floors down. No windows.

But one wall's on the outside of the house. Which is it? Which? He struggles to think what this means. Maybe there's holes in the wall like at home. Which wall? Which?

He takes the candle with one hand, runs the other hand along the walls, corners. Touching, knocking with his knuckles for hollowness. Stone, stone. Solid. *Not* like his house, ribs of wattle sticking through daub. From one room to another he goes. What's outside the wall? Nothing but earth out there, is it?

Fear snatches at his throat, his gut. Closed in. Closed up. He starts again. Feeling with big rough fingers. Peering behind the candle flame, especially corners near ceilings. Near the fire there's paper on walls. He touches plaster on others. His fingers grope under pictures. Gently. Don't let them fall and smash.

Into the small room again. Around the bath. Walls thick stone. *Can't* be. *Must* be. *Can't* be.

Sudden cold. He holds the candle to it. Flame flutters. Grating halfway down near the cistern. *There!* Curled iron-work flakes at his touch. Behind: narrow brick-lined shaft that goes up out of sight.

A cut of air slants down. He breathes it. Smells rust, leaf mould, morning.

Chapter 2

A KNOCK SIGNALLED the butler Jenkins, who announced Mrs Warlow coming to collect her money, as she had every Monday for the last few weeks.

He had been taken aback by her first appearance. He'd seen poverty of course, though not often, since he rarely went beyond the walls of his garden. Beggars cluttered London streets, but he'd never looked at them this closely. He made sure his servants were well fed and paid; every five years he made enquiries of other landowners, then paid slightly more. Fox was informative, too. Powyss reasoned that if they had sufficient food and wages they'd cause no trouble and he'd not waste time thinking about them.

Mrs Warlow was small, hostile, her clothes threadbare, torn, muddied.

She'd stood where he told her, by his desk, refusing to look at him, her arms clasped about her body.

'You have nothing to fear, Mrs Warlow. Your husband has everything he needs and can ask for anything else he might want. Do you understand?'

'Yes, sir.'

'You must come for this money each week and use it for food and clothing. If it is more than you have been used to, then no doubt the cobbler will benefit!'

She wouldn't smile. Had taken the money, walked rapidly down the room, been unable to open the door. He'd followed her over and she, in a shocking movement, shrank back, as if expecting a blow. He'd opened the door and called Jenkins to see her out.

Here was something he'd not anticipated, something he could neither brush aside, nor immediately forget. He hadn't expected to be *concerned*, only to give orders and record. He'd gone straight out to the hothouse, his place of relief. Where life demonstrated its resilience, where no pain was experienced, where death had no power to shock. Flowers died, fruit dropped. You began again.

The second week was no better. He contemplated sending Samuel with the money in future, but no, there was something he couldn't quite relinquish. Her look, never once direct, was yet startling. The colour of her eyes, he thought, but how hard it was to see them!

Since then he'd become used to her manner and noted at least less pallor, even a slight fleshing out in her face. Surely she and her children must eat more with the money he gave her and with Warlow not at home? He struggled to think about their previous life. Warlow, out in the fields all day, probably ate like a pig when he returned, and drank his wages in the Dog and Duck. How, then, had they lived? He'd never been interested in, let alone troubled by, someone's appearance before. Perhaps it was like watching a seedling, searching for signs of sprout or wilt, hoping for sturdiness.

Still she wouldn't look at him.

'How are you, Mrs Warlow?'

'Well, sir.'

'And your children?'

'Well.'

'Tell me something of them.'

She didn't reply; didn't know what he wanted.

'Tell me about your oldest child.'

'Jack.'

'What age is he?'

'Twelve year.'

'Is he a good boy?'

'Fair. He do scare crows with David and little John. For Mr Kempton.'

It was the most he'd heard her speak.

'And your youngest?'

'Mary.'

'How old is she?'

'Three year old. We do call her Polly.'

'Ah.'

In truth Powyss cared little about these children, just wanted Mrs Warlow to face him rather than the floor. This experience of apparently intimidating her was unpleasant. He gave her the money and walked to the door with her, opening it, calling out to Jenkins.

He went over to the north window. When he redesigned this room for his library, books filled the east side and windows were added at the north end and on the west side. Thus he greatly increased the light and could also watch the changing state of the weather. As his bedroom faced east, he began to read the sky when he rose and continued through the three windows of the library as the day progressed.

The great south window presented garden, fields and hills, the west the kitchen garden and trees beyond its wall. The north overlooked the back of the house. He watched Mrs Warlow hurry away from the door of the back kitchen.

*

She says to herself: I think on Mother. Got with child. Masters always take what they want.

It will be the same.

I shall scream out though it do no good.

*

He's glad of the porter. Has tobacco now. Thinks he'll ask for more beer. His notes work.

Pleas sen ter bacca
   Plaes   *John Warlow*

And there it was a few days later in a jar with four clay pipes.

Night is hard. He knows when it's morning because breakfast comes juddering down. Though what *time* that is he doesn't know. Past daybreak. He goes to the grating, smells dawn up the shaft well before the food comes.

Days are ruled by the waiter thing. Food down, plates up. Empty wood box, full pisspot up, kindling, clean pisspot down. Jingle bell, up. Down. Jingle bell, up. Down.

At night nothing. Home is noisy at night. Children stir, snivel, kick, whimper, cry in the other bed; Hannah moans in her sleep. Cats and owls screech. Rats scratch, running over their heads in and out of roof holes. Wind blows through broken panes, rain pisses into buckets. He'll never mend it, Kempton. Fall down around them first it will. Damned Kempton.

He's had three meals. It's evening. A day gone. He smokes till the fire dies. Ashes sift, soundless. It's night. Quiet. There's only ticking, ticking.

He's already stopped the chiming, like Powyss said. But it ticks. Tick, tick. Nothing else sounds. Not even distant thumps like in the day. Nothing. *Tick, tick.* Damn clock! He takes a stick of kindling, opens the glass, jams it under the big hand. Which comes off. *Damned infernold clock!* Can't read the time anyway. Tick, tick, tick. He unlatches a door in the side. Stop it *somehow*. Reaches in. Heavy pendulum slips off its perch, crashes through the thin wooden base onto the floor. Ticktickticktickticktickticktickticktickticktickticktick. Stops.

His head ticks in the silence. *Tickticktickticktick. No! Damned infernold ticking!* Must hear something else. He stumbles to the grating by the cistern. Something up there. Yes. *Listen.* Listen to the life he's given up. Up there, far away, a dog howls. Moreham dog. Howl! Howl away the ticking!

He stands, shivering. Stillness comes down the shaft. Cold tells of frost. He imagines the cracked crust of frozen earth beneath his wooden sole.

So far below. He's much lower than turnips, potatoes. Lower than moles and rabbits. Foxes. Brocks. Down where there's tree roots. Lower.

*

Powyss stood at his newly made cabinet with the sloping top. He was extremely pleased with this piece of furniture which contained ten thin, wide drawers built to his own design in which to keep his plans for the house and gardens. Now the top three drawers were given over to the folders of labelled and dated notes on Warlow.

To stand at it, write, think, was satisfying. Precise measurements had been taken to enable him to lean his elbows without incurring pain in his back. It faced into the room so that he would not be distracted by the scene through the great south window.

The library was fine, the shelves well stocked with classical authors, poetry, natural philosophy and the usual run of *Annual Registers*. The room was long, light, perfectly proportioned, but by no means elaborate. Although its ceiling sported a regular pattern of interlaced plaster octagons, hexagons and rectangles, he'd eschewed the endless pilasters and busts and urns in niches typical of the grander houses, where so much space was given to the demonstration of taste that little room was left for books.

From where he stood he could survey his books and engravings, his precious Apulian vases, marble bust of Aesculapius, the brass praefericulum for holding incense used in sacrifices, lumps of lava pocketed at the foot of Vesuvius. Three Dutch still lifes, bought for their wonderful similitude to fruit and flowers that he grows, not their moral. The set of globes made for him in London, the one of the world, the other celestial. He intended to obtain a small, portable telescope to observe comets and meteor showers, one that slotted into a six-inch brass column on a base that was also its box.

A copy of the advertisement for the experiment still lay on his cabinet.

Warlow had been the only man to respond. In a burst of lucidity he'd said he cared not for human faces, would be glad to be shot of them.

'Do you think you will be glad for seven years, Warlow?'

'I do think I shall.'

'And will you not be troubled by long nails and hair and beard?'

'No.'

'Do you have a family, Warlow?'

'Six childer.'

'You're a labouring man. Who employs you?'

'Mr Kempton mostly. Pulverbatch at harvest. I do take what I can.'

'You'll have no need to find work ever again if you stay the course. And you needn't worry about the war either. They can't possibly take you for a soldier. Nor your sons for sailors. I'll see to it. Not that they'd trouble to press this far from the sea.

'I shall take responsibility for the upkeep of all your family while you're here. I believe you have a wife living?'

'Yes. Her do weed the corn for Mr Kempton at sarclin time. Helps the wash. And gleanin.'

'She need not do that either. She can attend to her children.'

Thinking back to that interview Powyss recalls how Warlow didn't mention his wife until asked. He thinks of them both now, a Jack Spratt couple if ever there were one: Warlow a great, brawny man, too big to be of Welsh stock, rock-boned, his features crude; Mrs Warlow small in stature, overburdened, cowed. Jenkins, unasked, had intimated that Warlow beat his children. There could be little doubt he beat his wife, too. Perhaps it was better that they were apart; they hardly needed more children.

Mrs Warlow disturbed him somewhat, but he could help her with money. Her life would surely improve and then he'd no longer be troubled by her.

As for Warlow himself, Powyss was conscious that at the far end of this room, more than twenty feet down, the man could be standing right now, like himself, thinking, wondering. He hoped, rather, that he was sitting at the table writing his journal. Warlow's own written record was to play a major part in his paper.

How curious that someone should be so near in the room where he felt so agreeably far from others. Did it make a difference to his own sense of solitariness, he wondered? Knowing that someone else was also leading a solitary life, unseen, almost awoke a fellow feeling in him. That Warlow was there below unexpectedly enriched his treasured aloneness. It was as if he saw his reflection in a pool, quiet, unmoving. And yet of course, Warlow was as different from him as could be: a great bovine creature. Well, as long as he did what he'd been asked to do then it didn't matter.

He went to the end of the room with his notebook and pen, shifted the pile of papers, knelt and listened. Not a sound for fifteen minutes. He would try again in an hour. But he could smell smoke. He closed his eyes to concentrate. Lamp-oil smoke. And sweet, aromatic tobacco. He'd asked Fox's advice, ordered a quality Warlow had probably never encountered before. There'd been no complaint.

*

Bites on the pipe end. Scratches his beard. Which doesn't itch any more but he does it all the same.

He's struggling with the journal. Trouble is, he doesn't know the date now the clock's stopped. It told the day! But no, it didn't tell the month.

He knows the year. There's 1 7 9 3 in gold numbers on the spine. He runs his fingertips over them. Knows it were April when he came down. He reads what he wrote on the first page:

Aperl 1793

He tried to think of school then, didn't he. What did them write in school? Must have writ *somethin*. Went for three years. Then father were gone. Ground opened in the flood, horse fell in. Cart toppled on him, loaded with bales.

Crow scarin for him and his brothers after that. Dug ditches, hauled logs for their keep.

What did them write in school? Name of course.

J o hn   War lo w

What then?

I am   4 3 yer owd
I do liv in Moram

No! He remembers the joke – more ham. Morham. Only they never got any ham.

Now I do liv in Mr Powis seller. I hav plent to eat and smok.

That's days ago. He's proud of it. Done no writin since long afore. It's not *work. Him* calls it work! All the same, he puffs as much as when he's scythin down nettles. Think of the load of nettles he'd cut in the time it takes to write!

Can't be April no more. He smells less rain at the grating. But it's not warm. Each day he goes to sniff the outside world. Soil's still damp, he can tell. There are old leaves the other side, at the bottom of the shaft. He pokes them out with a fork. Thin, dry, been blowin down for years, sure to. Now there's spots of blossom dropped through onto the ground.

May
I did see a frog yest daye he cum down bhine the gratin. I did pot him in the sis tern.

He pauses, sucks on the empty pipe. Looks with pleasure at the last word – *sis tern.*

Rewards himself by filling the bowl with a good pinch from the jar and lighting it. Good tobacco.

He'd been about to kill the frog. Stamp on it with his clog. His fingers were covered in ink from writing; sand spilled all over the diary. He'd plunged his hand into the cistern and the frog jumped out, hopped off. He'd bawled at it. Gone after it. When suddenly, 'I did think no, didn't I?' He's begun to talk to himself. Tries to explain this. Thinks he'd have wrung a crow's neck in a trice; hung it from the ceiling. Crows is devil's birds.

'It were sorrow.' Young frogs fall down the shaft. Smell water. Struggle through the grating to the cistern. He knows there've been others.

On grown by the si stern   I did fine owd frog   skil
skilin   frog boans.

Stops writing. Done enough. Wipes inky fingers on his breeches, warms his arse before the fire.

*

A stream ran through the garden of Moreham House. Powyss's father, realising that fashion required him to improve his grounds, had begun discussion with a well-known and dogmatic landscape gardener. But old Powyss had died after only a ha-ha and a rustic cott were constructed. To the astonishment of neighbouring landowners, his son paid off the grand gardener, filled in the ha-ha, cut a track for carts, let out the furthest land for grazing and took off the door of the cott up on Yarston bank so that sheep could take shelter in it. He threw away the plans to make the stream even more serpentine than it already was, to construct zig-zag walks ending in obelisks and vistas thrilling the eye with a distant statue of Hercules. He enjoyed watching the sketch for an absurd Ruinous Bridge curl to ashes in the library fireplace.

Benjamin Fox had joyfully accused his correspondent of puritanism and Powyss acknowledged some truth in it. He hated Gothic effusion in gardening just as much as in writing and architecture. But nor would he tolerate classical pretension, which, together with Gothicising, his father had seen as a necessary badge of social arrival. A doric temple on one hill, a 'ruined' tower on the next would have made old Powyss happy. The obligatory Grand Tour, urged on and paid for by his father, had not been so inspiring that he might need to glimpse, daily, a temple of Venus on a half-distant mount. Nor did he want to impress his neighbours. He didn't much like his neighbours; avoided contact with them.

The two largest estates abutting his land belonged to

Sir Frederick Champney Baugh, Bt, and Valentine Tharpe. Baugh, older than anyone knew, seemed to have slept through the century, his house and land unchanged for decades, he himself reluctant to abandon his heavy wig that smelt of flour powder and old sweat, unaware how much material benefit his servants gained from his somnolence.

Tharpe took seriously his position as magistrate and patron of a London orphanage, but envied Powyss his collection of curiosities and suffered a scold for a wife who failed to hide an obscure displeasure. Other neighbours had known Powyss's father, so were best avoided for that very reason.

For all his study, his detachment, Powyss had a practical vein, shown in his designs for the hothouse, the mechanical lift, his copper-pipe listening device. It enabled him to fulfil his ambition to acquire new plants and trees. So much was being brought in nowadays from over the seas: America, Africa, New Zealand, China. Plants and trees carefully packed about with peat, seeds kept safe in stoppered bottles, beeswax or barrels. He'd once explained to Fox:

I desire that my garden display flowers each season, including winter, and in particular what has newly arrived on these shores from distant places. So I try out new strains as they arrive in the nurseries, discover which acclimatise well to the Moreham soil, the Marches climate. Of course I take pleasure in an ordered landscape through my windows, but my notion of order, of what is natural in a garden and beyond is only partly dictated by Claude. And Mr Gilpin is quite wrong. Even had I rocks and gorges I would not desecrate them with grottos and rustic knick-knacks and sham ruins. Sapientia prima stultitia caruisse. I have got rid of folly, though whether I have really begun to be wise is yet to be seen.

My horticultural experiments include trees, for there is a parcel of land to the west well suited and another with a warm wall which makes a perfect orchard. Vegetables, too, to which end I have my glasshouses, hothouse, hotbeds and a sizable kitchen garden. Pringle of the Royal Society said 'no vegetable grows in vain', I was pleased to read.

And who shall eat it all, you ask, for you know how I hate to entertain, being a convinced solitary. The servants and gardeners take produce back to their cottages and most likely sell it in the village. Do not mistake this for Christian charity. I do not grow fruit and salad to feed the poor. I grow it for my own studies in horticulture and send out the residue only so that it does not go to waste. Perhaps they are the only villagers in England to eat melon. The best is boxed and sent to you where, despite your proximity to market gardens, you make use of it for your social gatherings.

I have all I desire, Fox:

modus agri non ita magnus,
Hortus ubi et tecto vicinus iugis aquae fons
Et paulum silvae super his foret.

A little land, a garden, a stream and a bit of wood.

Of course that that was all he desired was no longer entirely true, for the *Investigation* now took his ambition beyond the confines of his estate. Recognition by the scientists and philosophers of the Royal Society was what he wanted.

The fields that he refused to turn into false Grecian landscape or even a ridiculous *ferme ornée* were rented out to Kempton and, in the lower reaches of the hills to an obscure man called Bloor whose shepherd, Aaron, roamed the hills with his flocks. Bloor would insist on setting the stubble on fire each spring, the better to encourage fresh greenery for his cattle. Punishment for such burning, which often spread, destroying nearby woods and coppices, was whipping or confinement, and so Powyss, who had a loathing of corporal punishment, had persuaded the magistrates to inflict a short confinement. Then sent Jenkins to Bloor with a bribe to desist from burning the next year.

He preferred not to surround himself with journeymen and apprentices, just as he kept his house servants to a minimum. The housemaids doubled as kitchen maids; the cook had housekeeping duties; Samuel the footman must turn his hand to all manner of tasks. Servants, like the expensive whores in Jermyn Street, were a disagreeable necessity. The country itself couldn't be run without labourers in fields, factories, unloading ships. You made sure there was bread, that there were poor rates. Then you thought about something else.

He employed two labourers and Price, a master gardener. Price trained the labourers to dig, hoe and weed with care. He was a Welshman, skilled, knowledgeable but surly. Or was it that surliness and discontent were becoming common, were spreading like ineradicable mildew in warm, damp weather?

*

A note comes down with the clean pisspot.

Send up your Linin

Linin? His clothes are woollen. Hasn't taken them off, hasn't wanted to. Except the coat in bed. He's seen shirts in a drawer in the bedroom. Linen. Not worn them.

It's summer. At the grating he smells warm air, warm rain, warm earth. Hears wood pigeons, the rasp of young crows. If he listens long enough he hears squeaking of fledgling sparrows and houseswifts. Wheelbarrows scrape along gravel for Powyss's garden – whiff of manure.

Corn'll be growing now, too tall to weed. Sheep's been sheared. Lambs taken from ewes.

Time lags between meals. He keeps the fire in. Drops crumbs into the cistern.

He's touched everything, handled, opened, closed, pulled, pushed, screwed, unscrewed, picked up, put down. Poked, patted, pressed, peered at, sniffed. Knows every damned infernold thing here. Sits in the high-backed armchair, watches the candle burn till the flame dances inside his closed lids. Candlesticks, snuffer, oil lamp on the round table, cask of oil. He's never used an oil lamp before. When he fiddles with it it flares, melts his eyebrow or singes overhanging hair. He curses soundly. Talks to himself often.

Looks at his legs stretched out. Toes hurt. Nails've grown through stockings. Needs bigger clogs. Turkey carpet's all patterns this way and that. He follows the lines. One goes all round the edge. Then there's pathways inside; he follows them up, along, down, round, back to where he started. Round again. There's shapes like stiff birds, trees, teeth, candlesticks. Eyes. He stares at an eye. It stares at him.

He glances at tongs, poker, shovel, brush, shelf of books, press with blankets, folded linen. Ah linen! In the *bed*. Why didn't them write *beddin*?

His eyes travel round the walls. Pictures of trees and lakes, people at a well: Bible story, can't remember it. Another with men in long dresses, bare arms. He goes over to the mirror. Holds up a candle. Sees a great big beard. Long, wide, black. Face recognisable only when he mouths at it.

'Me. It is me. John. John Warlow. Fifty pound a year.'

He feels the beard, hair at the back of his neck, shoulders. Thinks what he said to Powyss: he'd be glad to be shut of human faces.

'For seven years, Warlow? See nobody for seven years?'

'Yes.' Yes. Yes. Had no doubts.

It were the money. Fifty pounds won't make him rich as damned infernold Kempton. But *every year for the rest of his life!* That were it. It'll keep the lot of them. He won't work. Will he? Or if he do, he'll keep his wages to himself. Drink as long as he wants. All night. All day. That's Liberty. That's the word them do say in the Dog, isn't it? Or is it Freedom?

'For the rest of your life.' *For the rest of my life.*

The others were envious he could see. Though them said him were a fool.

But it's the truth about the faces. He'd rather look a horse in the face than see old Elias day after day. Thick grey dewlaps shakin every time him takes a swig. Dick grinnin. Grinnin whatever you say. Should've won a prize for it. Pound of tobacco.

'Dick, your dog's drownded.' Grins.

'Dick, your house's on fire.' Grins.

Wind blew, his mouth stuck. Suckin soaked crusts between his gums. Suck. Suck.

Perhaps them've gone for soldiers. Shootin French. No. Too old to fight.

'No woman for seven year,' them said.

He'll get by. Sure to. No cheer in Hannah. Niver were. Keeps out of his way. Often don't go to bed at all. In the mornin noddin by the ashes. Her do coddle the childer, them's always about her. Says her do love her childer every one, livin or buried. But her don't want *him*. Niver did. Thinks herself better nor him. All for her mother were a *lady's maid*! Thin as a skeleton, hates that in a woman. He could kill her easy rollin on top. Her gaspin for breath. The last time he hit her her arm broke. Hasn't done it since the girl were born.

Polly. He'll miss *her*. Her's got a sweet little face. But the rest. Good for nothin. Fightin, hungry all the time, have to knock 'em about. Like father. Knocked *us* about. Growls. Can't tell one from the next. Sometimes he mixes up names with the dead ones. Dick says childer is God's punishment.

*

July, and a letter from Fox arrived. One of Fox's many friends, a bookseller, Henry Clarke, had just been imprisoned for four years for selling Paine's *Rights of Man*. He was concerned about Clarke's wife and children. He wrote:

*The whole city is infected by a disorder of the nerves. Everyone
listens for treason, pounces like kites upon the tiniest mouse-
squeak of sedition. No coffee house, no tavern is safe from
spies and fools. There's an attorney just yesterday sent to
Newgate for 6 months __and__ an hour's pillory, all for speaking up
for equality in the Percy Coffee House. I pray God the crowd
takes pity on the man; too many have been killed in the pillory.*

*How protected from the world you are in your hills with
your endless supply of mutton! You might scarcely know we've
been at war with France since February.*

Fox had sent Powyss a copy of Paine's book a while ago,
but Powyss hadn't even cut the pages, let alone read it. And
now Fox was urging him to make sure he improved the lives
of Mrs Warlow and her children, rather than just 'cultivating
your own garden' as he put it. This double allusion to *Candide*
and to Powyss's horticulture was typical of the man.

His immediate reaction to any suggestion of Fox's was
always negative. It was an old habit begun and developed
in childhood against his father's orders and his mother's
demands. With Fox there was often a second round, however,
after the contents sank into his thoughts. Of course Powyss
actually cultivated his garden, but the experiment was not
equivalent to cultivating his garden in Voltaire's sense. He
was doing it for mankind, as he'd told Fox, firmly. But Fox
had a point: everything centred on Warlow. The idea of Mrs
Warlow and her children as an offshoot to the experiment, a
small, contained section, that might even merit a paper of its
own, seemed attractive.

He took a bound notebook from his store and inscribed it:
*Account of Lateral Effects of Investigation into the Resilience of the
Human Mind: Mrs Hannah Warlow and her Children.*

He found that he was looking forward to Monday. He
washed and shaved. Samuel had laid out clean undergar-
ments, hose, white shirt, his breeches, waistcoat and coat all

of black. Momentarily he admired his right calf as he pulled on the stockings, fastened the garters.

Usually he went out either into the garden and the orchard or to the greenhouses and hothouse after breakfast, but now, on Mondays, he delayed that until after Mrs Warlow's visit.

She barely replied to his greeting just inside the door, waiting to walk the length up to his desk by the window, past the shelves and glass cases.

Powyss stood.

'Come in, Mrs Warlow. I was looking out of my window, as I do each day. Come and see for yourself.'

She came, stood apart.

'This window faces south and so the sun has not yet reached it. But it is my favourite view. I can see my flower garden, some of my best trees, the fields, sheep, cattle, the hills. And today the clouds racing from the west. Is it not a beautiful sight?'

'Yes, sir.'

'Sit down please.' The day was promising, the experiment going to plan, he was pleased with himself. It was clear that Mrs Warlow was improving, though hard to say in what way.

He looked at her and she, refusing to acknowledge his glance, looked past him at the hastening clouds.

'Are the children getting any fatter?' he laughed, but it was misplaced. He spoke so rarely to the poor that he didn't know how to and resorted to jocularity.

'Fatter?'

'I mean are they eating more?'

'I do buy a bit o' meat.'

'Good. That's good. And have you stopped working for Mr Kempton now?'

'I did a bit o' cardin.'

'But there's no need, Mrs Warlow. You have enough to do as it is.'

'I agreed before. I keeps my word.'

'I see. I'd like it if your children would cease working too, and attend school instead, the village school in Moreham.'

'Mr Kempton must find other boys, then.'

'Yes, he can surely do that.' Kempton, a swaggering bully of a man, illiterate but sharp, who'd made himself rich mopping up small parcels of land on which tenants' dwellings rotted and in which widows cowered from his importunities. Even Powyss knew of Kempton's reputation.

'Jack do like his pennies.'

'Mrs Warlow. May I call you Hannah?'

'Sir.' She pursed her lips. It was another mistake, but he persisted.

'Hannah. Can you read?'

'Father did teach me.'

'Oh.'

'I were a help to him. He did have but one leg; were a soldier.'

'You didn't go to school, then?'

'No. He did teach me reading and names of birds and creatures.'

'I see. But let me tell you, this experiment with your husband is one thing. I have realised, in correspondence with an old friend, that it also enables me to be particularly helpful to the whole Warlow family. If I give you enough money it will be unnecessary for Jack or any of your children to earn pennies. Or you.'

'We all do weed for Mr Kempton. More now he don't have John to work. We all do join at harvestide for Mr Pulverbatch.'

'Please take my point, Hannah. Kempton, Pulverbatch and Bloor will each find others to employ. Your children have the opportunity for education.'

He felt her hostility. Apart from an occasional mild dispute with the cook, Mrs Rentfree, he wasn't used to opposition from a woman. He wanted to shake her, make her agree. Instead, he rang for Jenkins, she took her money and left.

It was only several hours later, after pinching out in the greenhouses, then checking for early leaf drop in the orchard, that his annoyance dissipated.

*

Find clean Bedlinin in Press.   Send up Bathlinin.
    Send up linin <u>Cloaths</u> like Undershirt and Draws.

Draws? Bathlinen? Not had a bath. Water too cold. No dirt, no mud on him. Washes his hands, face sometimes. Beard is so big, there's not much face to wash.

Them've sent down an undershirt, a shirt and drawers all of linen; woollen stockings. Pair of boots, not clogs.

He stands by the fire, slowly takes off his clothes. Took off their clothes when them were boys, to swim in the river. When a day were hot. Only ever a Sunday. Never done it since. Naked, he scratches his stomach, itchy groin. Shivers, hugs himself, rubs his upper arms. Sees long toenails like buzzard feet.

Pulls on underclothes and they're cold. Stockings warm him. The shirt cheers him.

'*Now* I'm a gentleman,' says to himself in the looking-glass. Stands on a chair to see his lower half.

He stuffs his old clothes into the waiter thing, rings the bell, pulls the cord. Never sees them again.

Gentleman's food. Gentleman's clothes. He will write in the journal.

Orgst
i do smell it is summe   it will bee har vist
i hev new

Seeks out the note that came.

42

Cloths   shirt   Und shirt   draws
i do hev but   1 frog now   hee do best lik bred crums

The others had jumped out of the cistern when he wasn't looking. Got lost in dark corners. Didn't write that he found one dead. Dried out. Flat, black frog shape. Took it to the table, peered at it under oil light. Tiny, dried webs and sinews. Broke to bits under his claw nails. He moaned and beat his head with his fists.

*

'Ah, good morning Mrs Warlow, Hannah.' Powyss was standing halfway down the long room, ostensibly searching for a book.

His own awkwardness was matched by hers. He wouldn't keep her long, today, but he must remind her. His *Lateral Effects* notebook was open before him, with the names and ages of all the children, the dates of each meeting with Mrs Warlow and the amounts paid over to her. There was almost nothing written under 'Comments'.

'The new term will begin soon. I hope to hear that all the children are at school.'

'Polly be too young.'

'Except for Polly, then.'

'Yes, sir.'

'I want only what is best for you and your children.'

'Sir.'

He held the money out to her and, as she took it, grasped her hand with both of his by way of insistence. She pulled away, perhaps thinking to hold onto the money, that he had changed his mind and would take the money again, and the back of his hand brushed against her breast.

'Ah!' he said, 'I'll call . . . ' but she rushed out before he'd had a chance to ring for Jenkins.

All he'd meant was to urge and even, perhaps, compel her to do as he said. He thought of the whores in Jermyn Street, tucking the new bank notes into their bodices as their breasts tumbled out. Their pert smiles. Yet now he couldn't forget that he'd touched this woman.

Chapter 3

CATHERINE CROFT FOUND IT HARD to rise early. She resented getting up before everyone else, had lost one past employment through oversleeping. Once up, however, she set about lighting fires, boiling water in the copper and opening shutters without thought, her mind still swimming in the night's vivid dreams.

The new housemaid, Annie Tayler, was young and very pretty. Everyone was alert to the girl's presence, she thought, even Mr Powyss, on the rare occasions when they encountered him. For a while Catherine was put out. She was twenty-nine, unmarried and her nose was too big. Combined with dark-ringed eyes, heavy eyebrows and straight, black hair she reminded one of a determined rook. And however much she pinched her cheeks and made mouths at herself in the looking glass she knew she'd never be described as comely.

For a housemaid she was unusually well educated, however, and could easily answer back when Joseph Jenkins reprimanded her, even if it wasn't a housemaid's place to be other than obedient to the butler. When Catherine was young her school teacher, not yet worn down, had noticed her spark, encouraged her, lent her books, even bribed her mother to let her stay on for a term. With such an example, Catherine had longed for nothing more than to become a teacher herself and move to the town, but her siblings grew in number to such an extent that she'd had to leave home and find work long before she'd wanted to.

She soon realised the pointlessness of envying Annie her looks; was compensated, too, by her higher status, much more by her own superior intelligence. She taught Annie with a briskness and rapidity of speech that made the younger woman gape. They scrubbed floorboards together with soap and sand and hot water; rubbed grates and fire irons with oil, brick dust and scouring paper; dusted, brushed.

'If we were witches we'd never be in want of brooms, Annie. I'm certain witches were only maids who brushed carpets, stoves, bannisters all day and blackened themselves with Servant's Friend.'

Annie giggled, learning quickly that that was the best response to Catherine's odd remarks. Catherine would nudge her heavily at Cook's continuous gin and water sipping and thrill her as they turned back Mr Powyss's sheets.

'This is the only company *he'll* ever have,' she said, thrusting the warming pan down the bed. 'Never taken a woman to bed, they say. Prefers vegetables.'

But now there was Warlow and Annie was shocked.

'Ooh, I'd hate all the dark down there.'

'He's got candles and lamps. He's not in the dark except when he wants to be. He'll get a lot of money, you silly thing. Think of it!'

'Him'll be lonely. I'd be so lonely.'

'Remember all the *stuff* he's got down there. That bed we polished up. Elegant furniture, pictures, a bath. Organ! All those books!'

'Books,' Annie said with horror.

46

'He even gets his pot emptied. Thank the Lord it's Samuel has to carry it to the cesspool, not us!' Shudder from Annie.

'And his food is the same as Mr Powyss's. We don't get so well fed. He lives in luxury, Annie.'

'Oh, I don't know.'

She became gloomy, stopped giggling. Catherine began to find her a trial and divided up many of the tasks so they didn't have to work together so much. Of course Annie had a point. While Catherine longed to possess the glass cabinet and brass bed, the books and chamber organ above all, she'd hate to live in the dark beneath the earth. What was Mr Powyss's experiment *for*? But Warlow had agreed to it, would do well from it in the end.

Meanwhile, Annie would sigh at the other side of the room and mutter 'poor man' over and over again.

And then the cook, Mrs Frances Rentfree, who observed more than anyone suspected, caught her tiptoeing down the stairs towards the lower cellars, hauled her back and sent the weeping girl to Jenkins.

Joseph Jenkins was briefly warmed by having such a pretty girl whimpering in his power. But he pulled himself together, lectured her harshly about getting bees in her bonnet, reminded her that any business of the master's should never be her concern even if it did involve the servants or other working people.

Catherine was appalled at the prospect of being bored by Annie's gloom for the seven years that Warlow would be below. They shared an attic room: Annie might pout all evening and sniff all night. So she reverted to jokes and diversions to educate Annie about human nature. Before long they were laughing in corners and trying Jenkins's patience in the way, according to his experience, maids often did if they were under thirty-two years old.

*

He read Fox's latest letter with the familiar mixture of mild curiosity and irritation. Had he finished the sixpenny *Rights of Man* he'd sent him? It still lay uncut under a pile of papers on the floor of the library. They'd guillotined the king in Paris and now, in November, the queen. Did Fox really think he never saw a newspaper just because he lived so far from the capital?

Hampstead, 21 November 1793
Or as the French Republic would now have it, 1st Frimaire

Dear Powyss,

I was reminded of Mr Warlow by the strange case of how some robbers treated a bank clerk after having removed a considerable amount of money from his pocket book. He was fastened to a plank with strong chains which were themselves fastened to the iron grating of a copper. However, within his reach they left a large mug of water, a bottle of brandy, some porter and a quantity of ham and bread, and a rug by his side. Such humanity!

But I joke, as you know, for of course you neither use chains nor relieve Warlow of his money. Quite the contrary. In this test of yours, should what Warlow endures be called <u>humane</u> suffering? You'll reply that <u>if</u> there is suffering (since you have provided so much comfort) it is for a higher purpose.

No doubt that is what they're saying in Paris this year, having done away with their king and now the queen (for whom a great mass was held in the Spanish Ambassador's chapel in Manchester Square and another in Winchester). You will rightly object to my saying this, and yet there is something in it.

Then came the wagging finger.

Do you remember how I once accused you, together with all gardeners and horticulturalists, of amorality? For you have no moral decisions to make about your plants, no dilemmas of conscience. You act with impunity. No bodies are hurt, no souls destroyed!

Now with your new experiment you have entered the moral world. Powyss, you must weigh your actions with care.

What did he mean? He'd thought out the *Investigation* with the greatest care! And as far as Warlow was concerned everything was in order, there were no further actions to be taken.

Mrs Warlow? Well, he fancied the awkwardness with the woman gradually seemed to be going. He made sure a basket of Ashmead's Kernels was taken to her and the Warlow children in time for Christmas, together with a bottle of Jenkins's elderberry wine. Though she still looked down whenever he addressed her during those brief weekly meetings, he strongly sensed her eyes upon him when his back was turned, or when he was searching through a drawer. The Bellissime d'Hiver pears would not be ready for a month, but when they were he'd give her a box of them himself and perhaps with such a gift he'd *compel* her to look at him.

*

Later, she says to herself: No. He be not like other masters. By now he would have forced me.

He did not mean to touch me for I am thin. A man do not like a thin woman. John did often tell me so.

Mother were comely they did say. More so nor I. Why Kempton did let us stay when she were widowed, couldn't pay the rent.

She did thrive on suckling. Were lucky with her bairns, until the illness took so many so sudden. Poor Mother.

I have buried six, as many as do live.

No, he do not want me. I were wrong to think he would take back the money. He is not like John. Nor Kempton.

But always he do want to make me do as he say. I think he will tell me not to come again and that be best.

*

D sember end
It have not snod   I no that from the   gratin   no sno hav falln
down   it did sno wen I cum in Aperl

He's become used to the journal. It passes time. He asks them to send a slip of paper with the new month when it changes. So, December.

Once, time were stretches of work. Stop to eat and drink. Another stretch. Orders from Kempton: plough Riddings End. Harness up. Walk horses across the common, up the lane. Plough half an acre of clay, him steerin, Dick whippin. Bread, bottle of cold tea. Plough another half. Horses back, brush 'em down, sackin over, keep off chill, hay to trough, water, lock 'em in, report to Kempton. December'd be diggin snow. Dig out sheep, dig out pigs. Home. Tiredness blotted with cider, bread, bit of bacon if she's got any. Up again, day-break. Hannah fussin the water to boil.

No work now. No day's orders. Kempton'd find other men.

Not tired. Tries yawning, can't. Keeping fire in is his work.

Not hungry. Stokes fire again. Meals descend. He rings the bell, hauls up greasy plates. Full pisspot. Distant clatter somewhere other side of the nailed door. Muffled thumps way above.

Powyss told him to write the journal. Each day. Not done it each day. But sometimes he does. Sits at the table, opens the book, grasps a pen, throws it down. Nails dig into his palm when he holds it.

I hav bit of my nales

He writes this guiltily. But it's not *cuttin*, is it!

Or I cannt writ
it wer Cri CHRISMUS Mr POISS did send mor beer.
Verri good Beaf Mins Pye

He experiments with capital letters. One day he opens a book, finds a picture like the man above the fire. Strange clothes, animal skin most like. No shoes. Two guns, sword. Hat like a church steeple. Opposite is writing in capitals:

THE
L I FE
AND
STR ANGE SUR PRI   SURPRIZIN
AD VENT   ADVENT URES ADVENTURES
OF
RO   BINSON   CR U SOE
Of YORK   MA RIN ER MARINER

Thinks he'll use letters like that. The book's a journal, sure to. Of this man Robinson. Thinks he'll read more another day.

No snow but it'll come. And cold comes down the shaft. He thinks of the children squeezing round the fire. Pushing each other till he whacks 'em back. Down here he's got the whole fire to himself.

Then all of a sudden he wants to be at home. Wants to fuck Hannah quick and hard while the children toss in the other bed. Make her not try to get away. Feels sorry for himself. Just like that. All of a sudden.

*

Powyss would attend church reluctantly at Christmas, but never invited the parson or anyone else to a meal on either of the two days. He always ate and drank more than usual because Mrs Rentfree would not tolerate cooking for a 'heathen'. 'If I cannot make Christmas food at Christmastide I might just as well give up the ghost,' she said every year, and insisted on a goose as well as beef and ham, a great mince pie, a spiced pudding, junkets and cider cake. Powyss didn't protest, and felt that the servants, though they were few in number, must be allowed their celebration. After he had eaten, they would gorge on Mrs Rentfree's feast, and drink primrose and dandelion wine until they were red and merry. Late into the night, after Powyss had gone to bed, they would dance to Catherine's spinet, bob for apples, play Snapdragon, and, when Cook was sufficiently inebriated and snoring, Pop.

This was the first Christmas that Powyss hadn't gone to church at all. The experiment was sharpening his reason, he told himself. Excellent! For years, without belief, he had attended Moreham church at Christmas and Easter as a regrettable duty he thought he couldn't abandon. It was hypocrisy. He would no longer do it.

Instead he planned a day of reading on practical matters. He would check through *The Gardeners Daily Assistant* to see if it was a suitable reference for his master gardener Price, who, he feared, had little reading, and assess for himself Winter's *New and Compendious System of Husbandry*, of which he'd read a most crushing review. After that he'd spend a couple of hours with Adams' *Essays on the Microscope*, which he'd purchased with his own instrument. Insect transformations particularly fascinated him, though this was not a good time of year to find specimens. He must content himself with a Peacock butterfly drawn to the warmth of his winter candle from hopeless hibernation.

To continue working his way through Gibbon, volumes IV to VI, would bring the day to an end, he thought, but after an enormous dinner he fell to drowsing and, whenever he woke he struggled not to hear the muffled merriment, wondered if below, Warlow was trying not to hear sounds that, he realised, might creep down through the lift shaft. Probably the man was asleep after so much food, extra beer and some of Jenkins's sweet wine. In which case that would be scarcely different from all other Christmases, through which he knew the village drank itself dry from the 25th till the 27th of December.

As a young boy Herbert Powyss had not much enjoyed Christmas. He'd recognised his father's bluster when landed neighbours came, had sensed its falseness, how sometimes his father said the wrong thing. He'd noticed the flash of supposedly discreet glances between guests. And been aware, too, of his sickly mother's anxiety at the social demands, her reluctance to celebrate. Events like these and at other times during the year had taught him to dread society.

He had always failed to respond satisfactorily to his mother's piety. At twelve he'd doubted the virgin birth, at fourteen the existence of the all-seeing God worshipped with such tedium for hours each Sunday. What boy with solitary tendencies could stand the existence of an All-Knowing, All-Prying? He kept these views to himself for as long as he could. When his mother, even in his earliest memories, died soon after his fifteenth birthday, he neither expected to meet her again in spirit form nor believed that the presence of the parson at her bedside during her last illness could have given her more than superficial comfort. He mourned her, missed her. Missed the rare sunburst of praise, even her aloofness fraught with disappointment.

He glanced up at her portrait above the fireplace. It was a Reynolds, commissioned at the peak of his father's wealth, and from which, even before his father had died though not before his mother's death, the paint had crumbled and fallen off in flakes. The red pigment had given out particularly fast:

his mother's ghostly white face gazed vaguely from an ever-blackening background.

No, Christmas was for others to celebrate.

*

Book's too hard. About the man Robinson. He raises his head from the table; candle's spitting to an end. Must've fallen asleep. Around him empty plates, jug, journal. He pushes them away.

Morning, is it? Night? Not Christmas no more – he drank all that. What'd he do at home when them'd eaten all his wages? Axe timber for Pulverbatch. Sick with drinking all them days, fingers numb. Same for the others. Wages cut when them didn't get on fast enough. Damned Pulverbatch. Damned Kempton.

He lights a new fire. Checks the grating: still no snow.

They'm axin, now, sure to. No, he tells himself, wishing to be there, no, I *work here now.* Fifty pound a year I gets. *Fifty pound for writin.*

He lights the oil lamp. Write journal later, after the next meal, he promises himself. Tamps tobacco into a pipe. Closes the Robinson book. Too hard. Schoolmaster never give us them words. There's more books in the case with the glass. He dreads them but makes himself open up the delicate doors. The first book he pulls out is words, all words. And the second. Rage begins like a pain in the jaw.

Then there's pictures. Animals. Look at that! – *horses, cows, bulls, goats, sheep!*

He pores over it. There's stoats, cats, bears. Dogs, hares, squirrels, beaver. There's animals they've made up – horse with stripes, bull with hair all over. THE BLACK TI GER. Glaring, about to bite. Can't get that out of his head. He reads the names, not the other words. Likes best the little scenes – the horse in the ferry boat, dog swimming behind. Boy riding a goat. Crow threatening a frog. Man shitting in bushes behind a wall, smoking his pipe, woman holding her nose.

But oh! Ach! His eyes sting with the staring and the fire is smoking, but here at the end he laughs in disgust, disbelief. THE SA RA GOY – a fox-rat thing with an open belly full of squirming bodies. *Ach!* THE FLYING OP OSS UM. THE RING- TAILED MAC AU CO. *Oh!* THE OR AN OUT ANG, OR WILD MAN OF THE WOODS. *Aah!*

He turns the pages with horror, with laughter. Hoots with amazement. THE BA BOON! Fixes finally on THE DOG-FACED BA BOON in its cloak of hair, staring greedily at a fruit in its hands. Be them *men*? Be them *devils*?

*

Early on a morning too cold for anything except a brief outdoor inspection Powyss decided to try a prolonged listening session.

'Jenkins, has Warlow breakfasted?'

'No sir. No dishes have been sent up from yesterday.'

'Sleeping it off I suppose.'

'Sir.' He invariably failed not to notice Jenkins's disapproval of the whole Warlow affair.

Later, when he gathered Warlow was up and about, he cleared aside the books and papers that disguised his listening hole and knelt upon the Ottoman, notebook at the ready.

So often he detected smell before sound; sometimes only smell, no sound worth recording. There it was, Warlow's breakfast. He'd always kept food smells out of the library, the room being well away from kitchen and dining room. Still, for the experiment he had to tolerate it.

He wrote the date, time, recorded smell but no sound and gradually his eyes closed with boredom. He dreamed that he was arriving at the Royal Society (only it wasn't the Royal

Society but some grand building in Paris) and was due to deliver his paper on the experiment at 10 o'clock. Rooting in his bag he found nothing but blank paper. The room was crowded with expectant men and he was forced to extemporise to mutterings and gasps from the audience. He raised his voice to drown them out, shouting above the hubbub and woke suddenly to real calls and jeers from below.

Warlow was making a whole string of noises though the words, unfortunately, were too indistinct to make out. There was a considerable variety of tone and he scribbled down everything he heard as fast as he could. Hums of appreciation or enjoyment, gasps of astonishment or disbelief, perhaps, guffaws, hoots, prolonged bouts of laughter that ceased abruptly.

The man must be directly below, sitting at the table. Was he dreaming? Remembering some past incidents? Or was he reading a book? He ran through the books he knew to be there. *Crusoe*? Possibly, but no, it was hardly funny, nor that shocking. There was only one writer who might make you laugh and gasp: Voltaire. Warlow was reading *Candide*.

*

There's tapping. He's counted three meals so it must be evening. Strong dark meat he didn't recognise, boiled celery, plum dumpling. Pint of porter. Cake from Christmas.

Scratches his scalp, beard, now down to his chest. Thinks he imagined the sound, but it's there all right. Tap, tap. Other side of the nailed-up door.

He doesn't move. Mustn't reply. *To get his reward he must speak to no one.* Then it stops.

Is it Hannah? No. Powyss said him'd take care of them. And what'd her want to say to him? Her's glad, very glad he's gone, he's sure of *that*.

Days later it happens again. In his new boots he creeps

over to the door. Pushes his hair away, presses his ear up against the wood.

Quiet, all quiet. Can he hear breathing? Or is it in his head? One of them flying creatures?

A woman's voice. Whispering.

'Mr Warlow? John? I know you're there. Other side of the door, aren't you?'

He jerks back, accidentally scratches the door with long nails.

'I can hear you're there.' He thusts his fingers into his mouth, gnaws.

'I know you're there, John. You poor man. Aren't you afeared? Aren't you lonely, all on your own?'

He's breathing hard. Mustn't reply. He's got used to saying his thoughts out loud. Likes the sound of himself: he's his own friend. *Don't speak now!* Perhaps it's a trap. To make him talk, lose the money.

'John?'

A young voice. Who is she?

'John? Listen to me. It's Annie. I work in the house and in the kitchen.'

He doesn't know her.

'You'll be so cold in there, John. It does snow now, right hard. There be drifts. The sheep are lost.'

'Not all of 'em,' he thinks, though he mustn't say. Her's a housemaid; what does her know of sheep?

'You'll be so cold.'

He wants to tell her he's right warm. And not to send any more fish. But no.

'Oh, I hear someone coming. Quick!' And she's gone.

Back again the following day. Tapping again. He's there at the door, eyes wide in the dark. Candle left behind.

'I know what you look like, John. What you *looked* like. I did see you once. I reckon you look different now. I reckon you've long hair and a beard?'

He listens to her waiting.

'You can answer me, John. I'll not tell of it.'

Her's just the other side, he thinks. He's pressing up against the door. Is her pressing up against it, too? *Pressing.*

'John. I could tell you things, John.'

He groans to himself. What things? He likes the sound of her voice. Her closeness. *But maybe it's the voice of the devil.* Ah now! Isn't that what they say? *The devil speaks in the voice of an angel to tempt you.* Temptation! That's what it is!

He moves away from the door, tiptoes back. His boots are soft. That's good. Gets behind the table to protect himself. It may break in, this devil. Thinks of the shape behind the door. Black it is, with cloven hoofs. Like the great hairy bull in the picture book. But standing on two legs, holding the end of a long tail. Fierce with flames and horns. And bubbies he'd like to squeeze and a lovely voice.

He says the name of Jesus three times. Then three times more. Three more. All his fingers except the littl'un.

Our Father, save me from infernold divils!

There's a scuffling, a man's voice.

'Come away! Stupid girl!' He recognises Jenkins. 'What are you thinking of? He's not allowed to speak.'

'It's cruel. Poor man! So lonely, all by himself. And his wife ...' Her words shut off as by a hand.

'He agreed to it. Didn't have to, did he? He must abide there.' All this shouted for his hearing. More scuffling. Steps retreat. Silence.

He sits down, sweating. Lights a pipe. No devil.

For some time he's buoyed by the episode. Recalls it again and again. *The girl is thinkin of him!* Her's kind. Young. Pretty no doubt. Annie. Pretty name. Strong too, liftin buckets, pans in the kitchen, sure to. He pictures her reddened by steam. Sleeves rolled above the elbow. Dress hitched. Meeting him in Horseshoe Copse. Eager. Greedy.

For he'll be famous when he comes out. Powyss said so.

He'll be a *wonder*. Them'll all want him. And Hannah? Tired her is. His mother was tired out in the end. When he comes out most like Hannah'll be dead. Once he wanted her. But that were long afore. This Annie'll wait for him. Will she? When he has fifty pound a year she will.

Yes, these thoughts buoy him up for days.

*

Jenkins marched Annie along the snow-cleared path to Powyss, occupied in the hothouse with Price. There, despite drifts blown up against one side, the atmosphere was pleasantly warm. Powyss, separating seed with a quill, waved them away, telling Jenkins to deal with her as he thought fit. Price gaped then sneered.

Jenkins knew it would be hard to replace the girl with another so fair, so shapely. In his mind he sifted through the young women of Moreham one by one, rejecting each, particularly if they were ill favoured. Not a single one was as dimpled as Annie, who in time might be persuaded of his worth despite their great age difference. He could do with a wife. Must be obedient, not like that Croft girl.

Yet she must be punished. She needed beating, but he knew Powyss wouldn't allow it. Soft, he is, not a proper master at all. Now if *he* were master, he'd keep strict order. Get rid of Price and Catherine Croft with her cheek. He reckoned if he made Annie give up her garret bed and sleep on a truckle in the kitchen, she'd be down at the nailed door all over again, so he settled for no pay for half a year and fifteen minutes of shouting and threatening to make her sob and snivel. He enjoyed that.

Catherine was not surprised. If Annie had looked like *her* she'd have lost her employment right away. But she wouldn't turn bitterness into a habit. Especially when she thought of Christmas, how she'd sat on Abraham Price's lap playing

Pop and, to her great surprise, he'd reached into her clothing when no one was looking. She never knew he had an eye for her. Thought he, like the rest of them, looked only at Annie. She'd enjoyed it till she saw Cook wake up from her gin and water doze and felt obliged to slap him. Later, Cook nodding again, he was forfeit and must take off his jacket, then waistcoat, then shirt and she saw how white his chest was below his sunburned face and neck. He stood up in front of them all and looked as though he'd crow like a cock.

It would probably be better to continue working beside Annie than put up with someone new as she'd have had to if Annie had been sacked. Some churchy, canting girl, perhaps. Annie was stupid, easily influenced. She'd shake her out of her mood. She enjoyed making her giggle. Besides, there really was the matter of Hannah Warlow. Between the two of them they could surely find out what was going on with her and Mr Powyss. *Something* must be happening during those visits, them alone together every week. She'd encourage Annie to make up to Samuel and get him to tell what he knew.

Chapter 4

POWYSS WAS NOT REALLY HAPPY with the listening tube. He'd placed a low stool to listen with greater ease. In fact he rather enjoyed kneeling on his Ottoman rug; thought he began to understand why the Turks did it five times a day; then accused himself of frivolousness.

The problem was that, apart from that one day, Warlow wasn't making much noise, and what noise he did make was indistinct. There'd been no repeat of the extraordinary sounds Powyss had recorded soon after Christmas. He'd been cheered at the thought of Warlow reading *Candide*, wondered how it might influence what he wrote in the journal.

He could hear him moving about but he couldn't always determine exactly where the man was. It was a mistake to have sent him a pair of boots instead of clogs. Even the carpet, a sizeable Ottoman, was a mistake, for though aesthetically pleasing it dulled sound. As he'd anticipated, Warlow was talking to himself but he could rarely make out the words, except for occasional oaths. Sometimes a few notes sounded from the organ, or he heard rhythmless surges of noise as

Warlow banged his hands up and down in imitation of a real player. There was whistling: bits of tune, always unfinished.

He'd recorded meals and knew now that Warlow disliked fish and venison and wouldn't touch sauces or pickles ('scraped to the side of the plate' it was reported). Junkets went uneaten; ice cream was returned, pools of delicate scum in porcelain dishes.

There'd been the matter of clothing.

'Mr Warlow has not sent any more clothes to be washed, sir. Only once since he went down,' Jenkins reported. 'That is many weeks ago, sir.'

'Yes, yes. Indeed. Then will you please send down clean linen together with a note. With *instructions*, Jenkins.'

'Would you like to see the note when it is written, sir?'

'No, but ensure it's easy for him to understand. I had wanted to avoid notes. Notes *from* Warlow are admissable. I told him that. But notes *to* him could easily turn into conversation, which would go against the spirit of the experiment.'

As to the clothes when they were finally sent up, well, no doubt they'd be feculent – he'd prevent Jenkins from giving him details, though it was clear Jenkins would relish doing so. He recorded the fact of what Warlow had not done, but there was no need for more. It was bad enough that one aspect of the experiment was not functioning perfectly. For his belief that a man could survive without human contact was dependent upon that man living well. The experiment was being jeopardised by Warlow's stubbornness or stupidity or whatever it was.

Then there was Warlow's request for notification of each new month. That meant that his sense of time was weak, his journal-keeping probably erratic and without precise timekeeping Powyss's paper would lack yet more strength. Powyss's longing for praise from the Royal Society lay in a drawer of his mind no longer secret from himself. It was true that the Society's annual *Transactions* had been shrinking both in number and quality. Too many members were merely honorary. All the more important, then, to produce something undeniably good.

So at present he had little to report to Benjamin Fox. No, he had *not* cut the pages of the *Rights of Man*, certainly not read it and he still felt irritated at Fox's implication that having 'entered the moral world' the *Investigation* might be immoral. It was easier to put aside Fox's letter than to reply to it.

And far more satisfactory to take himself off to the hothouse. There his senses rippled like cat's fur. This year cucumbers and melons were spreading great leaves, pushing out young fruit. He poked among them, counting, pinching out. Along the roof hung bunches of tiny grapes, acid-green.

Here, too, he recorded: temperature, germination time, quantity of water, production of fruit or vegetables per barrow-load of manure applied at the end of last year, rate of growth in hotbed as opposed to greenhouse.

Most days he met with Abraham Price.

'The seeds we put to soak, Price, has anything happened overnight?'

'Nothing. Another day, isn't it.'

'These need tying in, don't you think?'

'Maybe.'

Perhaps because of the frequency with which they saw each other they often spoke little. Would stand by a tray of seedlings, a dish of seeds, considering; move round a bed of young trees in the orchard nursery, inspecting Price's recent grafting. When necessary Powyss would issue an instruction or Price would bring him a diseased leaf, point to a barrowful of dug-out suckers.

They would walk together along a wall of espaliered fruit or a line of cold frames, wordless. Each grew to comprehend the meaning of the other's various hums, burrs, throat-clearings. In Powyss's view, Price's horticultural understanding was a fine one; he knew nothing of the surly Welshman's life.

'I'm pleased with *Magnolia virginiana*, Price, though her buds have yet to open. Do you have any worries about her?' He'd taken to the local use of the personal pronoun for objects when speaking to Price, though Price himself referred to everything as 'he'. He wouldn't know that *Magnolia* couldn't be masculine.

'No.'

'An American tree, you know, Price.'

'I know that. Tree of Liberty.'

He'd been taken aback by this remark and the sudden gruff singing that followed, *sotto voce*, so that he couldn't make out Price's words. He recalled the incident when guiltily filing away Fox's unanswered letter. Fox's Hampstead garden, small, walled, was entirely political. He had suddenly sprung an interest, begun planting it in 1792 with Tom Paine's exile to America. He grew only American plants, *for they have been born in the soil that now nurtures Paine,* he had written, causing Powyss an outburst of derision, which fell away when he realised that one of his favourite books was the enormous volume of Mark Catesby's *Natural History of Carolina, Florida and the Bahama Islands* with its wonderful illustration of *Magnolia altifissa.* And that many of his own best new plants came from America, such as the delicate *Dodecatheon meadia,* the *Ceanothus americanus.* The proud juniper that stood impervious to waves of winter snow.

*

It was a relief to put Fox's letter out of sight. Fox could wait. With his Unitarian colleagues, his radical friends (many of them the same), his reading of newspapers, new books, Fox had plenty to occupy him, didn't need constant letters from Powyss.

Powyss's own reading was extensive. A pile of books and papers waited by his desk. *The History of Philosophy from the earliest Times to the beginning of the present Century* by William Enfield LL.D. That would probably go straight onto the shelves together with *A Catalogue of engraved British Portraits from Egbert the Great to the Present Time*. The latest volumes of *Annals of Agriculture* – Arthur Young's *Travels* and Thunberg's *Travels* – also remained uncut; perhaps he'd get round to them later. Vol. 1 of Cartwright's *Journal of Transactions and Events on the Coast of Labrador* had been recommended by Fox for its account of Esquimaux women visiting London. There were several papers in the last two years' *Philosophical Transactions* that he'd intended to study more thoroughly – the remarkable failure of haddocks on the coasts of Northumberland, Durham and Yorkshire; Wedgwood's 'Experiments on the Production of Light from different Bodies by Heat and Attrition'; and especially Hunter's observations on bees and Dr Darwin on vegetable respiration. He hadn't given up on Sprengel's *Secret of Nature Displayed* yet. But since the beginning of his own experiment his concentration had gradually slackened. Often, his mind wandered to Hannah Warlow.

He'd only ever cared for plants. Every woman he'd ever slept with had been paid for, and to care for a woman you bought was like caring for a ripe fruit or a frangipane pastry. The pleasure was soon over, soon forgotten. Years ago, on his travels, he'd invariably encountered the demimonde, for in his youth loss of virginity, the alternation of flattery and mockery, the constant passing over of money were all part of the Grand Tour. He purchased a few moments of ecstasy, a dose of pox and pieces of antique statuary. The glorious trees and light of Rome mingled in his mind with mercury pills. And so it was easier after his father's death, his mother already dead in his childhood, to create rational beauty at Moreham, unmixed with either expectation or unpleasantness. What Catherine had told Annie was less malice than fact: he'd never taken a woman to bed at Moreham. He disliked the neighbouring women, wouldn't risk the maids because of the inconvenience of having to sack them and find replacements when they became pregnant. He became entirely absorbed in drawing up plans for the house and carrying out horticultural experiments. It was enough to visit Mrs Clavering's superior house in Jermyn Street every so often, sometimes treat himself to two or three whores at once, and occasionally, in the privacy of the library, study his collection of small erotic figurines stored in an unmarked drawer.

Since the unfortunate episode when his hand brushed against her he'd kept short his meetings with Hannah. Sometimes she appeared about to speak but never did. She would answer him of course, but it was always he who spoke first.

He was surprised at himself. Of course, speaking to a woman once a week these last months was much more than usual. Talk occupied little time in Jermyn Street. Physically the woman was no longer pretty nor painted like the harlots at Clavering's. Each Monday he'd noticed more of her appearance: the pleasing oval face with its delicate features, how her eyes startled, being sometimes grey, sometimes blue depending on the light of day. He'd overheard talk that her mother had been a beauty and perhaps *some* of it had come through to the daughter. The grace with which she carried herself was extraordinary for a woman of her kind.

But her continuing resistance, her suspicion challenged him. He'd tried so often to make her look at him and when at last she did, steady, critical, he suddenly felt desire.

After all these years could he really be more interested in her than his plants, trees and flowers? Surely not.

*

Catherine went to collect vegetables for Cook, for she and Annie were housemaids and kitchen maids rolled into one. Her attitude to Mrs Rentfree was ambivalent. She despised her for her utter dependency upon gin and water. Catherine's life had been determined by drunkenness, her father's. Each time he was too drunk to work her mother took in washing, however advanced she was in pregnancy, and Catherine had to help. The pregnancies were continuous, as were the lines of dripping linen, hung from the low ceiling of their cottage. Catherine's image of herself as a teacher, leading an entirely different life from her mother's, shrank into dreams. She still had such dreams. The closest she'd got to their realisation was the instruction of new housemaids in polishing grates and lighting fires.

Yet Cook was never incapable and Catherine admired a certain obstinacy in her. Though she could barely write (Catherine must help her with household accounts, notes, letters, as Powyss refused to employ a housekeeper), Cook knew when she could resist the master. While she was willing to prepare some of Mr Powyss's newfangled fruits, she refused to handle squashes, for instance.

'Ugly beasts, no Christian will eat them,' she said. Expressed her feelings subversively by serving salsify, so tiresome to peel, with far too much Jamaica pepper or on the contrary, broiling cucumbers with nothing to relieve their insipidity.

Every day a basket of vegetables and fruit was left for collection outside one of the greenhouses. Catherine had seen little of Abraham Price since Christmas, when he'd fingered as much of her body as he could reach during the game of Pop. Now he was there with an earthy basket.

'You've come for the dinner, is it?'

'Yes, Mr Price. Abraham.'

He stared at her meaningfully until she looked down. Then he said:

'I did like your spinit.'

'I learned to play at school. Sometimes I do without the music notes. It just comes to me.' Then she burst out: 'I only slapped you because of Cook,' and he, scowling, turned and stumped off.

Now she'd wrecked her chances. How stupid! How foolish!

She was furious at herself for sounding so childish, as bad as Annie. Putting herself at such a disadvantage. He'd despise her now. She sighed to herself. Probably he'd only acted out of drunkenness at Christmas anyway.

Who else *was* there? Samuel was far too young, Jenkins too old; the one timid, the other puffed up with self-importance like a toad; and anyway both had eyes for Annie alone. There was no one in the village even had she the time to go and look, and the labourers in the garden were beneath consideration. She was herself getting old. She'd like a husband, one or two children. She didn't want to wither. Or turn to gin and water.

*

Hannah puts the money in her pocket, sets off from the house. She's refused China tea in a cup with a curly handle. She didn't always refuse, especially in cold weather, but she dislikes the questions they ask in the kitchen.

She'd never had to do with them before, Mrs Rentfree and Catherine. But now she must encounter them frequently and they look at her in a prying way. Have begun to ask about Mr Powyss.

'How do you like the master, Hannah?'

'Quite well.'

'Has he shown you all them things in cabinets? Mr Jenkins say there be *all sorts* in drawers.'

'No, he have not.'

'You were a long time with master today, Hannah.'

'He did talk.'

'What did he talk of?'

'Oh, I forget.' Better tell them nothing.

It's a warm summer day. She thinks to walk by the orchard to see the young fruit. Goes through the gate, past glass-houses, glimpses men weeding in the kitchen garden.

The children have stopped asking about John.

'He's gone away to work,' she told them. They do as they wish without him there to use his stick or fists upon them, David, little John, George. Jack goes off. Hours at a time. Where to? She cannot stop him. Margaret is good, helps her with washing and cooking and Polly the youngest is growing now. They are all glad of more to eat. Shoes.

Without John it's like when she were a girl after Father were killed. Mother let us be, she reminds herself, no man to make us cry, except when Mr Kempton visited. I did always think it best to be a widow woman like Mother. She did love all her babies though she surely didn't love Kempton. I did like to help, feeding hens, yeanlings.

She thinks to get a few chickens now with the money; John were always too poor. The young ones can collect the eggs, George, Polly.

She imagines John living in a great big room like Mr Powyss's library, snoring on a bed with velvet hangings. But she almost never thinks of him. At home she lets Polly and Margaret sleep in her bed, the oldest and the youngest, to keep them from the fighting, kicking boys in the other. She sleeps as she's never slept before.

She thinks: Mr Powyss have no wife. They do say he never have a woman.

But he did not say to not come again. And I think he like me. That time. His hand did brush against me, he did blush.

Surely all masters do as they wish.

It is good with John gone. Like being a widow woman, like Mother. Except for Kempton.

Mr Powyss is a gentleman. I'm not his servant, but I takes his money and gives him nothing for it.

*

The tone of Fox's letter written at the end of August 1794 was sharp though ostensibly smoothed over with jokes. That was his way. He complained about Powyss's lack of reply, putting it down to his absorption in the *Investigation*, together with his solitariness.

You were always a man for whom numquam minus solus quam cum solus *most perfectly applied. Even when you were a boy!*

London was in a frenzy of war, he wrote, with volunteers marching all over the place and accusations of treason made at the slightest suspicion. It concerned *him*, for his friends were mostly radicals and yet more of them had been arrested. Annual parliaments, universal suffrage, Powyss couldn't bring himself to care about these things.

Of course events in France are hideous. They guillotined their own monster of reason Robespierre a month ago.
But our rationality is so unlike the Gallic. There is a wonderful growth of common sense among the people in the form of the London Corresponding Society whose huge gatherings in Hackney and Chalk Farm I have attended and observed closely. They have my namesake, the hirsute, grimy and brilliant Charles James to support them as well as Mr Sheridan, both excellent speakers. Yet the government is certainly afraid for they have suspended Habeas Corpus. 'Tis a government that throws crusts to the poor while paying spies great sums to listen at holes. I suppose it is something that good men, radicals like Hardy, Thelwall and my dear friend Horne Tooke get a trial at all.

And on and on. Powyss stuffed the letter into a drawer.

He was angry. He found himself thinking of Mrs Warlow too often. The slight figure of a woman who'd yet borne many children, her firm tread, the enquiring, still reluctant eyes he'd at last engaged. Her presence in his library had become exotic, irresistible.

But he'd heard her supposedly beautiful mother had been a feckless widow, giving birth to a stream of children sired by the despicable Kempton. (What *was* this, that he listened to servants' gossip!) Probably she was no better than her mother, who also went mad, they said. And in any case she was just a poor woman! One of the poor Fox was continually writing about, one of the poor who, according to Fox, needed more bread and the vote, for he even extended the franchise to women. Well, at least she was getting more bread. But that he spoke to her at all was an accident; he'd never have noticed her if it hadn't been for the experiment, and now he ought only to be interested in recording changes of an observable kind in her and her children for the *Lateral Effects* section. He turned from the window in disgust as though trying to turn away from himself.

But it was Monday and she came again.

With his notebook open and pen ready, he asked stiffly about her and her children. Wrote down little enough. What more was there to record from last week?

He gave her the money, her hands square and short-nailed. They would be rough-skinned but reliable whatever they touched. The thought aroused him.

He remembered having seen two of her girls run out of the kitchen garden, a tall one pulling the hand of a little, round-faced one. He asked about this.

'Mr Price did say they could get some sea-kale and carrots.'

'*Did* he now?' She was on her way out. They were halfway down the room, near to the beautiful globes at which she no longer stared in amazement.

'Seeing as how you do give us things. He did say.'

She could have as much sea-kale and carrots as she wanted, he thought, and better vegetables than that. Some fruit: cante-loupe, grapes, apricots. Price's gesture, however, he recognised as insubordination rather than generosity. He must keep an eye on him. It looked as though a pattern was emerging.

'Did you enjoy the kale, Hannah?'

'Oh yes, Mr Powyss. We be grateful.'

He didn't want such an answer, he wanted something else. She used that tone because she thought she should, or perhaps to protect her children. He preferred her resistance, even her hostility. Annoyed, he was about to raise his voice, recalled, in time, that Warlow beat her, so he didn't, but not before an image of Warlow rolling over her in bed revolted him into action.

He grasped her shoulders. 'Hannah, there's no need to be grateful!' Her eyes caught him; she moved out of his hold.

'Remember, it's part of the experiment that I support you and your children. You know that quite well.

'Let your two girls come into the garden. To look at the flowers. Remind me how old they are now.' He made as if to return to his notebook.

'Margaret be thirteen, Polly four.'

'Would they like to do that?'

'Oh yes. They'd be glad.'

'Good. Remember it's my side of the arrangement with your husband.' This was said as much to remind himself as her. He rang the bell to curb his impulse to pull her to him.

'I can do no less ...' he said, leaving the ellipsis hanging. Then suddenly as she turned he bent and kissed her clumsily on the cheek. Unsure, she lingered for a moment, but Jenkins came in and she left.

*

He always listens for Annie but her's not come back. Wonders if they've got rid of her. If her's gone her'll have no choice. No other work. He thinks of Moreham men enjoying her. Under hedges. In barns. Behind walls. Fucking in barns is best. How many threepences a day? Like Sarah Gibbs her'll do it for a penny. He groans. Scratches himself hard. Groans.

When he's not thinking of Annie he's listening. Listening. He's certain he can hear when leaves drop down the shaft. He'll hear new frogs next year when they fall, sure to. When it's dark you hear better. When you can't see much. Like now.

Always dark. There's candles of course. Candles! Sometimes he longs for the familiar smell of rancid rushes. Grease of bacon scummings fizzling. There's oil lamp when he bothers to fill it. But nothing's bright down here. Nothing moves either. No sudden birds. No trees cracking in a gale. No children wrigglin, fidgetin, pinchin each other.

Them as can't see hears like dogs at night. Thinks of the blind beggar in Moreham when he was a boy. Them ran after to taunt him. He always heard when them were coming, other end of street. Them'd tiptoe and he heard. Hid in bushes and he knew them were there. People said he could hear three mile away.

So he hears when they load the waiter thing two floors up. One day he decides to open the door to it, hear more. Can just make out, right up the shaft:

'He'll not eat that, Cook.'

'It's exact same as the master's, Mr Jenkins. That's the rule.'

'Oh, cut him another slice of beef. Mr Powyss'll not know.'

He never thought of that, did he! Powyss. That he'd *listen* up the waiter thing. So he keeps the door open when he sends up his used plates to the kitchen.

'Here's his plates. Left your strawberry custard, Mrs Rentfree.'

'Picks at his food! Don't know what Mr Powyss was thinking of. All cause of being a heathen. It don't say you should give away strawberry custard in the Holy Book. He don't read his Bible, do he. All them stacks o' books and papers, Jenkins do say. And no Holy Book.'

'He did put a Bible with the other books for John Warlow. Besides, some heathens are good people.'

A loud drawing in of breath. 'I'd give him a loaf a day and a piece of cheese. An onion. Stead of all these best dishes. Why should I cook for *him*?'

'You cook for Mr Powyss, Mrs Rentfree. He just gets a bit of that. And he isn't hungry. He's not doing any work.'

'What's he *do* all day long? Whilst we toil.'

He wants to bawl up at them. No. Better not.

'Don't wash hisself. That we saw from his clothes, did we not, Catherine?'

'Oh poor man!'

Annie! Surely!

'That's enough from *you. Hussy!*'

'Perhaps we should send some warm water. He's only got cold water to wash in.' That's Catherine again.

'And every day the *blessed pot*! If I'd ever've thought there'd be pots o' turds in my kitchen I'd never have taken the position.'

'Samuel whisks them away as fast as he can, Mrs Rentfree.'

'I should think so! Filthy, *disgusting* it is.'

He shuts the lift shaft door. Writes:

Send worm worter   lik you sed
*   Plaes*

It comes down in a bucket with a note.

Wash Yourself with Soap
*   You are Not Allowed to Listen.*
from Mrs Rentfree, Cook, Moreham House

This annoys him. He writes back:

Mr POWIS   niver did say no <u>lisnin</u>

But when he tries again there's always silence when they

74

take his tray off the waiter thing. The door up there shuts quickly. Voices are deadened. There's just distant bangs. Scrapes. He growls, kicks over the bucket.

*

She says to herself: he have kissed me twice. He have wanted it a long time, Mr Powyss. I am sure of that. I felt it.

John were always a rough man.

Surely it is not all he want, Mr Powyss.

*

Catherine could tolerate Annie as long as she didn't look at her. When she accidently caught that pose of pretty suffering, the pursed lips and loud sighing, she dearly wished to slap her, even throw a plate at her, not to hurt, mind, just for it to smash near her. Startle her into sense.

But she might be useful.

'How is it with Samuel, Annie?' she asked nudgingly, eliciting a predictable blush. They were alone in the kitchen. 'Did his onion sprout?' she said, laughing gaily.

Annie had tried the old trick of putting named onions to sprout in the loft to see who she'd marry. In fact the Samuel onion had not been the first to sprout. She smothered her embarrassment at Catherine's innuendo behind her hands and so avoided answering that particular question.

'He likes me, I do think.'

'Of course he do! Have you kissed him yet?'

'He's a quiet boy. He have no family.'

'Oh, I know that. It makes no difference. You must wake him up. *You* must kiss *him!*'

'Must I?'

'Yes. And make him talk when you've got him all bothered. *What does Mr Powyss do with Hannah Warlow?* Samuel's the only one allowed to dust the precious things in the library. What has he *seen*?'

'The master only do like flowers and that. You did say so yourself.'

'Annie! She's with him every week! She has no husband at home! And she has such airs just because her mother was a lady's maid got with child. How she do *look* at me! *She'll* want the master, won't she, much more than her husband.' But that was the wrong direction to go in, setting off a great warble of sighs and 'poor man'.

'Jenkins do know, I'm certain. He won't tell *us*, but he talks to Samuel. Tells him what to do all the time. You must make more progress with Sam.'

'He said Abraham Price do like you,' Annie said hastily.

'You say that to keep me quiet.'

'No. Abraham did tell him Catherine is a clever puss. A useful woman. He did say.'

Catherine was doubtful. At least he hadn't dismissed her as she thought he had but she didn't much like 'useful'. Probably he wanted her to write a letter for him.

'He do go to meetins, Samuel says.'

'Oh.'

What could that mean but getting drunk? As to Hannah Warlow, the fact was that Samuel was too loyal to the master to give anything away unless in the arms of Annie. He was far too shy of Catherine for *her* to have any luck quizzing him herself. She thought she might drop him a hint that Annie was pining for him, though there was a danger that would put him off completely.

They were roused from dreams of manipulating Samuel by shouting. The cobbler's son, Caleb Hughes, was looking for Abraham Price.

'Not here. Go to the greenhouses or hothouse. What is it?' Catherine asked.

'We stopped the post from London.' He was gasping for breath. 'Thomas Hardy.'

'There's nobody called Hardy lives in these parts.'

'Do you not know? He's tried for high treason.'

Abraham Price ran in.

'What news, citizen?'

'Not guilty!'

'Liberty for ever! Tom Paine for ever!' They hugged each other, danced about, making the women gawp.

Spying one of Cook's gin bottles under her empty chair, Price raised it to Catherine and Annie with a triumphant smile and whisked it under his jacket.

Then they ran out, leaving the women to chop suet.

Chapter 5

A LONG ACCOUNT ARRIVED from Fox about the radical leader Thomas Hardy. The man's pregnant wife had died of shock after a mob attacked the Hardy house, the mob instigated by the government, or at least that's what Fox claimed. Now Hardy was on trial and Fox had attended the whole thing.

Twice as long as the usual letter, Powyss would have put it aside for those minutes of faltering attention before he fell asleep. But he needed the distraction.

Accused of treason, Hardy had been acquitted, said Fox, defended by the brilliant, witty Thomas Erskine, who was capable of speaking for seven hours, an ability inconceivable to Powyss, who generally found it hard to speak for as much as seven minutes except, it seemed, to Mrs Warlow. Hardy had moved everyone in court with his dignity. Indeed the mob had pulled Erskine's carriage through the streets themselves and carried Hardy on their shoulders.

Powyss wondered briefly about the next paragraph. He recalled that Fox's bookseller friend Henry Clarke had been sent to Newgate for four years.

Mrs Clarke sat with me in the Sessions House on some of the days. She is acquainted with several witnesses and was there to see the jury's foreman sob as he announced 'not guilty'. She and I shed tears together on that last day. She is not a member of my church, indeed her husband professes atheism. But we have much to say to each other.

The friendship with his good friend's wife seemed to be growing. But Fox said nothing more and went on to conclude that the outcome of the trial proved no revolution like that in France would ever take place in England. Powyss knew he should agree and be glad, though he'd never been able to envisage actual revolution in these sparsely settled hills.

He felt the revolt of his own body. A man of forty-seven askew with lust, no better than a youth. Somehow, he must reimpose order on his life.

He saddled a horse and rode for several hours in the lower reaches of the hills.

*

He can sense daylight. Knows he's right when he hears the first meal begin its downward journey. Gets up, greedy for bread. Or doesn't. Them'll not wind up the dishes till he rings the bell. Can lie there as long as he likes. Imagine pressing Annie's bubbies, her buttocks. His hands in her skirts. Fucking her at back of Kempton's sty.

Bladder compels him up. Kidneys, lamb chops, white bread, butter, jam, the beer he asked for. Sits on the pisspot (close-stool! he snorts), scratching back, groin, behind the knees, digging into the skin till it bleeds. Sucks fingers, half buttons himself, lifts the pot, rings for its shaky ascent to where he cannot go. Clean one descends.

At the grating he breathes in dripping cold. The world's still there. He grips the flaking iron, shakes it. If he loosened it, what then? More leaves'd blow through, more frogs'd get in. Shakes it harder, harder. Won't budge. Far too small for him to get through. Not think about getting out.

Checks traps. Several. Since he wrote:

I need rat trapps   plees   5 trapps

Builds a new fire, burns the corpses.

No frogs this end of the year. Air smells like end of year. He did try putting frogs back between the curls of rusting iron. Them couldn't jump up. Too high. Couldn't get up the shaft. Once fallen them're stuck. Drawn to the cistern, lured to its lifeless water.

The futility of their life troubles him. When he found the last one floating bloated on its back he was depressed for days.

Then he thinks what if he puts a live one under a dish-cover. Send it upstairs. Laughs at how the women will shriek as it springs off the dish. Have to send a note to stop them killing it:

pt frogg in pon   pleas

Have to be next year. When new ones come.

Now the long gap of morning. Sometimes he opens a book and flicks its pages as if this time it will make sense. There's the animals of course, especially the horses, sheep, dogs. Bulls. But the ones at the end of the book give him a turn. He forgets the journal for weeks. Writes notes when there's something to ask for. Chews. Spits. Cracks flies creeping among crumbs. Picks at wallpaper, damp-bubbled. Peels off long strips, chucks them into the fire, but they almost put it out they're so wet. Stands by the nailed door. Hears far-distant kitchen sounds. Annie hasn't come back down. Sits again. Scratches the webs of his fingers. Kicks off his boots, pulls off stockings. Scratches the webs of his toes. Skin flakes. Sores bleed.

Seasons pass. Behind the grating, dusty leaves in summer. Then scores more gust down. Ash keys rattle. Smoke-smell of fog. He hears hail's clicks, soundlessness of snowfall. Hooves, wheels, boys shouting, bells. Cocks, pigeons, rooks. All noises shrunken as from a tiny country.

He labours in his mind: mud, seed, weeds, grain. Plods up a furrow, down the next, hands calloused with grippin, shoutin to Dick to straighten the horses. Hitches on the bush harrow: easier nor ploughin. Herdin, thwackin flanks. Tugs warm udders. Scythes, sharpens, scythes, mows, head drippin, body drippin with heat in a roke. Chews bread while the horses rest. When he thinks of hot earth he longs to get out and shit among the leaves at the wood's edge.

But it only occupies minutes. His mind grinds down like a windless mill with no corn. Great stones, weighted, waiting.

He scratches his lice-thick hairiness. Curses. Thinks how to burn off some hair. That's not *cuttin*, is it? But how'll he do it without settin his head alight?

Feet hurt. Toenails like horn. Digs at them with fingers; but he's gnawed *those* nails down. Tries forcing a foot into his mouth but his body is stout, stiff. Can't bend. He topples off the chair; lies on the patterned floor bemused. Why move? For what? Until he gets cold.

And when the meal comes creaking down it disgusts him. Pieces of soft fish hidden in thick, winey sauce. Unknown vegetables. Freezing *ice cream*. Don't them know he never eats that? Powyss somewhere above, eating the same meal, thin fingers. Sipping wine. He scrapes the food into the traps. Them'll eat it.

More blank hours. Fear runs across his mind like black beetles. He closes his eyes, dozes. Dreams prompt memory. Them thought he was a fool. Be them right? Fifty pound. *Fifty pound for life.* He wants someone to tell him he was right to agree.

81

Mother were always old, working, never still till the end. Had no time for any of them. He'd never've asked *her*. Hannah's already like her. Worse.

What would father have said? Nothing, most like. Beat him. Then him were gone. Arm and hand sticking out from under the cart. It were good when him were gone, couldn't beat us no more. Not good us had no horse, legs broken, meat for dogs. Cart smashed to bits.

Only Mary looked at him without loathing or annoyance. With sweetness. His older sister Mary. Named the little one after her. Only we do call her Polly. Hopes she grows up kind.

Mary. Oh Mary. He refuses to think of her end. She, now. She'd tell him he's right.

*

Catherine couldn't get the image of Abraham Price and young Caleb dancing in triumph out of her head. She'd never seen anything like it. It was not drunken pleasure for they were not yet inebriated. It was something else.

She went for the basket in the hope of finding Abraham, saw him in one of the greenhouses, hands in pockets, staring up through the roof.

'I've come for the vegetables and fruit, Abraham.'

'Him's out there. Didn't you see?' She had seen the basket but pretended not and shrugged her shoulders.

'Them says you write a fair hand, isn't it.'

She'd guessed correctly: he was going to ask her to write a letter for him. She was pleased and disappointed.

'Yes.'

'Come here.'

She walked towards him along the brick pathway between rows of winter-empty pots on benches. Horticultural excitement was all in the hothouse this time of year.

'Who's it do *govern* us?' Darting eyes scanned her. His

bark-brown face was lit from within, she thought, certain he was right. But it was neither the question she expected nor wanted.

'Why, Mr Powyss do govern us.'

A Socratic self, slow to germinate, now quick to sprout, emerged from Abraham Price.

'Hah! I'll tell you. Them governs us in par–lia–ment.'

'Oh, I know that.'

'And who *sits* in par–lia–ment? Do you know *that*?'

'Mr Pitt. And. And other men of parliament.'

'*Members* of par–lia–ment. And who *are* members of par–lia–ment?'

'I don't know.'

'Them as has money to buy theirselves a seat. Them as knows one another, isn't it. Them as kisses each other's arse. Them's friends. Them's sons.'

'Ah.'

'And do us vote them there?'

'There be elections, that I do know.'

'And do the likes of us vote in them elections?'

'No, I suppose not. *I* never did.'

'You! You're a *woman*! *Women* can't vote. Uni–versal suf-frage, that's what us wants in the Society. *Them* won't allow it.'

'Ah. No. What *is* it, universal suffrage?'

'That do mean every man do vote.'

'And every woman?'

'Women can't vote.'

'But I can read and write.'

He waved that away. 'Oh, back to the kitchen with the basket now isn't it.' He'd seen Powyss coming. 'Come tomorrow,' he said out of the side of his mouth. 'I'll tell you more.'

She lowered her eyes and bobbed as she passed Powyss, aware that she had touched something hidden, alive and powerful. As if she'd caught a glimpse of great writhing snakes in a pit nearby that Powyss didn't know about. She wished she might talk to Abraham somewhere less exposed than a greenhouse tomorrow, but it was better than nothing.

And he must have had a similar thought for when he handed over the basket the next day he told her to call on him in the evening in the tiny master gardener's cottage that Powyss had built onto the stables.

*

For Powyss the glasshouses were a refuge. When he was a boy, before they'd been constructed, he would rush out of the house whenever he was in dispute with his father, or his mother's demands became too great. His mother, scathed by stillbirths, removed herself from her marriage bed and resorted to piety. Her one surviving child, Herbert, was to accompany her journey towards ever greater spiritual purity, but his education, in that small establishment attended by Fox and run by a parson rapidly losing his faith, made it impossible for him to do as she wished. In any case what boy, however bookish, however sensitive, would willingly conform to a life of prayer and abstinence? But even before that, he'd failed to understand why the good God had allowed all of his siblings to die and his mother, steeped in sadness, to retreat from the world, to turn away so often from her son to her prayerbook.

He came now to the hothouse, its hot-water pipes clinking pleasantly, the sea-coal boiler well stoked. Dismissed Price, despite the need to discuss the careful nurturing of his newly arrived blue-flowered *Lupinus nootkatensis* seeds.

He was exhilarated and furious. Weeks after having kissed Hannah's cheek – well, he'd done so twice – he'd embraced her. Put his arms round her, held her to him, kissed her hard, saw her eyes open in half-sceptical surprise, blue-grey, kissed her again.

Those accounts of experiments with electricity he'd read,

84

Galvani's frog or the cadaver with its sudden violent movement, told him that his realisation was like a shock. He wanted her. Wanted this entirely unsuitable woman and couldn't stop himself.

Ach! It was infatuation! Had she been a woman of his own kind, with or without a husband, there'd have been no difficulty, he'd have found a way. In fact both married and unmarried women had approached him in years gone by, and he'd turned them down each one. Knowing, overblown, manipulative, they'd have wrecked his life of pleasurable solipsism. The neighbouring women had all wondered about him of course. No wife. No mistress. Was he like Pitt, they asked each other, interested only in port and parliament? But then they heard how he travelled to London and someone came across him walking down Jermyn Street, so they made the correct assumptions.

An affair with a woman of his own class would have been acceptable if carried out with discretion, especially if the husband was notably complaisant. An 'arrangement' with Warlow's wife would be despised. Not that he cared either what the villagers thought, or for the neighbouring landowners' views, though he never forgot how unpleasant it was to catch the satirical glances that passed among the guests at his father's table. But in his own mind he could see that it was out of place, disorderly. Even the injustice to Warlow, who could never afford to take him to court, unlike rich cuckolds, irked him, however much he disliked the man.

The worst thing was that it would muddy the experiment. The paper he intended to write and deliver to the Royal Society would be tainted because he'd have to exclude information.

Yet all these reasons against it merely conspired to entice him further. How much more did he want her than any of the powdered, chattering, flattering women of the neighbourhood who'd dropped sly hints in past years! Champney

Baugh's niece, stately, ambitious, so sure of herself, whose name was soon linked to the Prince of Wales and then his friends; numerous urgent-eyed spinsters; even the unfortunate Mrs Tharpe, whose attempts to attract him took the form of insinuations about his London visits and incessant complaints about her husband.

Oh, but wasn't the whole thing absurd? That he should actually want this woman who was no longer young nor beautiful, and yet, and yet irresistibly attractive to him, her grey-blue eyes daring, drawing him. It was preposterous. He must get over it.

He hovered near a hot pipe willing himself to think rationally. Here among seeds and seedlings, delicate graftings, where so often he'd exerted order and precision, used good sense and experience, where reason had ruled, *surely* he could determine what to do next. Yet nothing came to his clouded mind.

*

She thinks: he did really kiss me. At last. I did know he would one day.

I am married so it is wrong. Not even a widow. The commandments, number seven I think. But many do it, for sure. I think John have not been true.

How many babies Mother did have. Kempton it were.

He did let us stay when Father died. We had hens, a few sheep, we did never starve.

She did love all her babies even though Kempton's. I do love all mine even them that died, even though all be John's.

I do take Mr Powyss's money and his gifts. He is a gentleman, not like Kempton, but he is master. Surely he will want me to comply and I must do it. I shall take his money for my children as Mother did for hers.

1795 began bitterly. Surrounding Moreham, white hills met white sky. In London ice thickened the Thames, though not enough to prevent men falling through and freezing to death. Filling their boots with brandy which froze. Mobs on the streets kept themselves warm with fires and demolition of crimping houses where press-gangs as good as imprisoned young men for the fleet.

But gardeners looked to spring: Fox had taken to gardening his small plot in Hampstead ever more earnestly. After some nonsense about 'the fellow in the cellarage', he wrote:

> I should like your advice on Helianthus atrorubens *and* Dodecatheon meadia. *I have recently purchased seeds of both. No doubt you will scorn the reasons for my choice but shooting stars and sunflowers suit my present mood. Both originate from America of course and I am told that the* Dodecatheon *will fire off in the spring and then lie dormant while the* Helianthus *gazes forward with its striking dark eye. Have you grown these plants and do you think they will survive in my modest garden and in soil I have only recently begun to cultivate? Of course the temperatures are higher here, being both more south and east than Moreham.*

As usual he left the main point of his letter till last, but this time it wasn't a criticism of Powyss; if anything he seemed to expect *Powyss* to wag the finger at *him*.

> *I am daily encouraged in my gardening enthusiasm by Mrs Clarke who is very fond of flowers and who has also accompanied me on buying expeditions to Chelsea. As spring matures we intend to visit Kew, I with my notebook. Mrs Clarke and I have come to an understanding. I might say that our friendship has become a strong plant. Yet of course she*

*is not a free woman and her husband languishes, though she
visits him whenever she is allowed. Her children are schooled
nearby. My frequent meetings with them have resulted in a
fine mutual affection.*

Fox wanted the opinion of his friend, Powyss, as 'a confirmed bachelor and freethinker'.

How extraordinary! A man so steadfast in his moral position, so certain in his faith. Powyss supposed he'd have to reply, on both matters, to respond to a new hesitancy in Fox, whose authority appeared to be wavering.

For years now he'd felt an inferiority in his friendship with Fox. Of course he knew a great deal about plants and trees, could boast of all the improvements he'd made at Moreham. But Fox wrote of higher things, of government and God. He was a man who knew his own mind, was steady in his beliefs. Once, Powyss had written to Fox that in his letters he felt *like a papist confessing trivial sins to my confessor.* And Fox, amused, had played that role exuberantly and paradoxically, from his Unitarian viewpoint.

Now, this imbalance had reversed. Fox asked whether Powyss thought a good act could have bad consequences. Clearly he was worrying about his position with Mrs Clarke, but he was certainly also thinking of the Warlow experiment.

Months before, Powyss had begun a letter but put it away. He brought it out again. Perhaps he should send it. It was a reply to a question of Fox's about the *Investigation*.

*Do I see my experiment as an act of pure goodness? No.
Experiments are neutral, they lack a moral dimension. Acts
of pure goodness are for God alone, if there is a God. I suppose
that we do good as far as we are able. My experiment began
as science, though I admit it now answers to science and to
charity.*

He made a move to strike out this complacency, but left it for the moment. It couldn't help Fox in his dilemma, which, remarkably, was so close to his own.

Your question as to whether a good act could have bad consequences does not apply to my experiment, since, as I say, experiments are neutral. Of course ill could come out of a good act, though surely it would be inadvertent. No one can intend both good and ill. That defies logic as of course you know.

This wouldn't help Fox either. He probably hadn't intended to start something with Mrs Clarke, but rather had merely wanted to help her and her children while her husband was in prison.

He chewed on his pen and gazed through his window. In the lower reaches of the hills stood ewes fat with unborn lambs. Mist hung over the tops.

He would not tell Fox about Hannah. He was not obliged to respond in kind to Fox's confession despite some similarity in their situations. Indeed he was not obliged to reply at all.

He'd certainly not reached that sort of 'understanding' with Hannah. Instead, he longed for her with a desperate thirst. There was reluctance still; she held herself back from her own not quite hidden desire. He longed to crush her to him, to absorb her, to fuck her till she was his. But must not. That's how it was. It would be wrong to take advantage of a woman whose husband could not prevent it. Even such a woman, such a husband. Most importantly, the experiment would be jeopardised if he did.

At the very beginning she'd probably been merely glad of the money, perhaps awed by his books, the long room with its grand windows. But she'd distrusted him, resisted. Then, gradually, he thought that like a plant she'd become acclimatised. He began to perceive something of what she had endured. So many births, no doubt deaths. Poverty. Warlow, big, wilful, barely articulate, his movements propelled by bulk. Unlikely that kindness was a quality Warlow knew, so that she had turned to it like light; her arms, tendrils, reaching up for life.

His upbringing told him what he did was wrong. His reason argued that, on the contrary, kindness was a virtue, though kindness was by no means all he had in mind. He sensed she would accept whatever he had in mind.

Whenever he'd wanted a woman he'd been able to purchase her. Always it was a transaction, though sometimes he hadn't desired those he'd bought. He gave Hannah money, certainly, but didn't think it was the same.

Desire pulled against a certain tenderness for her. He was entranced by this woman who was so different from the impertinent girls he paid to remove his breeches, lick him erect, smother him with their breasts. She'd be laughed out of Jermyn Street were she to appear there, and yet how inferior to her they all were!

He thrust the letter to Fox in a drawer and went out. This utter confusion of mind was intolerable. He paced the flower garden and woods, stood rooted in the hothouse, staring, not seeing. And became alert to danger when he suddenly recalled the irony in Price's tone, the secret smile of the maid Catherine.

Back in his library, he willed the distance between him and the man beneath to increase. Two floors down was as deep as the middle of the earth. He stopped using the listening tube. In any case he heard so little. The pile of papers placed to cover it lay to one side. Uncut books, unread pamphlets stood about the long, light room, unnoticed.

*

Abraham Price wanted Catherine to write a bill to tie onto the market cross in Moreham. Actually, what he really wanted was to stick a bill on the church door, but he knew the time for such acts was yet to come.

'Come now, clever puss! Ink, paper and pen's here. Write big letters. People must *see* the words easy, isn't it.'

'But I'm not used to writing in great big letters.'

'Try now. Liberty. Write Liberty.' Her spelling was good: she wrote it slowly, the letters decreasing in size as they moved across the page. Underneath came Equality.

'Now,' Price said, 'write Fr–ter–nity.'

'I don't know that. What does it mean?'

'It do mean brothers.'

'What have brothers to do with equality and liberty?' She remembered all her brothers – the unfairness of her life as a girl, even if they did get beaten.

'It do mean us are all brothers.'

'Oh. Even you and me?' She glanced at him under her eyebrows. Humour, she was beginning to realise, was not one of Abraham's strengths.

'Yes. O'course.' But Frternity went off the page. She began again and again but there was never enough room left on the paper for everything else he wanted written.

The arrangement between them was this: she helped him improve his very limited reading. Books and pamphlets were sent by the London Corresponding Society to the Moreham Disputing Club which, so far, had not been closed by the magistrates. And occasionally she wrote a letter to his mother for him (someone would read it for her back home, he said). He instructed Catherine in the latest radical thinking and inspired her with his rhetoric and fiery eye. Ideas flamed up in her head like dry kindling. Young Caleb, the cobbler's son, was sometimes present after the club meetings (which ended with the singing of the last verse of Paine's 'Liberty Tree'), but the reading lessons were always unattended and Price's undoubted progress was regularly matched by advances by hand within Catherine's bodice. These she found extremely pleasant and not at all brotherly, but she always insisted he read two whole pages first. Then of course she must return soon since Annie might be lonely in their attic room and would certainly talk if she stayed out long.

There had been an extraordinary cold spell, mid-June. It was reckoned 120 sheep, just shorn, died in fields around Moreham. Catherine, caught in a sudden hailstorm on her way to Price's cottage, dried her hair and shook with cold. With his encouragement she removed her soaked stockings and he rubbed her feet and ankles, her calves, knees. Clamped her thighs with his gardener's hands.

But though she felt her will weaken, Price would not forget his other goal – to read all of Paine's *Rights of Man* without help. So, for an hour or so the balance changed while *he* submitted to *her*. And her sallowness reddened in the pleasure of the task. How much more satisfying to teach this irascible man with his sunburned face and seedsman's fingers than instruct pouting Annie the correct way to melt leaf gelatine.

Some weeks later summer righted itself. Heat reclaimed intentions. Heat drove the street in London. Price's connections brought him news of riots in Charing Cross. With increasing passion he told Catherine how the people smashed Pitt's windows in Downing Street, dismantled a recruiting house near the Obelisk.

'Them sent the horseguards and trampled them.'

'Oh, oh! Were they killed?'

'Some smashed, some killed. But more men come next day and them did gut the crimping house like a fish, isn't it. Bones, innards, them drags everything out. Piles up the furniture, every stick. Heaps and heaps it up and lights a spark and burns it all in one great big fire! Mag–ni–fi–cent!' He grasped her to him and by splendid analogy, in minutes demolished her thin resistance to his other cause.

*

Yesterday he puked. Went to bed cold, soaked with sweat. Slept and slept.

Now he feels good. Needs a piss but pot's full of puke. Fires out so he pisses into that. Opens the lift door. Flies crawl over his untouched meal from yesterday. Piles the dishes to make room for the pot. Rings bell. Hauls up.

Down comes a clean pot, a small box and a note:

Mix spoonful Rothwell's pouder in water.
Will we send for Surgeon?

No he begins. But there's almost no ink. Spilled it before, didn't he. Nib scratches into the paper:

I am hungr e   incs dri   send mor   pleas

First, breakfast descends. Then a clean shirt, ink bottle, sheafs of paper.

He scrapes out the ashes, makes up a new fire. Today he'll not think about Mary. Her's a shadow anyway. Can't *see* her when he closes his eyes. Her face. What did her look like? What colour were her hair? Her eyes? Her were there before dawn, at dusk. Always dark. He tries to make the picture in his head clearer but can't. Fades all the time. Just her smiling left. Come a day her face'll be blank.

Mustn't get gloomy. Remember that miller. Miserable man, never laughed, never smiled. Drank though. One day he were gone. They found a note: *Jacob Cole lies in the mill-dam.* Writ it hisself afore. Sat, smoked a pipe and writ it. Then drownded hisself.

Opens the other book. Not the animals. Hates the baboons. Worse is The   Ter   nate Bat. Wings like cloaks, skeleton arms, teeth, claws. He puts it in the back of a cupboard behind candle boxes so it can't get out.

Rob   inson   Cru soe. Did *he* get fifty pound a year?

93

Stares hard at the man. Must have been cold with no boots.

Who lived eig   eigh   oh yes eight   and twenty years all alone

Ah! And him's only to live *seven*. And not yet that much! *Those words were not hard. Read more*:

all alone (Yes!) in an un in hab habit   habit ed   unin habit ed (what's that?) is   land island on the Coast of AM ERICA, near the Mouth of the Great River of OR   OO   NO   QUE

Makes no sense.

ORO ONO

He gives up. Flicks through for more pictures. None. Will Powyss write a book about *him*? Is that what him meant? When I write it up, send it to the something, him said.

He holds the book open with one hand. Copies into the journal:

THE
LIFE
AND STRANG   SUR PRIZIN   ADVENT URES
OF
JOHN
WARLOW OF MOR HAM PLOW MAN

He draws a man. Crosses it out. No good. Takes the candle to the glass to look. Eyes, yes. Nose. The rest is beard, hair all round his face. Where's his mouth? Can't see the faces he pulls. Sticks out his tongue to find his mouth.

Back to the paper. He draws a bigger circle, two little ones for eyes, another for nose. Scribbles hair all over. Doesn't look good next to the picture in the book.

Starts again on a new page. Gives himself a body; tries for a linen shirt. The Robinson man looks like a sort of gentleman in his suit of skins, his guns and sword. The Warlow man holds a candle. Around him he shades in blackness, more and more blackness.

*

Late summer brought great quantities of fruit. The labourers turned their hands to picking, then pruning under Price's guidance. Baskets of plums were lugged to the kitchen to be bottled, turned into pies and jam. Damsons were simmered for hours, sieved, simmered again for more hours, solidified on saucers, compressed: damson cheese. Apples were laid out on slatted trays to last two seasons in the pantry or packed into boxes with pears to send to Hampstead. The more fruit Powyss sent to Fox the less he felt obliged to write. The letter he began in February still lay in a drawer.

Strolling beside the herbaceous bed he met Margaret and Polly. He'd seen them from the window occasionally, the younger bending and poking among the flowers, brushing them for their scent, the older pulling her away.

He was surprised they didn't run off. The older one wouldn't look at him, a heavy-featured girl, perhaps resembling Warlow. He was hard-pushed to remember what Warlow looked like. Hannah said the girl was motherly.

'Good morning,' he said.

The older child bobbed a kind of curtsey, looking down.

'Be you Mr Powyss,' the little one asked him. Her face was round, placid, slightly curious. He saw Hannah in her, fled the thought.

'Yes, I am. You are Polly. And you are ...?'

'Margaret.'

'Margaret, yes. Which flowers do you like, Polly?' He was drawn to her.

'Them big white flowers. I likes them.'

'*Eucomis autumnalis.*'

They stared at him.

'Spikes of pineapple flower. Look closely. What do you see?'

'Stars. White stars.'

'Yes.'

Margaret, resenting his lack of interest in her, bobbed another curtsey and pulled Polly away.

He walked on. The espaliered Catherine pear had failed again, its leaves curled and blotchy, its fruit small, dropping before their time. He thought he'd try a Grosse Mignonne instead. But whenever he began to make up his mind to write to Loddiges Nursery the thought seemed to slide past and out of his head.

Into the denuded orchard. A labourer up a ladder was receiving Price's barked commands. Price was too keen to cut.

'Go easy with the knife, Price.'

Price's reply was obscure. 'Rather axe the root would you, Mr Powyss, *sir*?'

'Certainly not. What can you mean?'

'You'd axe the Tree of Liberty.'

He'd suspected Price of revolutionary tendencies for some time. It was one thing to read such language in Fox's letters, quite another to hear them from a man in his employ. There'd been a strong indication a while before when he made it clear to Price that he was a lodger in his cottage not a householder, that as he didn't pay rates he had no vote.

'Ah!' Price said. 'But I've a hearth on which I boil my pot, isn't it, and my own door.'

Powyss had to hasten to the law. There he found a quibble, surely not worthy of him but usable all the same.

'Now, Price. Although it's true that you do indeed have access to the cottage without having to go through another property, it's nevertheless not access from the *street*, since the cottage opens onto the stable yard.'

Price growled at this, walked away and Powyss had thought no more of it; but since then there'd been these odd remarks and he sensed a festering.

'But this isn't the tree of liberty,' he now said. 'And if it were, you'd surely not want to cut it back to this extent, Price. Plums need little pruning; and apples, well, it's almost autumn now, not winter; they need little and careful cutting. I hardly need tell *you!*'

'Growth is stronger after the knife,' Price replied darkly and Powyss walked off.

*

Catherine was reading aloud to Cook and Annie. Samuel hovered in and out of the doorway biting his nails.

'On the occasion of his majesty's going to the House of Lords, the Mall and the Parade of St James's Park and Parliament Street were completely choked up with spectators. They at least amounted to 200,000.

'The earl of Chatham, duke of Gloucester, etc. were hissed, and the duke of Portland was very much hooted.'

'What's this?' Jenkins walked in and sat down. 'Begin again, Miss.'

'Oh, it's the king going to the lords, Mr Jenkins. Thousands of spectators hissing and hooting.'

Jenkins grunted with annoyance. 'I said begin again.'

'Let her read on, Mr Jenkins, for heaven's sake!' said Cook.

'About twenty minutes afterwards the king left Buckingham House, and was violently hissed and hooted, and groaned at the whole way, but no violence was offered till he arrived opposite the Ordnance office, when a small pebble, or marble, or bullet, broke one of the windows.'

Mrs Rentfree took a swig from under her chair while all

97

were concentrating on the report and burst out: '*Bullet!* It's the Irish. Rabble. Papists. Thank the Good Lord we have nothing like them *here!*'

'Read on!' Jenkins commanded.

Catherine continued: 'In returning, the crowd pressed closely round the coach, and his majesty, in considerable agitation, signified, by waving his hands to the horseguards on each side, his anxiety that the multitude should be kept at a distance.'

The listeners were silent. There was no sound in the kitchen except for a low bubbling from a large pot on the range. The room was steamy.

'A considerable tumult took place when his majesty was about to alight, and one of the horses in the state coach took fright, threw down an old groom of the name of Dorrington, and broke one of his thighs, but it proved fortunately a simple fracture. His other thigh was considerably bruised, but not dangerously.'

'Poor man!' cried Annie.

Jenkins glared. 'Don't *you* interrupt!'

'A few minutes after his majesty had entered the palace, the mob attacked the state coach with stones, and did it great injury. In its way along Pall Mall to the Mews, many things were also thrown at it.'

'Tut, tut, tut,' from Cook.

'What things did they throw?' asked Samuel.

'What difference does that make? Stupid question,' Jenkins said.

'It don't say,' Catherine said to Samuel and read on: 'After a short time the king went in his private coach from St James's to Buckingham House; but on his way through the Park, the mob surrounded the carriage, and prevented it from proceeding, crying out, "Bread! Bread! Peace! Peace!"'

Catherine sat back in her chair, but raised the paper hastily before her face lest the others should see the sparks firing in her mind. How Abraham would long to be there with the mob! How she longed to be among the crowd herself, hissing, hooting, crying out! Her whole body stirred and she thought to get out if she could, take the newspaper and find Abraham.

'Read on, then!' commanded Mrs Rentfree. 'Did they arrest 'em, the papist mob? Throw 'em in prison? There'll be hangins, just you wait.'

'It says that three or four persons were apprehended.'

'*Three or four*? Three or four *hundred*, more like. Three or four *thousand*!'

'Three or four were apprehended on suspicion of having thrown stones, etc. at the king and one of them was charged with having called out, "No king", and other such expressions.'

A heavy drawing in of breath, another swig.

'Disgraceful!' Jenkins growled. Cook looked sharply at him lest he meant her.

'The king, through the whole of the riot, displayed the cool magnanimity for which the family have ever been distinguished,' Catherine read to silence Cook and Jenkins. 'But,' she couldn't stop herself from saying, 'it said before that he showed *considerable agitation*, so *that's* not true.'

'Read on, miss!' Cook and Jenkins accidently spoke together.

'Confident in the attachment of his people, notwithstanding the alarms of the preceding day, the king, accompanied by her majesty and three of the princesses, visited Covent Garden theatre, and at their entrance was received with the usual burst of applause. "God Save the King" was sung twice, and by a considerable part of the house overzealously called for a third time; this in a corner of the gallery, provoked a few hisses, which however were soon overruled, and one or two of the most active of the turbulent party were turned out; after which the performance went on.' She threw down the paper in disgust: 'Surely, those dumplings will be cooked,

Mrs Rentfree? Quick! Let us take them off the fire before they boil dry!'

*

He's proud of his writing. SUR PRIZIN   JOHN WARLOW OF MOR HAM PLOWMAN

Picks up the book again. About the man like him. Rob Robin Robinson

Couldn't niver write so many words. Look at all them pages!

Creaking. Dinner's coming. He lugs the tray to the table. Meat under the cover, what is it? Picks it off the plate: *pheasant! Oho!* Niver ate a pheasant that weren't stole.

A note on the tray:

Mrs Rentfrew says His Majesty the King do like apple dumplings

Under a smaller cover an apple dumpling. Puts his finger in a jug of cream and licks it off.

He thinks he'll write back: *I liks appl pye.* But he doesn't bother.

Best is apples off the tree. No cookin. Pinchin apples from Swaine's orchard like we did. Early in the mornin or just when dark were comin. Throwin sticks and stones were no good, best climb up. Quick! Fill your pockets, throw down to Joe, the others, stuff 'em into *their* pockets. Whistle when you see Swaine.

Caught us many times got a thrashin, but he couldn't thrash us all at once could he! One took the beatin, the rest ran off. Nex time another took the beatin.

They'll be pickin the late ones now, sure to. Mashin for cider. Sun'll be low. Ploughin. Cold's begun seeping in, he's felt it.

He's eaten every bit. Drunk up the ale. Eyelids heavy, but he lights a pipe. Try a bit more about the man Rob like me.

Oh can't read all that! I'll pick a page. Like old Mrs Cattle did with her Bible. Funny name she had, Hez, Hezzy somethin Cattle. Pick a page, she said. That'll tell you what'll happen when you's growed up.

Stabs a page; nail rips a strip.

my dog   two cats

Can't see no frog. Dogs wouldn't like it down here. Stabs another bit. Looks easy can read that.

But to   re   turn   return to my   new   comp   compan compan ion   my new com panion

Companion?

I was great   greatly de   light   delighted   with him teach him

What's all that?

make him speak

Can't read all that.

It was very   pleas   pleasant for me   to talk to him.

Oh.
There were someone. Someone there. Robinson were speakin to someone.

Now   my life be   my life began   to be so easy

Oh.

Not like him. The man is *not* like him. Has a friend.

His eyes close. Pipe's out. He smells rain beginning, nods off.

*

She thinks: the rain have poured down. It is November. Lane did flood, bridge by the ford were swept away. I could not get home after I went for the money. I did worry about the children. Jack so wayward. Turning bad I do think. Margaret do like to take my place, tell them what to do. But I cannot be from them long.

He did want me to stay but they will talk he said. I like him though I do wish it were not so.

I must wait in the kitchen till the rain stopped. They did question me but I said nothing. They are not friendly.

He have a small room with instruments, a tube to see things closely. He showed me. I looked through the glass and saw a butterfly wing.

He were pleased when I did name it. Father did tell me many names of butterflies and such.

Then a grasshopper. Did use to catch one so it jump inside my hands; watch it hop away. This one were dead.

He have a telescope do show the stars he said only if I be there at night which I cannot.

He have kissed me many times. Many. But that is all. Not like Kempton and Mother. Perhaps it is a fortunate thing as I surely cannot live another birth. In any case I do think I am too old to bear more children.

Maybe he only like to kiss, why he have no wife. Maybe I am not clean enough. I shall wash my gown once more, my hair.

Part II

Chapter 6

HAD HE BEEN ASKED, Powyss would not have said the experiment had broken down. Warlow was still there, after all. In April it would be three years.

One of the principal attractions of experiments for Powyss had always been their neutrality. You set them up (would the Chinese *Daphne odora* survive better on an east- or a south-facing wall; how much greater is the production of melons in the hothouse compared with the melon bed; what degrees of warmth and moisture are required for the germination of this or that seed), you detailed the origin and number of the plants or seeds, laid out the conditions of soil and climate, recorded the outcome carefully, day by day, then you drew your conclusion, your thesis thoroughly tested. Even when you lost plants, or seeds refused to sprout, or the experiment failed entirely, it always remained neutral. No emotion was involved.

He'd begun the *Investigation* as if it were another horticultural experiment, though much bigger, more important. But it hadn't turned out that way.

And he went about it differently, now. Minutely detailed records, sometimes several a day were no longer necessary.

He knew exactly what Warlow would and wouldn't eat. His tastes were becoming more finicky perhaps; he was eating less. Powyss had refused to increase three pints of beer a day, though Warlow had asked for it. Tobacco and fuel supplies remained the same.

He recorded only the unusual when reported to him by Jenkins, ignoring the butler's undisguised relish: the possible illness, a request for yet more rat traps. If the man became really ill and required a surgeon then the experiment would certainly be at an end. The condition of Warlow's clothes when erratically sent for washing was no longer unusual. That Warlow was not cleaning himself was apparent but Powyss ignored complaints from Mrs Rentfree conveyed to him by Jenkins. In truth the business of recording had become tedious. The promise of a week of fame in the Royal Society following the delivery of his paper at the end of the experiment, perhaps 1801 by the time he'd written it up, had begun to blur. As if there was an aberration in the microscope lens or as if he'd failed to adjust it. But he didn't *want* to adjust it. The quest for fame had begun to seem wearisome.

He abandoned the listening tube completely and laboriously described and explained its failure for incorporation into the final paper. *Investigation into the Resilience of the Human Mind Without Society.* He still took pleasure from the title. Crucial to the experiment would be Warlow's condition when he emerged in 1800, his frame of mind and what written evidence he brought with him, and there was nothing Powyss could do about any of those things now.

What had gone was neutrality. And surely it had been obvious from the start that that would happen. There never *could* have been neutrality. Yet *if* it had occurred to him then, he'd swept it away as inconvenient.

He did his utmost to keep Warlow from his thoughts. Yet there was ever a sense of a presence below, even that far down. A presence he'd begun to resent, at times to hate.

When Jenkins announced Hannah each week he awaited her by the south window, knowing that that part of the room was not above Warlow's cellar. He handed her the money, announcing it in a voice loud enough to be heard at the keyhole, and then he'd lead her quietly into his small instrument room with its botanical and entomological specimens, its table for the microscope and the portable telescope perched on its brass column. Beneath he knew there was merely a corridor, not Warlow. And of course, were Jenkins to interrupt, initially they would be hidden from sight.

There he held her, kissed her face, her neck, for all like a youth, guilty, unsure. He longed to explore every part of her, but couldn't, mustn't. In time her fingers began to caress his neck, her diminutive body to press against his. And yet they remained celibate. Was it the room perhaps, so many shelves of books, the scientific instruments and priceless objects that oppressed them, held them back? How many men would have such scruples as he, he asked himself? As master of Moreham House he could do as he liked. As author of the *Investigation*, explorer of the solitary human mind, he couldn't.

'Shall you come to my house?' she asked him one day.

'No! No. I shan't do that.'

'I cannot leave the children.'

'No, of course not. I . . .'

A loud knock and Jenkins entered the library.

Often, for what short time they had together before she must return, he simply talked to her, rapidly, frenziedly, as though to shut out the clamour of his lust. He drank in her expressions, their changes, how she would listen to him, colour, how in her eyes seemed to lie an expectation of enjoyment. The *Lateral Effects* section of the *Investigation* approached dissolution. All her earlier resistance had gone; they stood on the edge.

He thought of Jermyn Street. Over the years he must have

occupied every over-furnished room at Mrs Clavering's, each hastily smoothed bed. The girls whose names he could never remember varied in appearance and skill: that was part of the reputation of the house. And they were sometimes high-born, girls who'd fallen or been plucked from not unknown families. There was even one whose exquisite voice pampered a wealthy, leering audience with Handel arias.

They were paid to please, not to be pleased. That was the difference.

His reply to Fox's last letter remained unfinished, unsent. More than a year had passed, yet phrases from their correspondence would recur. This was not surprising given that Fox was the only direct voice from the outside world to which he'd ever listened. Despite their many differences and despite his new hesitancy of tone, Fox had an authority Powyss had occasionally welcomed, for it was a measure against which he could hold himself. Though they were the same age, he had thought of him, at times, as of a father whose ideas he respected.

But he found himself bored by Fox's 'understanding' with Mrs Clarke. He envisaged them making their arrangements to shop, visit, dine together, all so civilised, all quite humdrum. Was he envious of Fox for finding himself a mistress from his own sphere? Did he envy their freedom in the sophisticated metropolis, meeting privately without lurking servants, for Fox's household was small? Perhaps he did.

He couldn't have explained himself to Fox anyway. This was not love: he didn't know what that was, suspected it didn't exist, was an invention of poets and Gothic novelists. No, it was desire that had something of the excitement and sensuous pleasure he felt when he brought back a tree from Chelsea or Hackney, some new, unusual specimen, barely known in this country, wonderfully rare. He'd plan its ideal site, dig a capacious hole. Untie the rope, unwrap the sacking. Gently disentangle the roots with his fingers, spread them out, place them in the earth. Water them generously. Crumble good mould, rich with vegetable and animal manure, pressing with both hands, firming, until the sapling stood without his help.

Or it was like the sensation of seeing an antique piece, unusual, fascinating, knowing he *had* to buy it, to own it, to hold it whenever he wanted.

More than both of these it was his body's unbearable heat, stoked by restraint, that he couldn't imagine restraining much longer.

He had told her how much he liked her, how he wished she were free. She had looked at him with a kind of sceptical contentment, said nothing. That was good: it was better he shouldn't know her mind.

*

Catherine's preoccupation with Abraham Price had the additional advantage of relieving her of hours of Annie's company. However, if she was to keep the full nature of her activities with Price concealed from Jenkins and Cook she must keep Annie sweet. Whenever she could, she would drop comments about Price's much improved reading and had begun offering to write letters for others as part of the disguise.

'I have written a letter to old Mrs Price,' she'd say to Cook. 'Shall I write one for you, then both can be sent to post together?'

One evening she was lying on her bed. At least she didn't have to share a bed as she'd once had to do in a previous employment. She was halfway through Paine's *Rights of Man Part II*, borrowed from Price's Disputing Club. She wanted to keep ahead of Abraham and had indeed got much further than he. She struggled with the dry matter of constitution but laughed at the image of the monarchy hidden behind a curtain. Chewed on phrases for days as she polished or sliced: *it has put down the dwarf to set up the man; a flame has arisen not to be extinguished.* That last, for someone who lit fresh fires each day, was especially enjoyable.

Now her attention was interrupted by Annie's noisy rummaging. Two padlocked deal boxes stood at opposite ends of the attic room they shared, marking out each woman's cramped territory. Catherine's was decorated with strips of wallpaper she'd garnered over the years: oak leaves, geranium leaves, loops, lines, sprigs and shells rioted all over it. Theft was unheard of with the present complement of servants, and yet Annie must needs check through her belongings daily. Perhaps after a day of cleaning someone else's house, preparing someone else's food, the familiarity of her own things – her best gown and shifts, her little watch and ring – reminded her small self of who she was. And after her six months' punishment of no pay, the money she possessed was ever important to her.

Tonight she took each article and laid it out on her bed. Catherine closed her book.

'Will you never tell me how you came upon the silver teaspoon?' she asked.

Annie blushed and wouldn't. Then she held the watch to her ear, shook it, listened again.

'Still not going?'

'No. When I shall save enough I shall take it to the watchmaker.'

'There's no watchmaker for miles about here.'

No reply. This dialogue had taken place many times and always ended there. Annie began to count her coins.

'Now what does Samuel say, Annie?'

Over the months Annie had made some progress with Samuel. He admitted to liking her and would sometimes plunge out of the blacking room off the corridor that led to the back kitchen and kiss her fiercely, anxiously. What he really wanted was to take her into the knife room where, in his leather apron, he rubbed knife blades with bath brick and powdered limestone. His own room.

His family had been poor tenants in London. When he was twelve, the old, neglected house in which they were crammed collapsed, as such places did periodically. Samuel was squatting in the jakes over the yard. Neighbours and passers-by scrabbled through the rubble looking for survivors; laid out Samuel's parents and siblings in the road, dusted white like ghosts.

From an orphanage patronised by Valentine Tharpe he arrived in Moreham, where loyalty to Powyss was the greatest certainty he'd known. Now there was Annie to think about. However, he wasn't completely sure what he'd do with her once he did get her into his room and in any case knew she'd not abide the knives; had already complained of the violence with which he embraced her.

'Sam says nothing.'

'Annie, that will not do. I'm certain he knows everything about the master and Hannah Warlow. He lays out the master's clothes, is the only one allowed to dust his precious vases and that.'

'He will not tell against him. I do think he do worship the master.'

'You must *make* him tell. Resist him, then relent only when he's told you something.'

'I do scoff at him all the time for he is so eager. He do pinch my arms so.'

'Don't *scoff* at him! That's not the way. Let him kiss you and put his hand about you. And you do the same to him. Then stop suddenly and promise to resume when he tells you.'

Annie held a shift against her face in embarrassment, rubbed the skin prickling up and down her arms.

'He is callow. You must teach him.' Annie was further shocked by what she heard as 'tallow'.

And when Catherine said: 'Or we shall need to take matters into our own hands', Annie thought she meant all three of them tangled up together in the blacking room.

*

Hampstead, Ides of March, 1796

Dear Powyss,

Whilst I am entirely thankful for a Christmas greatly improved by quantities of apples, pears and slices of damson cheese from Moreham (for nos numerus sumus et fruges consumere nati), I am sorry to have received nothing in writing from you. How fares your testing of the old mole?

I live in hope that you are not dismayed by my friendship with Mrs Clarke and make bold to assume that your silence is as fruitful as was my Christmas.

Powyss yawned and walked to the window in the hope of catching sight of Hannah. It wasn't Monday and he dared not ask her to come more often. He knew the servants suspected something. In one sense he didn't care what they thought, but in another he dreaded the disorder, the contumacy that might ensue. But Hannah might walk along the lane beyond the garden wall towards the village and he might glimpse her.

Would she? He had no idea of her life, what she did and when she did it. Preferred not to know. He wanted to have her *here* among his best possessions, exotic, unexpected, to touch, to hold at any time of day. In her sordid daily life she might seem different, might disappoint him.

In the distant Marches you hardly will have noticed the repression we now endure in the capital since the absurd

stone-throwing at the King's coach last year which was
without a doubt the result of ministerial conspiracy; I am in
good company believing that. The worst cases of repression to
my mind are the fining and imprisoning of booksellers whose
livelihoods are ruined by the new bills.

With disgust Fox added that the Prince of Wales's debts had just been liquidated *to the tune of £50,997.10s. And the people cry for bread!*

Finally, to Powyss's astonishment, he announced that he'd left the Unitarian church, partly under the influence of the agnostic Mrs Clarke. He now regarded himself as a simple Deist like Paine and accordingly enclosed both parts of Paine's new work, *Age of Reason.*

Good lord, how the man was breaking out, Powyss thought! He added the two volumes to one of several piles of unread books on the floor before returning to his place at the window. Perhaps Fox's church had expelled him for his adultery with Mrs Clarke, he wondered vaguely.

He didn't see Hannah that day.

*

He lays out the journals to count the years: 1793 1794 1795 in a line, then 1796, the new one, underneath the others. Not writ in it. Not writ much in any except the first.

He knows it was April a while ago. He got extra tobacco and a note written with loops and curls:

Congratulations John Warlow! You have lived for 3 Years
Underground!
Joseph Jenkins, April 1796

Suddenly by itself came a plate of gooseberry jam tarts with no note. He suspects Annie. Thinks of her fingers pressing the pastry. Imagines her licking jam from her lips, her chin; her tongue darting in and out. He bites up the tarts.

There's frogs again, which pleases him. He had a stroke of genius in the winter. Once he'd seen a thing at a fair: not spectacles, but a glass on a handle. He writes:

plees send   glas   it do mak thins big er

It comes after many days. In a box. *Magnifying Glass*. He touches the velvet on which it lies. Takes it out, holds the glass up to his eye. A blur. Looks down. More blur. He holds it at arm's length and sees:

M a g ni fy   ing   Glass

Then tries the journal. Blur. But then:

1 7

9   6

And a claw – his great, yellowed nail. Curved, a beak. Huge fingertips sooty from candle nats. Skin like wood grain. The weave of his cuff, grey-edged, spotted with meat grease; *big stitches* of his sleeve: ropes, like a field of ropes.

Fly bodies red-staining the tablecloth. Legs. Wings. Tiny hairs. Others not flattened shining blue, green. Drops one into the spider's web over the mantle. Waits, glass in hand, waits till at last the spider darts and grabs and he goes too close and the glass is sticky with web.

For days he peers at everything. Everything is lines. Neat like on fish skin (*still* they send it down!). Paper is lines. First, it's rough like short grass. Then you see it's lines. Some things is dots. Bread is dots and holes. Wood is scratches, scratches and lines. His skin is scratches and lines; this way and that they go, criss-cross. He stares for hours at his hand. Pushes the skin on the back of it and it's like ripples on a pond.

He roots out the animals book. Cows all stripes, bear wavy strips. THE OLD ENG LISH HOUND. And the terrible bat. He dares. Shuts the book quick, stuffs it back in the cupboard.

Little grey lines all over the man Robinson. The book's spine cracked black like a burned beam.

Takes the glass to the fruit picture. No good. Can't see no worm inside. Bad bit's not soft.

He thinks he'll look at a frog. Builds a pen of books to keep it. In it goes, but jumps out before he can look. He makes the sides higher. Then it's too dark in the pen to see it. Cradled in his fingers, he lowers it to the floor, takes a candle, heaves himself down to where the creature sits. Its sides blowing in and out, panting. He reaches for the glass and the frog hops off under the cistern.

He wants to see it close. Especially he wants to see its feet, its face. Its slow eyes.

*

Catherine found an opportunity one Saturday when Mr Powyss was out riding, a rare enough occurrence. It was a fine afternoon; he'd have plenty to inspect in the orchard and glasshouses. It was not yet time to go to the kitchen. She and Annie were sweeping the hallway.

Broom in hand she knocked at the library door for form's sake, poked her head round, beckoned to Annie then pushed the hesitating girl before her.

They stood inside the door, unsure which way to go. Although lighting the fire on cold mornings and brushing the carpets were their tasks, they were not allowed to touch any objects in the room. Only Samuel had that job.

'Why he thinks Samuel's more delicate-fingered than

us I don't know,' Catherine whispered. 'Just because he's a footman and we're only housemaids. Look, I heard they go in here.' She darted to the instrument room.

'Come *on*, Annie.' But the girl could only stare in terror and fascination as Catherine inspected the upholstered seats of the two chairs.

'No stains. She must have used scouring-drops after. That's a telescope on the table I do think, but there's not a thing else, look. No bits of dead butterflies and beetles and spiders like Jenkins said there were.'

'Oh Catherine, quick, afore he come back!' Annie said in terror at the spiders.

'We can always be *cleaning*, silly.'

'There be nothing here. Come away!'

'Nothing means he did clear the table to make room for them *on* it.'

'Oh!' Annie drew a shocked breath.

'But nothing there either. They must have wiped it clean. That's it, yes. Ah but look here.'

She ran back into the main room. 'On the floor here. These papers in fallen heaps. *There* now. I'll push them away.' She was on her knees searching back and forth. 'But this rug has so many squares and lines and squiggles I can't see the marks!'

'Quick! Someone's coming, I'm sure of it.'

'Nonsense! Look at these stains. Come over here.' Annie darted over, darted back.

But Catherine was sure she had enough evidence now. They tiptoed to the door. Annie ran out and Catherine took one last look. Yes. *That's* where they lay. Just like her and Abraham on the mat before the fire. Who could blame them?

*

She ran straight to Abraham, leaving Annie to pod peas in the kitchen and hope Cook wouldn't bother about her absence for a bit. Price was delighted by Catherine's description of her invasion of Powyss's library.

'Clever puss!' he said.

Her account was not kind to Annie and made Price laugh hoarsely. She enjoyed that for he rarely smiled, while she would find amusement wherever she could.

'Show how you did inspect the carpet,' he said, and when she got down on her hands and knees and gave a comic rendering of herself he pounced on her and shoved her over onto her back.

'I be Mr Powyss!' he said, of a sudden, pulling his mouth down into a ridiculously serious expression.

'Oh and I am poor Hannah Warlow, even though my mother *were* a *lady's maid*,' Catherine squeaked merrily.

'Her were no *lady* isn't it. I am Mr Powyss your master. And you pulls up your shift, isn't it,' he said frowning and pulling open his breeches.

'Oh, oh. Mr Powyss. Oh. I am all pale and sad and all I can do is pull up my shift for you!' And she cackled and he fucked her quickly, she having to get back to dress the fowls.

'Adultery isn't it?' Price said.

'What we do?'

'*No. Them.*'

'Why yes. But he is master and she is nobody; he can do what he will.'

'Her's a married woman. It is a sin. A sin in the church court.'

'Will you go and report him then, Abraham?'

'I have heard them do pro–se–cute for adultery. And in–con–tinence, too, it is called. No, there's better ways for us.'

'What do you mean?'

'I mean your writing, clever puss. Us'll write him a letter, isn't it. Tell him us knows what him does and us'll tell soon enough.'

'Not a letter from *me*!'

'Anon–y–mous, silly woman. And you do disguise your hand. Tomorrow I'll get more paper from the club. I'll say it, you'll write. And you'll lay it on his desk in the morning while him's still abed.'

*

He's back to thinking about Mary again. When father beat them she'd get him behind her. He never beat *her* with his knobbed stick. Once Joe ducked. It caught his head, stunned him. Thought him were dead, but no.

'My rod of iron!' Father'd roar. 'Even as I received of *my* father!' That be the Bible. Someone finds the stick under the cart when it topples. Not broken. Not like him, crushed flat.

With him gone they work for Kempton. Kempton's father, *Old* Kempton. Up before crows wake. Runnin, he this side, Joe the other, flappin arms. Crows themselves. Hoarse with shoutin. 'Cept crows don't go hoarse. At day's end, Joe runs ahead, is gone. Mary's twilight shape limps towards him.

'Art cold?' she says.

'Yes.'

'Art hungry?' Takes somethin from her apron, holds out her hand.

'Yes.'

Nob of bread. Better than all *this* from up there! *Gentleman's dinner.*

'Don't tell.' Her voice is low. It's their secret, just them. 'Don't tell mother.'

His eyes fill. He covers them with his hands and sobs. Mary! Grinds his palms into his eye sockets.

There's murmuring. Close to him. He's a boy. And there she is, talking in her low voice.

'Don't tell, John. Say nothin.'

'*Say nothin,*' he promises.

John Warlow 9 yers owd

Murmuring. He hears her.

It be undertide. Dark. Can't hardly see her face.

Feels her arm round his shoulders. She hugs him to her hip; his arm rests on her waist, not long enough to go round it. She murmurs to him. They walk. Slowly, slowly. He rocks up and down with her limp. Smells the damp roughness of her skirt. Always thinking *don't get home yet. Walk slowly.* Up and down.

Come back! Come back! Mary, here's my hand!

Murmuring. Murmuring.

But it's *two* voices. Two! His head jerks up. He listens. *Two* women's voices. He's been dreaming.

Feet run. A door closes. *Above!* Voices came through the *ceilin*. But he's two floors down! *How?* What's up there?

One candle's alight. Lamp'd be better, but look *now*. Find out *now*. Can't see much. Must be hole in the ceilin, must be. Climbs on the chair, the table, reaches up. Feels with big hands, black from no washing, dried scabs. Beams, crumbled plaster, lath. He yelps as a splinter jabs into his flesh. His hands run over plaster lumps – fruits and leaves.

Then metal. Metal *hole* in the middle of the fruits. He puts a finger in it. Nail clacks against metal.

He clambers down heavily for a broom. Climbs back. Panting. Thrusts the handle into the hole. Up it goes, up till there's nothing but bristles in his hand.

That's it! Pipe in the ceilin.

Why?

His pulse, his wits race. Powyss! Watching me through the hole. *Spyin!* Shove the broomstick in his eye! But no, what'd him see? Hole's too small. Couldn't see. That's not it.

Powyss *hears* him through this hole! *I* heard *them. Them* hears *me.* Powyss put it to *listen* to *me!* Damned Powyss. *Listenin. All this* time.

Powyss! Damned infernold dog! *Powyss* hears *everythin.*

Hears him scrape the ashes, scrape the plate, scrape the pen on the page. Hears him eatin, fartin, scratchin, groanin, cursin, shittin. *Damn him!*

Heard him sob just now, did he? And the *women?* Listenin to him sob *with two women*, were he?

'Damn you, Powyss! Damn you! *I knows you're there!*' he bawls up at the ceiling.

No sound. Nothing. He puts his ear to the hole but there's nothing.

'Damned dog, Powyss! Him shuts me down here. Never says him'd be listenin, spyin.' He gets off the table.

'Powyss! You said . . . what were it? *Science* you said it were for *science*, you said,' he shouts. 'What's that mean, Powyss? *Science*, what's that?' Waits. No answer.

'It mean, it mean *No Freedom*. Yes yes. *No Freedom* it mean. That's what.' Phrases remembered from the Dog bubble up like gas.

He yells: 'Them as have money takes all. Takes bread from mouths. Damn to Powyss! Damn infernold dog! Damn to the government! Damn to the king!'

He stalks about the room restlessly clenching, unclenching his fists, can't be still, shouting, bawling, searching for something, something. Then he understands. Yes. He is like the others even down here. Yes. That's it. The others stirrin up before he came below. The others grumblin in the Dog. More and more. Men scrawlin on the market cross. Liberty. *That's* it. And that other word. Men shoutin, thumpin the table. Once them did shoot at an effigy. Who were that? Them say them chops heads off in France.

He tires. Throat hurts from the bawling. But he can't stop seeing Powyss in his fine black velvet coat. Listening through the hole at every moment. Smiling. Proud. *Of all this!*

He snatches up the shovel, whacks it on the table bang bang bang bang bang break! – but it doesn't. Flings it across the room. Then the tongs against the iron fireplace clang onto the hearth. He waits, listens for a moment, but nothing stirs. Nothing up there. So he heaps coal out on the floor and slams the scuttle with both hands hard against the grate, the mantle, smashes the man in the skins. Let him hear that!

'*I knows you're up there!*' Quiet. No one's *listenin*, are they?

But wait. He's got *fire*. He can fire the house. Tonight, when Powyss has gone to bed. He'll stuff paper in the hole. No, strips of linen's better; he's already ripped a shirt for a length to tie his hair. Smear that butter on 'em – that's good. Push 'em into the pipe. Light a spark. Blow the bellows! Them'll catch fire, up the pipe, to boards, carpets, furniture. *Whole house!*

He knows men do it, pull down houses, fire them. He's heard about it in the Dog. Bands of men. Birmingham, them said. But *he*'ll do it himself. On his own. Them'll praise him in the village. Not the fool them said he were.

Flames, big flames, tall as houses, lickin up chimneys.

He's seen it. Houses on fire in Moreham when he were a boy. Hot ember began it. People and animals jumpin out of windows, screamin. Streams of rats, mice pourin out. Huddles stood and watched. Someone counted. Two souls missin. All but the end house burned to nothin. Two bodies in the cellar. Nails torn with clawin. *In the cellar.*

'Aah. Aah!' He bangs the table with his fists. His head.

'How can I *do* it? Cannot get *out*. Must get *out*.' He moans. Moans become howls, a dog baying.

No! He feels a surge of strength in his back, his shoulders, arms; overturns the table at one go. Everything crashes off it. He heaves the armchair backwards and jumps on its back. Stuffing oozes. Hurls things at walls: candlesticks, jugs, boxes, lamps, roaring like a goaded bear. He runs to tear things down: glass shatters from pictures, the smashed looking glass. Plaster frames break; he stamps them to powder. Pulls, twists, yanks. Skeletal doors hang from bookcase hinges. Ripped books shower their shreds. Endpapers, boards bend under his boot soles. Pens crack like bones.

His voice, mocking, squawks falsetto *'pump with your feet!'*
He levers off the hinges of the organ doors, pulls out pipes
which ring metallic notes where he flings them, slams his
forearms hard on the keyboard so that howling sounds
crowd out at him. He takes the chair to kill it, the poker to
stab, wreck, he wrenches wooden shards of the case with
his hands, bloody with cuts, shouting, stamping, yelling,
yowling, bellowing.

Suddenly crumples, falls. Exhausted. Great bulk on bed of
splinters.

Sleeps.

Wakes to the creak of the dumb waiter. A meal descends.
Half a roast fowl, bacon, peas. A salad. Redcurrant tart. Pint
of porter.

*

Powyss summoned Hannah. He saw from Jenkins's expression that they all knew, had all heard. Had all listened. He
used to look at Jenkins rarely. Now he read every word on
his face.

'I shall walk with Mrs Warlow in the garden.'

They might peer through the windows but at least they
wouldn't hear what was said.

August. Plum tree leaves are ragged.

Fox had written about the election which failed to unseat
Pitt, despite all the work of his favourite radicals and their
alliance with Whigs. He quoted his namesake Charles James
Fox to whom he had listened on the hustings: 'A more detest-
able government never existed in British History,' Fox had
declared, 'It has destroyed more human beings in its foreign
wars, than Louis XIV; and attempted the lives of more inno-
cent men at home, than Henry VIII.'

Powyss felt as if he were reading about himself. He had
only heard the end of Warlow's rampage, but that was bad

enough: the endless wrecking, the terrible baying of an animal in despair.

He had caused it.

'Hannah. I shall free Warlow. Your husband.' They walked apart beside long flower beds, where the child Polly had run her fingers, bent her head to sniff. *Aster, coreopsis, phlox paniculata.* Red and pink, late summer's blood and flesh.

She stopped. He remembered the first time she came for the money, when she shrank back as if expecting a blow. How much she had changed since then! Yet always there'd been a strength in her and now resistance spoke in her silence.

'I see you don't want that, Hannah.'

'No.'

'We can speak freely. They'll be watching but no one can hear us. No keyholes! He's had a kind of fit, Hannah. It was extraordinary. He was smashing things, shouting, cursing.'

'They did say.'

'No doubt, but don't tell me what they said. All I know is that he must be brought out. The experiment has gone wrong, Hannah. Perhaps it *was* wrong. I thought I could observe Warlow like I observe the growth of a plant. I wanted to see how he'd survive in certain conditions. I didn't think he might become mad. I thought melancholy possible, but not this. Perhaps his explosion is only temporary. Yet who knows what destruction he has wrought? And were it to happen again it might be worse. I cannot be the man's murderer, Hannah.'

She flinched; said nothing.

'He must come out before it's too late. He must return home and life will resume as it was.'

'Life?'

He refused to think what her life had been before.

'The agreement will be broken of course. He signed a contract. I cannot pay him £50 a year if he hasn't stayed below for seven years. And I shall no longer support you. If I did, everyone else around about would make a claim.'

'The children are well. They will be poor again.' It was a cry.

'And I have taken advantage of you, Hannah.' *Rudbeckia*, black-eyed.

'I am yours,' she said, and it fired within his veins like laudanum.

They had reached the end of the flower garden, where a rose hedge, blooms long gone, led into the orchard, fleckered in shade. Out of the watchers' vision. He clasped her to him and they held each other with the force of finality. He felt himself burn, sear, wanted her *now*, for her to be his.

And to master Warlow. Yes, to master the brute who *owned* her, who would take her back. To fuck her now would be to crush Warlow.

He pulled at her clothes to free her neck, her small breasts. Oh, he'd wanted this! On the ground, in long grass, his hands sought her skin, her limbs, found the surprising warmth of her birth-stretched belly. And, as he'd anticipated, she moved towards him, with him, searched for him, found, took him in and cried out with relief.

He was certain, pitiless. Dug his nails into earth. Groaned, himself, from the relief of it. At last, at last, his release before Warlow's.

Then, in the orchard a crack. Something skirred. They heard a throated sound, a cough, a jeer. Broke apart as at a snake beneath them.

He drew her skirts down over her thin, reddened legs. Helped her up, wrapped her fallen shawl about her naked shoulders.

'Quick, go home! That way.' He indicated a gate in a far wall; watched her tremble and hold her clothes together with fingers he yet felt on his body, run towards the gate, through it, without looking back.

Stood, himself dazed, shaking, thwarted.

Turned his back on the sneering watcher, whose identity he guessed, and went to the hothouse. Ashen. Wretched.

He wanted a woman who was not his to have. Had wanted her all this time and now it was over. A woman of few words, serene as a tree new-found in a foreign land whose fruit he'd never taste again. Desire for her had grown, a convolvulus, winding, charming him with its strength, its fragile blue beauty, ineradicable. It had smothered all till he could think of nothing else.

And now!

Melon leaves shrivelled in the heat, their great growth over. He began to clear cucumber haulm. Stopped. Wrenched at the fleshy stalks. Frantic desire tore at reason. Yet he knew the experiment was ill conceived, the results blurred by his self-ishness. He must cut it down, clear out the wayward growth.

The night's expected storm was violent. Hailstones shat-tered the lower lights of several greenhouses. The valley flooded. His mother would have accepted the clear sign of punishment. But he abhorred superstition. If God exists he cares no more for us than a captain for the mice on his ship.

Still, he stood at the window watching the storm, listen-ing to the distant destruction of glass. Saw lightning split an indigo sky.

Bowed his head to reason.

Tomorrow he would release Warlow at midday. Instruct Mrs Rentfree to pack two baskets with provisions for the family, instruct Price to find a month's labour for Warlow until Kempton took him on again.

*

She tells herself: John will come back.

He says he have done wrong. Mr Powyss. But it is too late to think so now.

John will be angry when he do not get £50 a year. He will strike the boys, though not Margaret nor Polly, he will spare them, surely. I must keep out of his way.

The servants will talk. Tell John. They will say all manner of things. Especially now.

In the garden I could not tell him, though he wanted me to speak. I could not say. It is hard for me. He has given us money. I cannot ask for anything more.

I think I do love him.

Someone were watching us. That evil man I think. And so it were over when it had only begun.

He did say he will think of me always. But we cannot meet ever. I do think it be untrue then, what he say.

Chapter 7

HE WAS WOKEN by Jenkins coughing.

'Mr Powyss. *Sir*.'

Powyss had fallen asleep in the chair by the library window. Instructions were needed about storm damage. And Warlow. A letter had arrived from Fox.

'Return in an hour, Jenkins. No, I'll breakfast later.'

Everything came back to him; he felt exhausted, sick. His coat smelled of sweat. Fury and fear surged in his gut. Such utter disorder, how it revolted him! Yesterday he had decided. How so easily? How at all? And why now had he given himself a mere *hour*?

Confusion drove him from the library and out of the house, unwashed, in his foul clothes, unseen as far as he knew. He avoided the hothouse and greenhouses where he was likely to encounter Price, whose snarls he couldn't face. No doubt it was he who'd watched them in the orchard yesterday. All his refuges were useless. Labourers were in the gardens; a smirking maid might dash past at any moment.

He set off across the fields and up Cold Hill. The ground was dry and smelled of sun-baked sheep droppings. Berries of twisted hawthorn rusted; clusters of curling yellow leaves gathered beneath.

He walked without stopping, the strenuous movement seeming to consume his fear. Blood beating in his head kept out voices.

For a moment near the summit of the hill he thought he was being watched once more, turned and looked back: it was only the eyes of the house. Moreham House, small yet pleasing in its symmetry and ordered grounds; within it a fine collection of books, curiosities, scientific instruments and a crazed labourer, filthy and violent; a set of servants not to be trusted. And he the master, infatuated with that same labourer's wife. Obsessed by her.

Clarity. He must find a solution. He climbed higher, higher, right onto the brow. Moreham was behind him out of sight. He crouched down among the whins, until his shins ached and he fell forward, his hands clutching at his head as if to crush the thoughts within.

I won't give her up! I won't. In his mind's eye he saw her running from him through the gate in the wall. Felt still the ferocity of their coupling before it broke, again and again the heat of her skin under his hands, her bones against his. And she was glad, yes, glad!

Clarity! What had happened to reason? His ordered life, his run of experiments and minor achievements. *I will not be thrown off course like this!*

Yet, why must I have this woman when I could buy one tomorrow?

He removed his coat. There were no dwellings within sight. Hills spread away and were absorbed into sky. He saw clouds change, colours shift.

A cow bellowed in the distance. Or was it Warlow bellowing underground?

What was once resentment was now hatred. Warlow had lived with Hannah for years; Powyss had known her for so few. Warlow had maltreated her, aged her, beaten her, no longer deserved her.

And he had tasted Hannah. Knew he had to again. The longer Warlow remained below, the more he wanted her.

But surely this was a distortion? Perverted reason. Not reason at all. Warlow would have to be freed and he must stay away from the woman for her husband would certainly kill him.

And the experiment, what of that? He'd admitted to Hannah that it had gone wrong and perhaps it *was* wrong. The conditions below were ruined. The experiment itself was ruined. He had lost it all.

He sank down onto stones, his face scraping hard, woody stems; he pressed dry earth-dust, his fists clenched like a child in tantrum.

Silence rang in his ears. Birds were quiet at this time of year; not even the mew of a buzzard. His eyelids closed. He dozed, perhaps for minutes only, enough to cut his mind adrift.

And woke to a stroke of cold air.

Thirst. He cast around for the spring nearby, bent, drank and standing again, felt black anger rush back into his blood. Now he must go home, must give orders that would leave him filled with loathing and despair.

He took up his coat against the chill, saw Fox's crumpled letter about to fall from his pocket. Slit it open with his pocket knife.

I have been thinking about your Warlow, it said halfway down, after news of the latest government outrages.

Of course, the man doesn't know what's taken place.

As you will have perceived, I have had some doubts about your under-earth experiment. But of course it is not Warlow alone who is affected. Have you thought how his bruised children may hate you when you finally release him?

For you have raised them above their lowly state. Relieved
Mrs Warlow of her slavery of fear. We certainly should
attend to the rights of woman as to those of man. The spirit
of God lives in each person (I still maintain that Unitarian
belief), but in this case the advantages for six children and
their mother far outweigh seven years of minor deprivation for
their father. Greater good thus drowns out evil.

You once accused me of being your conscience, Powyss.
But on balance I commend your experiment.

He read it twice. This was the glass through which Fox saw the situation, clear like a new-polished lens, trained on a species of animal life caught and presented to him by someone else. Fox's sum was simple: the good done to a woman and six children was greater than the evil done to one man.

Fox's voice was the cut of clean reason. He knew nothing of Powyss and Hannah. He needn't know.

It was evening. A wind stirred the stunted plants at his feet. Concentration, tension had stiffened his limbs. He moved awkwardly, startling some sheep who ran away in a rush, then set off a different way back, penning a letter to Fox in his head as he strode down.

*

'Sam says they never did,' Annie told Catherine in a hushed voice, proud of herself that she'd both extracted this indelicate information and actually pronounced it. She was preparing fruit; Catherine was rubbing butter into flour.

Catherine was cross. She didn't like to be wrong.

'How do he know?'

'You *said* he were the one to know!'

Cook stomped out of the pantry.

'Gossip, tattle! There'll be pips and peel and maggots in the pies!'

They continued when she returned to the pantry with a bottle barely concealed under her apron. Did she really think they couldn't see, didn't already know perfectly well?

Annie bent over the apples. Sam had sharpened the knife so much she was worried there'd be blood in the pies, let alone maggots and peel.

'Sam have looked at all the clothes. His drawers in particler,' she added in a small voice.

'Ooh! Annie!'

Annie was overcome with blushing and went out to the back kitchen ostensibly to fetch more fruit.

In fact, since John Warlow's outburst Catherine had not been thinking about what the master did with Hannah. And she didn't believe what Sam said. However, it was something to take to Abraham.

''*Course* they did. *I* know,' he spat. 'And do not say *master*, Catherine,' he added tetchily.

'Oh, and why not?'

'Him's no better nor us. Him's more money but him's *born* same as us.'

'Not so! He were born in the big house whereas I were born in a hovel. And you, too, I should say.'

'Him were a naked baby, just like us. *Did not he that made me in the womb make him?*' he added lugubriously.

'Abraham! I did think you despised religion!'

Price grunted with annoyance. He never felt embarrassment.

Catherine said: 'That's like when Tom Paine says m*en are all of one degree.*'

Price ignored this; *he* was the expert on Paine. 'Him'll die same as us, will Powyss.'

So, she must remember to say Mr Powyss, not master, though Price himself omitted Mr as well.

'Him have put John Warlow in a prison, isn't it.'

'No, Abraham. Warlow *agreed* to live down there. Think

131

of the food and clothes he's given. The money he'll have when he comes out. It wasn't a prison when Annie and I got it ready. You forget I have *seen* it down there. Everything you could wish for. All new. Better than anything you or I have. It's an underground palace!'

'Silly girl you, Catherine. He did try to excape, isn't it. For him it's a prison. Warlow is Powyss's ex–per–i–ment. Powyss must let him out.'

Catherine knew he was right, of course. She and Price had not heard the worst of Warlow's day of destruction, for they'd been busy aping Powyss and Hannah on Price's floor. But she'd heard from the others and she had imagined. A great bear of a man who beat his children and his wife, laying about him, bringing everything down. All that lovely polished furniture. All those beautiful pictures.

'And now him do fuck his wife!'

Catherine noted to herself that, from Hannah's point of view, as far as *that* went Mr Powyss would certainly be preferable to John Warlow.

'And I says nothing!' Price groaned. '*And I do his work!*' The corners of his mouth turned down and for a moment she thought he might cry.

'Then I shall write the letter about adultery.'

'Pah! Adultery! *Sin!*' He sucked his fingers, earth-brown and hard like twigs. 'Letters is not enough.'

'What can you mean?' Catherine often felt she was one step behind Abraham. Sluggish his reading might be, but his thoughts shot about like mad stars.

'Ponder him in thy little head, clever puss,' he said, pulling her hair back and biting her neck till she cried out.

*

Hampstead, 8 May 1797

Dear Powyss,

*I was greatly relieved to receive a written communication
from you in addition to an edible one. I was mighty glad
of the Christmas fruit of course, but I have missed hearing
about Moreham. And I am grateful, too, for in the inclusion
of the half-penned letter you say has lived in a drawer for a
year. Reading of Warlow's outburst and of the intimations
of subversion from your servants, I understand how you have
been occupied. I must reiterate my previous computation: that
the greater good for Mrs Warlow and her children outweighs
even the <u>fortissimo</u> suffering of Mr Warlow.*

*Here, in the seat of government, subversion is dealt with
with vile severity. Even a whiff of complaint sniffed out by
carbuncle-nosed spies means imprisonment without trial.*

*Yet in the public mind treason has been usurped by
war. People talk of nothing else, especially since the French
invasion attempts in Devon and Pembrokeshire. People
demand <u>peace</u>. I attended a meeting with a friend who is an
inhabitant of Westminster (has there not been such a meeting
held in Hereford?). You should have heard the great cries of
Peace! Peace! that rose to the skies. And to the skies it was as
they had been <u>shut out</u> of Westminster Hall and were obliged
to meet in Palace Yard!*

*The speakers rightly made much of the outrageous, wicked,
delusive conduct of ministers, their corruption and iniquity
for eight years ever since the storming of the Bastille set them
aquiver in 1789. From 1792 they have cast our enemies not as
those against whom we fought abroad, but as those <u>at home</u>.
They have increased the numbers of military in preparation
for putting down <u>domestic insurrection</u>. Worst of all they
have sent about a <u>rumour of famine</u> to raise the price of
corn prodigiously so that honest labourers and industrious
mechanics should save themselves by joining the army!*

Perhaps this information will distract you from your troubles. I am myself troubled by the imminent release of Mr Clarke. While I am pleased that a good man, wrongfully imprisoned, should at last retrieve his freedom, I am concerned for my friendship with Mrs Clarke and tremble at the prospects before me.

Yours ever,
Benjamin Fox

*

Warlow had been sent buckets of hot water, more brooms, rags for cleaning and a note supposedly from Jenkins to ask if anything needed replacing. There had been no reply. At first the entire household held its breath. Then, when meals were evidently consumed and full pots for the cesspool appeared, a disgruntled normality seemed to return.

In fact Price wasn't the only person to think Warlow should be let out, though nobody else's methods were likely to be the same as his.

Bottles of sherry were piling up in Joseph Jenkins's pantry. His theft from the cellars was in direct proportion to Powyss's loss of authority, each bottle representing an action or utterance of which Jenkins heartily disapproved. He'd known a handful of masters in his time, but none as spineless as Powyss. Damage to the master's authority had a way of damaging his own rule, he found. That Croft hussy, for instance, with her pert replies.

He drank little of what he stole. An occasional glass at the end of the day or after a particularly tiresome event was all he ever took. Quite unlike Mrs Rentfree, who was bosky as a stewed fruit. Rather than being for the purposes of consumption, he saw what he did as rightful possession on account of the master's failings.

Not that he didn't admire some of Mrs Rentfree's qualities. Her beef was never overcooked, her plumcake never sad. He enjoyed the way she lashed those worthless maids with her scorn. A harsh puritan childhood and a little learning informed Jenkins's attitude to his fellow men, most of whom he despised, but he was certainly not a revolutionary. Toppling Powyss never entered his mind. Order was what he required. Order was all.

'He should be made to clean the place up and got out. Send him back where he come from. And the wife. Thinks she's better than everybody because her mother was a lady's maid. Her mother went mad carrying all Kempton's bastards.' He was standing in the kitchen doorway after decanting some wine for Powyss.

'Disgusting,' said Mrs Rentfree.

'Should never have let the woman into the house.'

''E never goes to church. 'E's no religion, the master.'

Samuel leaned up against the wall, having served the first course. He bit his nails fiercely.

'You'll be wanting to leave us, Mr Jenkins,' Mrs Rentfree said, cutting and doling out slices of pie.

'I can't tell if you're guessing or hoping, Mrs Rentfree.'

'You've been complaining for years is all I say.'

Samuel dared to speak: 'Mr Powyss is a clever man. He read books.'

Cook exchanged a glance with Jenkins and handed Samuel the master's portion and a jug of crème anglaise. They ignored the footman's remark.

Warlow's dishes appeared at the top of the shaft, Catherine and Annie unloaded them and placed a second course and a small dessert of nuts and fruit on a tray, Cook tutting loudly.

'Powyss don't eat much these days,' Jenkins remarked. 'He's thinking about something else and we know what *that* is. Won't look at me.'

'You should tell the master your mind, Mr Jenkins.'

'It'll all come to grief in its own time, mark my words.'

'You're wrong!' Samuel said in a sort of strangled shout. 'The experiment's an important thing.'

'What do *you* know about it, you whippersnapper? Just because the master lets you dust his *knick-knacks*.'

Laughter from Cook, and Annie tittered, not exactly sure why.

'It's *you* as don't know,' said Samuel, galled by the women.

Jenkins grabbed him by the collar. 'Telling *me* are we? Think you know what you're talking about? You know nothing, you little rat. And don't go running off to the master and telling him everything we've said when you're laying out his *breeches*.'

More laughter. Samuel raised a fist but Jenkins caught his wrist.

'Hit me, would you? There's insubordination for you,' he said triumphantly to the others. A favourite word, its syllables strung out grandly. 'I'll haul you over if there's any more of that. *Get out!* And don't you whimper, Miss!'

He put his face close up to Annie, who backed away, not knowing whether he might bite or kiss her. She hated the thought of either.

*

Powyss had posted Fox a carefully incomplete account of Warlow's explosion so that Fox's reply, drawing an analogy between subversion sniffed out by 'carbuncle-nosed spies' and put down by means of imprisonment without trial, and what had happened in Moreham annoyed him greatly. He crumpled the letter and threw it on the floor.

Perhaps Warlow's behaviour *was* domestic insurrection. But were he to analyse the discontent in Moreham House, apart from wreck underground, he wasn't sure what he could give as evidence. Jenkins and the other servants continued their routines. His clothes were laid out, meals were cooked, the house was clean. Work in the gardens and grounds was maintained. And yet he sensed a hint of revolt. His orders tended to result in a fractional hesitation. He'd seen the maid Catherine come out of the library more than once without cleaning apparatus, a smile slipping from her face. He couldn't help hearing Jenkins's heavy emphasis on 'Mrs' every time he announced Hannah's arrival. Samuel, whom he trusted more than the rest, who was willing to do anything he asked, looked anxious all the time.

A few days later Jenkins handed him a note from Warlow, apparently written with his finger on paper torn from Defoe's *Plague Year* – he recognised the list of deaths from fever, spotted fever, surfeit and teeth that Defoe gave for the first week of August. Scrawled along the margin was:

I   no yor lisnin

He felt the steel edge in Jenkins's stare as he read the crude letters.

The irony was that he'd not used the listening tube for months. But Warlow must have found his end of it in the ceiling, which had provoked his outburst, he supposed. He could reassure him about *that* at least.

However, if Warlow were indeed to remain below, the terms of the arrangement must still hold.

'There's to be no *direct* reply of course, Jenkins. Please find something to plug Warlow's end of the tube. By now, I take it, you yourself know about my copper device.'

'Sir.'

'Ask Samuel to cut a piece of cork; he should be able to remember the original measurements. Send it down with a sheaf of fresh paper, ink and pens. Evidently he has destroyed his pens.

'After that I should like you and Samuel to transfer some furniture, books and so forth upstairs into the small sitting room. I shall make a list and give it to you in the morning.'

Moving upstairs placed another floor between him and Warlow, but his relief at this was swamped by revulsion. It was inevitable that he'd hate Warlow – *proprium humani ingenii est odisse quem laeseris* – he could hear Fox's pen scratching Tacitus at him. Of course he'd recorded the explosion and all that was known about it. But the whole experiment was now a shackle, heavy, painful, irremovable. It was as if all that ambition to enter the world of natural science, inchoate as it had been at first, then finally focused, had withered, blackened, died. And now rotted and stank. It sickened him to remember. Moving up a floor removed Warlow further.

He stood by the window in the upstairs sitting room. His young *Magnolia virginiana* was on the point of flowering, its candle blooms firm, serene. He was expecting Hannah shortly.

This room was far less satisfactory than his library. He missed the presence of his globes, his Apulian vases, the cabinet with the sloping top, the possibility of consulting any one of hundreds of books. The view from the window was the same, only smaller, confined and he had to stand to see certain plants and trees of which he was particularly fond. On the other hand it was a pretty room, light, comfortable, pleasing with its delicate, pale-green geranium-leaf wallpaper. His essential books were there, the desk, his microscope and telescope, not that he'd gazed at the night sky for months. Of course he *could* use the library if necessary, find books, reorder his drawers of curios. But he wanted to be in that room as little as possible.

And nowadays almost the only book he actually used was Miller's *Gardeners Dictionary*. He would always need to refer to the dictator of English gardening, but concentrated reading on any other subject was something he failed to do now. His eyes slid over pages of words, his mind elsewhere.

Books would thud to the floor as he fell asleep over them, often followed by the shattering of his brandy glass on the hearth.

He held on to the authority of Benjamin Fox's arithmetical logic. Repeated the formula at moments of greatest doubt, like a daily prayer: *the happiness of Hannah and her children is greater than . . .* Otherwise, he almost never thought about Fox himself. He could not recall the content of the last letter from him.

Jenkins knocked.

'*Mrs* Warlow, Mr Powyss, sir.'

'Thank you, Jenkins. Please leave us.'

*

He kicks paths through the debris. From bed to pisspot to lift shaft. Most days he lies in bed wrapped in the smell of himself. Won't light a fire. Listens to vermin back and forth beneath the bed, infernal buzzing of flies.

Sleeping, waking, there is little difference. Dreaming. Not dreaming.

Is it morning? He lights the stump. Walks the path to the big room. He'd pulled the table back up from where he over-turned it, but a leg's broken. Dishes slide. Liquid slops. Now he sees plates on it. Congealed lamb's fry. Empty beer jug. His full pot on one of the lift shelves. He'd returned to bed, not rung the bell. Must have *been* morning.

There's no path to the grating. No debris there: couldn't smash the bath or the cistern could he. But he doesn't go to the grating anyway. Cares not for the outside world. The tiny, distant outside world.

When buckets came down, the thing creaking again and again, he put his face in the warm water. Pulled at his beard with his claws. Scratched out lice. Threw it all in the bathtub. A lake for frogs. Except there are none.

The roar of anger has gone out of his mind. He tears a page from a piece of broken book and scrawls with a nail dipped in ink. But only to remind himself:

I no yor lisnin

Puts it next to the full pisspot. Forgets about it.

He looks at the mess. He's glad he smashed everything of Powyss's, but he never thinks of that time when he did it now. Powyss can go to hell. They can all go to hell. Hannah, children, the others. To hell.

His heavy body occupies him. He picks, scratches, gnaws. Pinches biters out from under his vest, squashes them hard. Rubs where they get him in his sleep. Presses on sores that hurt, that weep. Goes back to bed.

Summer passes.

*

She says to herself: When I think on Mother it *cannot* be the same. She surely cannot have wanted Kempton.

In Herbert's room the bed is soft. So soft! It have sheets and pillows and beautiful cloth about it. It is warm.

The man Jenkins always do take me upstairs, not the library. He smile harshly into my face but I look away if I can. He wish me ill, though not as evil as the other.

John will stay.

When it do seem wrong I try to think if John changed place with me and I were below. He would sure to God take another woman. Many. He did complain of me often.

I know it is not an answer.

But he will get the money, that will please him. He wanted the money.

He were always a rough man. It is true he did save me from Kempton. And Kempton then be always hard on John and never mend our house. But after, John did come and take me himself: were no better than Kempton. Worse. Did crush me often almost to the death.

I do wonder what will happen when John come out. I dare not ask Herbert.

Sometimes he do groan then I think he be sorry I am there. He drink too much brandy. And the cordial. He do call it the tincture.

*

Something was happening to Abraham Price and Catherine wasn't sure what to make of it. He'd become more impatient and quite unpredictable. He'd leap up in the middle of his reading, which progressed but haltingly, grab the household mending she'd brought with her, cursing and ripping it before she could prevent him. He would pace around angrily, thumping furniture with his fists till she had to tell him to stop, for it made her dizzy. But that only angered him more. She wondered if it was because he was displeased that he still stumbled when he read and did so in front of her. Accordingly, her corrections were often hesitant. Or was it simply that he was fired by the news of the great gatherings there'd been in London. He'd tell her what he'd heard of the meetings, of the huge numbers of people. He'd repeat fine stirring phrases in a loud voice, waving his arms, then suddenly rush at her, bending her back onto the table as though she were a recalcitrant sapling.

It had been a mistake for her to quote at him once more, but she'd been delighted to read of Paine's February walk in the country, his finding a bud on a twig, that *though the vegetable sleep will continue longer on some trees and plants than on others, though some of them may not* blossom *for two or three years, all will be in leaf in the summer except those that are rotten.* How delightful, she thought, how Abraham will like this, and she read it aloud, but he dismissed it with a wave of his twiggy fingers. Metaphor didn't move him.

She already knew never to laugh at him even though to laugh was her way, her tendency. She'd pointed at his mud-encrusted clothes one day.

'Do you live in the ground?' she said, amused at the thought. 'You look as if you've come out of the earth to visit me!' He was, she thought to herself, something of a goblin, from the world of nature, likely to appear or disappear without warning. She remembered his look of malice more than the fact that he had struck her.

Then she was foolish enough to suggest that they might marry and live a respectable life.

'Abraham, do you hear me? Would that not be a happy thing, and then, you know, we might ...'

'Get out!' He slammed the book down, jumped out of his chair. 'Get out! Never say that again!' She ran out before he could reach her.

Two weeks later he opened to her timid knock, but she was careful and made sure to bring an offering.

It was a newspaper she had taken from the library. She and Annie still cleaned there even though Powyss hardly ever used it. She would look along the shelves sometimes and wish heartily the books were hers.

'Mr Powyss, he do have so many books, Abraham. If only I had some. Then I would not need to listen to Annie every night.'

'Take them. Him'll not miss 'em.'

'I couldn't take books.'

'You did steal his newspaper.'

'That's nothing.'

'Him'll never notice. Him's with Mrs Warlow all day long, isn't it. Everyone do talk of it in the village.'

'People exaggerate. She's not often there. But he have begun to drink somewhat, Jenkins said. Bottles of old Mr Powyss's brandy laid down years ago.

'This newspaper, now, Abraham. It is two months old but it tells about the seamen's mutiny. You did mention it one time. When all the sailors in the fleet refused to sail.'

'Read it, read it then!'

She was glad to have pleased him, though she knew the report would stir him up, make him roar and thrust her to the floor.

'"The mutiny among the seamen broke out on this day with greater violence than ever; owing, it is said, to a misrepresentation of certain parliamentary discussion on the subject, and to an idea that the concessions granted to the seamen would not be adhered to."'

'Who trusts par–lia–ment?' Price shouted. '*See*, do you, Catherine?'

'Yes, but let me read, Abraham! "In the morning of that day, the signal for sailing being made by Lord Bridport ... "'

He snorted.

'Abraham! This is the important part. Listen! "... the seamen again refused to weigh anchor. Some of the delegates from the ships at St Helen's coming alongside the London of 98 guns, Admiral Colpoys, that officer declared that not a man should come on board; and on their persisting to enter, an affray happened between the officers of the London and the ship's crew, which ended in bloodshed, several on both sides being killed and wounded."'

'Do it say how many them did kill?'

'No, it don't. But *listen*. "The sailors having overcome the officers, the former immediately confined Admiral Colpoys and Captain Griffiths, their commanders, for whose lives, for some time, great fears were entertained."'

'Confined their commanders! Oho!'

'It finishes: "In the sequel, they were released; and this alarming mutiny has since happily subsided."'

It was not what she expected. Instead of banging about and cursing, grabbing her and ripping her dress in his haste, he sat silently in his chair, picking at his fingers and biting his nails. He was brewing something. Catherine's left foot was at the ready lest she need rush to the door.

'Us'll do it, then.'

'Do what?'

'I'll tell the men. Them'll bring what them has. You do tell no one.'

'Abraham, what do you mean to do?'

'Why *confine* Powyss of course! Amos have a pistol, isn't it. Us all has staves and forks. Us'll confine him! Force him!'

'Then the constables will come and the militia and there'll be bloodshed and you'll be hanged. Abraham, no!'

'Him'll not call the militia if he be *dead*.'

'No, you must not!'

'Him must be brought down. Everyone be against him! Him fucks another man's wife. And keeps that man in prison!'

'Abraham stop!' She felt chaos, disaster roiling up. He might act at any moment and all would go wrong. She should never have brought the newspaper, how foolish to have tried to please him! She must try for all she was worth to control him. For who else could?

'I have a better idea,' she said rapidly to prevent him from speaking. 'Listen to me. Sit you down and listen. We shall release John Warlow. *I* shall release John Warlow.'

'*You?*'

'I can do it easily. I'll run down when Cook and Jenkins are asleep. Annie sleeps like a log. Sam in the back kitchen. I shall let him out. He'll go back to Hannah and that will be the end of it. No more experiment for Mr Powyss and no more Hannah for him, else Warlow might kill him.'

'Ah!' Price relished that thought.

'No bloodshed. No *hanging*, Abraham.' The word seemed to have its effect. He must have seen a hanging.

'Him'll tell Powyss it were you let him out.' He thought he'd trumped her.

144

'What crime shall I have committed? It's not murder, nor theft. I shall speak to Mr Powyss if I have to. I'm sure I can convince him it's for the best.' She'd glimpsed his face, tired and frowning just this morning, felt sudden pity for him.

'*I'll* break down the door first.'

'*No!*' She stood. 'That will waken everyone. I can do it. I'll steal the key from Jenkins, prise off the bars myself. Don't you see, Abraham? This way we can free Warlow *and* wreck Mr Powyss's plans without any trouble.'

Price ground his teeth.

'Let me try. And look you, if it fails, *then* you can get your men together.'

'Clever puss,' he sneered, 'I'll *consider* it,' and tore her clothes with such violence that she had to creep up to her room and had much sewing to do before she could appear again downstairs.

*

One day he slips on the board of a ripped book. Falls heavily. Lies in the refuse, the wreck, groaning. His wrist and foot pain him. Soon it's cold on the ground. He should light the fire; he's not far from it. But it's too full of ash. Won't draw.

Candle goes out. More candles in a cupboard other side of the room. He touches the debris around him to feel where the kicked path to the cupboard begins. Hauls himself slowly. Feeling, feeling his way. Don't want glass splinters in his hands, his knees.

There's a skittering on the table. Let them! They'll keep off him if there's orts and mammocks to gnaw.

The cupboard has no doors. Good. He takes out a candle but he's left the tinderbox near where he fell. Stuffs his pockets with candles, crawls back, dragging the hurting foot. His hand sweeps carefully before him like a delicate brush.

Tinderbox. It's hard to strike – nails too long. Still, he's kept his right thumb and forefinger chewed, so he has a pincer. Middle nail's too hard to bite off. Balances the box in the palm of his left hand with its beak-claws. Grips the steel with pincer fingers and strikes on the flint.

The candle flares; he sits on the floor, panting. Melts the ends of two more, sticks them on the ground, lights them. He looks at his legs; the ankle is swelling. Left wrist aches. Hears the lift thing creak up then down. Taking up the food he doesn't eat whether he rings the bell or not. Sending more. He won't eat it. Won't eat that slop. The thought of it makes him want to vomit.

He sees the board he slipped on. Among swathes of dust, blackened dottles, shards of organ case, cracked magnifying glass. A tear of paper, shred as big as his thumb. Words. He peers through the lens. Rubs off smears to see better.

My skin is bro ken

It is that man from before. What was he called? He was like him, wasn't he? Rob   Robin. The Strange Ad ventures. He picks the paper up, holds it near a flame. Pinched between forefinger and square thumb that blots out half the words.

My flesh is cloth   clothed   My flesh is clothed   with worms and clods of dust

He sits back, astonished. It *is* so! He scratches out lice from his sleeve. In bed the biters crowd down from the walls. What parts of himself he sees are black with dirt. Feet, hands. How can that be when he's not trod in mud for years?

my skin is broken,

yes, yes it is,

and be come   loath   some become loathsome.

The words are *not* about the man. They are about *him*. Him. John Warlow. It *is* him. Sores don't heal. His skin is broken all over his body. Lice bite, bite.

He shifts the paper. There's two more lines. The words are not hard. The words are speaking to him.

My days are   swift er   than a   wea ver's shutt   shuttle, swifter than a weaver's shuttle

Oh. Have they gone so fast? He doesn't know one day from the next. Has he not been here for? For how many years?

and are spent with   out   without hope.

The words are about him. He found them *here*, on the ground next to him, this scrap of paper. They are for him. They tell his life. His life now. Broken. Loathsome. Dust.

He is borne down by the words. Sadness whelms him. Without hope, without hope. He cries in gulps like a baby. Great gulps.

Through tears he pinches out two of the candles. Crawls with the other slowly, slowly. Stops, sob-racked. Moves again, ox-like. Pulls himself up onto the bed, snuffs out the light, curls into darkness.

*

'I think you cannot want me much longer. I am not a lady. I know nothing.' Hannah, entranced by the touch of fine linen, warmed by a well-stoked fire, felt with awe her inadequacy.

'No! No, you are wrong.'

'My mother were poor, always with child so I must help her, not go to school.'

'You said your father taught you.'

'Yes. Then they did give him a peg leg and sent him back to fight. He were killed in America.'

'I heard say your mother was a beauty.'

'People always said. She were a lady's maid till master got her with child.'

'Ah. Were you that child?'

'No, it were stillborn. When Mother were a widow four of her bairns did die, all Kempton's and her mind did wander. She were never the same after.'

Powyss lay next to her, exhausted by the energy that always possessed him when, politeness over, they were alone in his room. Her mother's story seemed barely to touch him. He envisaged her life as here, only here, in his bed.

'I think of nothing else but you all day.'

In fact he sometimes thought of the Harriets, Anna-Marias, Sophies at Mrs Clavering's, though he could never remember a face to fit each name. Wondered if, in recalling their attractions and what they used to do, he might resist this fatal compulsion. But it was hopeless. For always when he'd finished in Jermyn Street he would feel nothing but a little bruised, forget which girl it was who'd exerted herself. The hours there were not memorable. He would look forward with more eagerness to a long discussion with the nurseryman on the morrow. Useless. Hannah's was the body he wanted, incessantly.

He was obsessed. Besieged by exigent lust and rage. Racked.

'I cannot understand you. Herbert.' She used his name rarely, uncertainly. 'You are a gentleman. You do as you wish. But I have no learning. Nothing.'

'That doesn't matter, Hannah. I cannot understand *myself*. All my life I have despised everything except the life and work of the mind. Now my plans, my interests have vanished. I care about nothing except you.'

And he could see no relief. Lust and rage. The two were indistinguishable. To fuck Hannah was to destroy Warlow. Over and over again.

'I did say it before: I am yours. I will be always.'

He bowed his head with the weight of this sad honour, and she raised up his face with both hands and dared to look into his black eyes.

'It's no good,' he said, 'we can do nothing while John Warlow lives.'

'There be folk live not married.'

'But it is impossible that you live here with me. You and all the children while Warlow seethes below! There is always Warlow!' he said, raising his voice and grasping her hands. 'Always down there in who knows what frame of mind, while we take our pleasure.'

She looked away. Pleasure. A word she'd never used. It was exactly what she felt.

'Can *you* stay him from your thoughts. Hannah?'

'I have decided. It is best. While we can.'

'But you are married to him. Did he court you, Hannah? Did you, did you want to marry him?'

'John did save me from Kempton. When the illness came and Mother were not herself no more Kempton did turn to me. I were a girl. John did black his eye, break his nose.'

'Warlow the hero!'

'But then he did take me himself for his reward. Jack were his child, so then we must marry.'

'He is a wilful man. He get his way. He did want the £50 a year though others told him not.'

'So we punish him for his wilfulness?'

She didn't answer.

'It helps me to think of you. Your children. You look so well now, Hannah. There is a beauty in your face that was hidden when I first encountered you. You wouldn't let me see your eyes! Grey now in this firelight. You have sent out blossom after years in the dark.' He held her head and smelled her skin, her hair. Could Warlow *ever* have known her as he did?

'And your children are surely well. Aren't they? It's a while since I've met them in the garden. Little Polly, who likes flowers, is she in good health?'

'Yes.'

'That's good then. And yet. And yet we cannot forget him, can we? He is *our* punishment. And now the servants are against both me and you because of him. And I began it all!'

There was nothing she could say.

'This may shock you. In my whole life I have only ever paid for women. When I was young, in Athens, Rome, Naples. In London I pay expensive harlots.'

'Oh.'

'You are like none of them, Hannah. I want to keep you. Like treasure.'

'Then you shall keep me in your library in a glass cupboard!' she said, laughing.

He was pleased to see her laugh, acknowledged the dart of truth in what she said. For that's what he *would* do, if it were only possible: keep her, a precious piece in his collection, to touch, to have whenever he wanted her.

Sometimes it occurred to him that he should protect her from the lust which now he had begun, near drowned him like the brandy and laudanum. Hadn't he always shrunk from physical violence? What he did sometimes seemed like violation, though she didn't complain. Before long it might crack her innocence. She might begin to resemble the older whores.

He needed a drink and poured another glass of brandy.

'I do think you must not, Herbert.' She touched his face. 'It will be a harm to you.'

He downed it quickly. Smiled at her concern.

'Someone at the door!' she suddenly said.

The bedroom led off from the small upstairs sitting room.

On the other side of it was Powyss's dressing room, so that, wedged between the two, they were always assured of privacy. They had never yet been disturbed. Without being instructed, Jenkins knew he mustn't. Until now.

Powyss buttoned his breeches, pulled on his coat and shoes.

'Don't worry, you are safe in here. I shall deal with this in the other room. It must be urgent.'

He closed the door. The knocking increased on the sitting-room door.

'What is it? What is it at this time of night?'

Jenkins appeared, flushed, annoyed. Powyss saw that his clothes, too, had been hastily pulled on. Jenkins didn't have a wife. Did he fuck the maids? He knew nothing about the man.

'Sir, there is an attempt. Catherine Croft has opened up Warlow's door. There is a commotion.'

'Damn, Jenkins! Can you keep *no* control of the staff?'

'Sir, it is night. All were asleep.' He looked accusingly at Powyss.

'Has she let him out?'

'She have tried to. I don't know if he be gone.'

Powyss hesitated, distracted absurdly by the collapse of Jenkins's usually correct grammar.

'Go and find out. I shall come down shortly.'

He stood, uncertain what to do. If Warlow was out, it could be disastrous, given his probable mood. There was no likelihood he'd not hear about Hannah and him and then she'd need protection. He'd have to keep her here. But of course not! There were her children, would they come too? All of them live in Moreham House terrorised by Warlow?

The experiment was over, that was clear. He heard his father's voice thanking God, with that laugh that made him wince. He'd have to bribe Warlow heavily to compel him to treat Hannah well.

For she would return to him. Must. And life for them all would resume its past condition, except that the Warlows would be richer and he ...

He would lose her: No! No. How could he possibly abandon this life he had with her? That tormented him when she was not present, overwhelmed him when she was.

He saw himself reduced to glimpsing her through windows. Strangling acute desire with plants, books, brandy.

He uncorked the phial in his coat, smelled the kindness of cinnamon and cloves before the opiate struck, went back into the bedroom and sat by her.

'Hannah. Jenkins tells me that someone has opened up the door and let out your husband.' He saw her eyes gape with shock, her hands fly to her face.

'Fear nothing yet. Put on your clothes, but stay here, in this room. Stay until I return. I'm going down to see what's happening.' She pressed both fists against her mouth, her eyes wide with terror.

As he closed the door there was more knocking.

'Yes?' It was Jenkins, as expected. 'What now?'

'I have apprehended the maid Croft. Cook has hold of her. No one has seen Warlow. But sir, a visitor has arrived. Mr Benjamin Fox. Shall I bring him straight up?'

Chapter 8

HE WAKES TO THE THROB of blood in his ears. And another noise. In the other room. Different. Not rats. Not the creaking. He sits up, pulls a blanket about him, hunched. Holds the ends together just under his nose; ears free to hear.

The door into his place. Outside it. Against it. A tool against it. Wood screaking. Someone's prising off the planks.

He doesn't move. Noise stops. He breathes again. But he's too far in to hear everything outside. Strain hard. Listen. *Listen!*

Key in the lock. Turning. Squawk of thick-rusted iron.

He is rigid. Someone is there. Someone has come in. Someone! His hearing, refined by years of silence, begins to pinpoint the sounds. Each movement.

Someone is there. Crunching on debris. He hears a gasp.

Steps stop. Scuff through it. Stop.

He imagines it looking round. Is there one? Or *two*? Lookin for him. He mustn't move. They don't know where he is.

No sound. Then: 'Are you there?' A *woman*'s voice. Woman! Them wouldn't send a woman. Why a woman?

'John? Mr Warlow?' Doesn't recognise the voice. Dreamin.

Not dreamin. It's comin closer, comin to get him. Comin. The devil comes in the shape of a woman. He knows this.

'You can come out now,' it says. It is a trap. Mustn't reply. Not speak. He hears it scuff about the room. Hears it move away to where the bathtub is, the grating.

Hide! He'll hide before it comes into this room. Hauls himself, prickling with sweat, off the bed, down onto his knees. Bed is high off the ground, there's room for him. Bends, but he's stiff. So many pains. His head hits the sharp edge of the bed frame. He ducks in. Twists. His limbs like great roots bursting out of a bank of earth.

He's scared off the rats under the bed. Wants to laugh. Devil won't see him here. Can't. Can't take him away. With its devil claws. Tail! Tail like an eel, great eel whippin. Whippin him down to hell.

'Where are you, John?' A trap. A *trap*! A blanket hangs off the bed. He pulls it down further to conceal himself completely. Just in time. Steps are coming closer. He presses up against the wall, holds his breath.

'Are you in bed?' It's lookin round the door, not come in yet. Quiet. It's lookin, is it? Lookin. Seein nothin. He takes tiny sips of breath.

'John?' it whispers.

His leg's stuck. He moves it and cramp shoots up the calf. He kicks out his foot; can't stop himself.

There's a shriek and it rushes out. Out and away. He kicks again to break the pain and hits his shoulder. He hears the steps, the scuffing, crunching, smaller shrieks. Gone.

But *has* it gone? Wait, wait. Don't come out now. It'll pounce.

Cold under the bed. He grabs at the blanket which falls. Pulls it in but there's no room for him and it. His ankle throbs, wedged beneath him. He rubs at the cramp. Cold seeps into his thigh and hip, yet it's stifling. Can hardly breathe. He sneezes.

More noises, far off, distant voices. Them'll try again, sure to. Come and get him. Drag him. He hears his father's voice, worse even than the knobbed stick: *devils'll drag you to the bottomless pit.*

*

Jenkins showed Fox into the upstairs sitting room. Puffed, for he was somewhat overweight, he was unsettled by the butler's apparent grumpiness, wondered if this was the 'mild grumbling' about which Powyss had written.

Powyss locked the bedroom door behind him.

'Fox!'

'Powyss!' They shook hands. 'I must apologise *profusely* for this descent upon you. Unforewarned! Unasked for! And at such a time of night! I have had untold trouble with travelling, I can barely begin to tell you. But the reason, the reason for my appearance, you see ...'

He broke off, suddenly aware that despite his surely unexpected arrival and the news he was about to break to Powyss, the man was only half attending. He was listening to something else, perhaps in the room he'd just left or downstairs. There were indeed voices beneath, but that was the ill-mannered butler, Fox conjectured, giving orders for his room, for some refreshment, which, after the awful journey, he was ready to eat immediately.

'I'm sorry to hear ...' Powyss began.

'It has become too hot for me in London. I am fleeing to you in your fastness, Powyss. Please take me in! Mr Clarke is out of prison as I told you. He is frail, for which I pity him. But he has rich friends. And they ... in short, Powyss, they have urged him to bring a charge against me. A charge of criminal conversation with Mrs Clarke. They would *try* me.'

'Ah. Fox, I must leave you for a while. Please make yourself comfortable. I shall send up Samuel to light the Argand lamp

155

and bring you some cold repast. Forgive the poverty of my welcome, Fox. It shall be explained. Oh. And you shall tell me your story.' And he rushed out.

Fox was amazed. 'Your *story!*' Did Powyss imagine it was a tale of once upon a time? But he'd always been odd. At school he was uncommunicative, solitary. Conned his lessons obediently, wandered off whenever he could. The restrained growth of their epistolary friendship had been unexpected, quite remarkable. And here now the man seemed barely able to speak, was distracted, utterly thrown by Fox's surprise arrival.

A footman came to light the lamp, which cast its shadows on the pale green walls. One of these newfangled things, but elegant.

'Mr Powyss says to tell you a room is being warmed, sir.' Fox noted some Cockney tones. The man put down a tray of food.

'What is your name?'

'Samuel, sir.'

'Is something happening that draws Mr Powyss away, Samuel?'

'Sir?'

'Hardly have I arrived and Mr Powyss has rushed off. Why is that?'

'I can't say, sir.'

A loyal footman; or a well-paid one, thought Fox.

'I will take you to your room after you have eaten, sir.'

Fox was extremely hungry. Although cold, the food was delicious – evidently there's a good cook here at least, he thought. There was a bottle of port, claret being impossible because of war with France.

Fox had known he'd never persuade Fanny Clarke away from her husband. He'd certainly never wished to offend Henry Clarke, who, after all, had been his friend. Nor, of course, had he sought out scandal. Once he'd admitted to himself the attraction he felt, and as his ties to Unitarianism became threadbare, he thought merely to enjoy himself for as long as he could. And to cheer dear Fanny in her straitened condition. Fox smiled. Poor woman! Her life had become dreary, wretched, with her husband in prison.

It was not she who gave away the game. Fox considered just how erratic friendship could be. A friend, mutual to both him and Henry Clarke, one Beeston Neave, whose opinions in all other respects were admirable, had not only distressed poor Clarke, newly released from Newgate, with his tale, no doubt luridly told, but encouraged him to punish Fox through the court *and* provided him with the means with which to do it. For certainly Clarke had no money, having lost it all through imprisonment. Neave's motives were obscure, unless he had designs on Fanny himself. If, finally, a summons were taken out, Fox would have to return to face trial.

Oh, he thought, who is there to trust, if one cannot trust one's friends? Blushed when he realised Clarke would surely say the same of him. Well, anyway, he'd decided to trust Powyss. For the moment he would live here, at Moreham, pleasingly far from London. If necessary he would pay Powyss for board and lodging, though he didn't imagine Powyss would require it. His stay would undoubtedly put their friendship to the test. But perhaps he could help him with whatever was happening, Fox thought, though he found it hard to imagine what difficulties a rich, atheistic bachelor who preferred plants to people could possibly have.

*

When Powyss arrived in the kitchen Jenkins was standing over Cook, who was assembling a tray of food for Fox, while Samuel waited impassively at the door. Annie had been sent to prepare a room for Fox, and Samuel was to help her shortly. The sound of hysterical sobbing gradually died away somewhere in the back kitchen where Catherine had been confined.

'Jenkins?'

'Catherine has been frighted, sir.'

'Has Warlow got out or not?'

'Catherine has not said.'

'Oh?'

'She will not speak of what she saw.'

'Before I go to speak to Warlow – which would signify the absolute end of my experiment – I want to know if he's still in the apartments or not. Someone must look.'

Jenkins was not happy. He'd certainly not demean himself. 'Samuel?' he turned to the footman, half ordering, half questioning, hoping he'd refuse and there'd be no one to go but Powyss.

'I must take these victuals and help Annie,' said Samuel, torn between loyalty and fear.

Powyss was becoming impatient. 'Jenkins, you will please to go down now.'

'I must supervise the others, sir. It is not a task for me.'

Cook, a shawl wrapped over her plentiful nightwear, burst out in a fury: 'Such feebleness! A body would think Warlow's a monster. The girl had a silly fit – she cannot stand a bit of dark. I shall myself go and look. And speak my mind to him, too. Living in idleness and luxury! Taking money for nothing!'

'I'd prefer you not to speak to him, Mrs Rentfree. There is a small chance the experiment might still continue.'

'Sir! The girl Catherine have already spoke to him. Wait, Samuel! Here's a cantle of fruit pie for the visitor.' She surveyed the tray. 'That should be sufficient unless he be a greedy man. Now take it!'

She wiped her hands on her apron, tucked another shawl about herself, then her cloak on top of it all and without embarrassment took a considerable draught from a bottle, which she replaced in the pocket of her skirts. She carried a lamp with her and set off, while Jenkins and Powyss stood looking away from each other, lily-livered conspirators. Powyss fingered the phial in his pocket.

All was quiet as Cook descended. After a while they heard her loudly call 'Mr Warlow!' Silence. Her voice became a muffled booming as she made her way further into the apartment, presumably still calling his name. More silence.

Powyss wasn't sure what he wanted her to find. It was most probable that the man had escaped soon after the servant Catherine had opened his door but while her back was turned, and that she had *imagined* she saw him. Once more he thought how dangerous Warlow might become once he heard about Hannah. How could he keep Hannah and the children safe from their violent husband and father? He could hardly have the man locked up. And now there was Fox! Why was he here? He had barely heard Fox's explanation. Yet the man had seemed to fill the room just as he'd done that one time in the house in Hampstead. He loomed.

How he longed to run from it all. Longed for the soothing warmth of the glasshouses, the feel of rough stalks and leaves, of cutting cleanly into a stem with his clasp knife. He turned away from Jenkins, uncorked a mouthful.

Suddenly there was a new sound, a smothered, distant shrieking like a pig being killed across the valley. Powyss and Jenkins ran down the stairs to the apartment door expecting horror.

Cook came out with her lamp, hugging her cloak about her.

'He be in there. A disgusting sight it is,' she said and walked away from them up the stairs.

'Jenkins, lock the door. He must stay till morning when I decide what to do.'

Back in the kitchen he asked Cook what she'd seen.

'He were hiding beneath the bed. Screamed at me that I were the devil and he could see my cloven hoofs. Hideous noise he did make. Like an animal. Not human it were, Mr Powyss. Said I had come to take him down to hell! But, sir, it is like hell down there already, all broken and ... '

'Don't tell me, Mrs Rentfree. I am grateful to you indeed for going. Now please return to bed. Jenkins, ensure Mr Fox's bedroom has been properly prepared. What do you intend to do with the other maid?'

'I have locked Catherine in the dairy,' Cook interrupted. 'Let her stay till she come to her senses. If she choose to eat butter she'll feel much worse.'

'Will you please cook for three from tomorrow,' said Powyss, 'for the duration of Mr Fox's stay. However long that is. Now we should all go back to bed.'

*

She says to herself: he did take me home for it were very late. In his garden were Abraham Price. He did run from there when he did see us. The same as before I am sure of it. An evil man.

The children were asleep. Margaret be a good mother in my place. Most times the boys do what she say. Polly give me a kiss when I get into bed. She is a sweet-natured child. Except Jack, the children be consolation to me.

Herbert told me John have not got out still. But I must not go to the house until he send a message. He said he shall always think of me. Even though he pay harlots he think only of me.

But John will come back and then it is the end.

*

Powyss didn't go to bed at all that night. After he'd taken Hannah to within fifty yards of her patched cottage, its roof sprouting tussocks of grass, and watched until she'd gone

160

inside, he returned, poured himself a glass of brandy, then several more. Emptied the phial in his pocket without numbering the drops, and unlocked a particular drawer for another.

He should have released Warlow after his rampage. But no, the man was in a dangerous mood then. And he'd not have had these last weeks with Hannah. He'd abandoned the previous pattern of her visits once a week, in fact he'd abandoned all form, insisting she come to the house each night. He existed in a stupor during the day, his mind in dissolution, lived from dark till dawn febrile with lust and rage, the only certainty.

Fox would tell him he should never have set up the experiment in the first place. Should have been content with his bland life, the highest points of which were the successful germination of rare seed, the production of perfect fruit, the planting of exotic trees. True, he had been free to read or not, to buy new plants or not, to look through his microscope, admire his vases, his globes, search for shooting stars, think of no one else. Uncrazed.

All his adult life he'd been free to choose, restricted only by the demands of the seasons. As a boy his life was ordered by his father of course; his mother compelled him more subtly. There'd been school. But always he'd found places to run to, to breathe in, be soothed by.

Now, now, and his eyes swam with self-pity, his familiar places of refuge were useless and each decision he made, each action he took bore vile consequences. He was obliged to consider the lives of others: Warlow, Hannah, even the servants, who'd revealed aspects of themselves he'd never cared to notice.

Warlow's children. He'd encountered the child Polly in her dress too big for her. Alone in the garden, she'd been brushing the scented peas to release their sweet smell.

He'd asked about her sister and brothers.

'Jack do go to meetins.'

'Oh yes?'

'Jack says damn to the king.'

'How old is Jack?'

'Sixteen year. He says Father did say it and he be right. But he is dead I think.'

'Ah. Now Jack will get into trouble if he says such things about the king. Don't tell anyone else, Polly. It does no harm to tell me.'

'Mother says you be a good man. Jack says damn to Mr Powyss, too.'

'Who is right, do you think?'

'Mother of course! Jack is bad. He do hit me.'

'Enough now. On your way.'

Another source of trouble: Jack Warlow.

Sitting at the desk Powyss lay his head on his arms. Figures crowded into his imagination, clamouring for attention: wasps, hornets they were, which, once he placed them under the microscope became individual, each with its oddities: its missing leg, crooked antenna, bigger-than-usual abdomen. They were not all the same. Observation, unsought before, revealed existences he could no longer deny, existences which affected him even without his wishing it. They buzzed, whined, crawled through his hair, up his sleeve, stung.

He was overwhelmed with tiredness but could not sleep; emptied the bottle of brandy, opened another, smiled at the liquid's scorching warmth, wept as it wore away.

He began to feel sick. Fox would expect an explanation tomorrow. He must find a solution to it all before they met up again. He dreaded the man's booming voice, his wit, his spurious authority. The very size of him was exhausting. He must get rid of him! Perhaps he could delay dealing with Warlow until he'd gone back to London. Surely he'd go in a day or two? That was it! Leave Warlow for the time being. Show Fox his improvements to the house, walk him round the gardens, woods, glasshouses, then see him off.

His thoughts reeled round to Hannah, now asleep in a mean bed in her broken-down dwelling. The hovel wasn't his to mend, belonged to Kempton. He had never been inside, preferring to think as little as possible about that part of her life; it was enough to provide money for food and shoes. Hannah. The serenity of her features and manner, illuminated by pleasure. She'd not been dazzled by his wealth, his knowledge, his priceless collection, and he always held back from trying to impress her in the face of her clarity of mind, her intuitive simplicity. It wasn't that she lacked words. Had she been educated she'd never have been prolix. And the lines of life on her face and body. The smile that lit his desire for her. Oh, he was beleaguered!

A wild scheme entered his mind. He would leave Moreham and take her with him. They could travel abroad, to Italy, say. He would buy her clothes and they would live as man and wife. No one need know her origins. Warlow could be released after they'd gone and he'd leave money with Jenkins to dole out to him at suitable intervals. Ah, that was what he must do! He was certain she'd want it. The plan sounded within him its great opening chords. Sunlit scenes from his youthful travel ran before his eyes, the accompanying loneliness and humiliations of those times forgotten.

And even as hopelessness rose in his throat, for Hannah would never leave her children; Jenkins would fail to control Warlow; the servants driven by Price would riot; his gardens turn to wilderness; he took out his pen to sketch a route, rose to fetch maps and collapsed on the floor.

*

Fox awoke when the maid came to light the fire. Short of sleep after the interminable travelling, he was anxious to confirm arrangements with Powyss. And curious, too, to discover whether there *was* something afoot or whether, as he suspected, Powyss, in his social iciness, found Fox's actual presence less welcome than his epistolary one. He was ready for a tour of the house and estate of which, over the years of their correspondence, he'd heard so much and which he'd envisaged so often. It would be amusing to test the degree of precision his imagination had employed.

The maid was uncommonly pretty, he thought, when he opened an eye and saw her as she darted out of the door, having lit the fire. He sat up ready to address her when she returned with hot water.

'Tell me your name, miss.'

'Annie, sir.'

'Good morning, Annie. How is your master today?'

'I have not seen him, sir. Samuel do prepare his room.' She blushed as if she'd told him something rather wicked.

'And is all well in the house today?'

'Nobody know.'

'What does nobody know?'

'Nobody know what will happen next.'

'Ah, indeed. What of Mr Warlow, Annie? What can you tell me about *him*?'

'He be there still. Cook did see.'

'Cook *saw* him, did she? But that breaks the rules of the experiment. Why did she do that?'

'The master did tell her to look, after Catherine have tried to let him out.' Suddenly she became voluble. 'Poor man I always did think. But Catherine did not agree. But now she must have, for she have done this and they have locked her in the dairy.'

'Good Lord!'

'Catherine were daring. Poor man I always did say. Lonely under the ground and Mrs Warlow, his wife Hannah, sir, and the master they …' Blushing from the shock of having said this much she bobbed a curtsey and rushed out.

Fox was taken aback. Well! If it were true – and everything

164

about Annie's manner suggested it was – then Powyss was in a thorough pickle. Samuel knocked to ask if he might lay out Fox's clothes, but of course, would not be drawn on any question.

In fact it seemed to Fox that he'd arrived at exactly the right moment. On the one hand Powyss could shelter him until, as he hoped, the fuss in London died down. And on the other he, surely, could help Powyss in return, for he suspected his friend entirely incapable of unravelling this knot of human complication. He had a veritable riot on his hands! Until recently Fox had had much experience resolving difficulties with the Unitarians at Newington Green, so he believed he could certainly help now.

Intrigued by these possibilities, he dressed and went down to breakfast, but there was no sign of Powyss. Jenkins, short-tempered, showed him into Powyss's library, where he whiled away the morning in quite the wrong mood to enjoy its admirable and extensive contents. He was looking through the great long window with its view of ever-receding hills and vast sky making him wonder how he had survived so long with nothing but a pleasing wall against which to grow his struggling new plants and the glimpse of two fine trees beyond, when Powyss came in.

'Fox, I trust you slept well and have been attended to?'

'Certainly, my dear friend, and I cannot apologise to you enough for my precipitate action, but I hope, indeed am sure that when you hear the full story you will understand its cause and permit me to stay.'

'Yes, of course,' he said, 'but it is I who should apologise for my inadequate welcome last night and shall explain.'

He looked white and unwell, his black, staring eyes filmed, indistinct. He told him the story Fox had already heard from the maid though with more detail, greater coherence and the complete omission of Mrs Warlow's name.

'I must confess, Powyss, that already, this morning, I have

been given a very brief, fragmentary version of these events from the maid Annie, though from no one else.' Powyss went even whiter and gripped the back of the nearest chair. 'There was some mention of Mrs Warlow.'

At which he flashed a look of such ferocity, even madness that Fox took a step backwards.

'Very *little* was said, to be fair to your maid,' he hastened to tell him, 'but perhaps I am right to infer that your situation is not completely unlike my own with Mrs Clarke.'

Powyss's anger dropped. Tired beyond resistance, he sat down as if his legs had given way.

'I should like to be of help, Powyss. Would you listen to some advice?' For a while Powyss didn't move. Then he closed his eyes, raised his right hand in a gesture of vague permission and the next moment his head nodded down onto his breast and he snored.

*

Abraham Price had difficulty mustering the number of followers he wanted, and in the end just five men hammered on the door of Moreham House that night with their staves and a pitchfork. Among them Jack Warlow, freshly fired up, wielded a scythe found in a corner at home. Price held a flaming brand in his left hand.

When he'd heard Catherine was locked in the dairy he had crept down to its window grille and extracted the information he needed from her. He ignored her teary squawking that he go away and never come back again. Two imprisonments were enough for his purpose.

'Open up! Open up! Us'll speak with Powyss!'

But Moreham wasn't Birmingham. There just weren't enough people living round about; his dreams of a mob tearing down the house, as they'd done in that city – of great burning stacks of window frames, furniture, wainscotting, the carting away of stone in mass celebratory theft – had gone. Instead he fixed on the description of the mutiny Catherine had read from the newspaper, the confining of the officers. For that, a group of five sufficiently armed men was adequate. He anticipated only the most puny resistance from Jenkins and Samuel, and indeed from Powyss himself.

They beat the door again. Price had imagined they'd gain immediate entry, and envisaged storming through the house straight to that library Catherine was always talking of.

'Strike harder, citizens!' Knobbed sticks and a hayfork were only a small part of the men's weaponry. Caleb Hughes had stuffed a cobbler's knife into his belt, and there were mattocks, a chisel and two brummocks, their blades vaguely Ottoman in shape. Amos's pistol had been a boast.

Price stepped back to inspect the front of the house again. All the windows were shuttered, so even were they to smash the glass they'd not get in that way. And there was little to fire. The house was stone, its portico also. Only the door was made of wood, so massive that scorching was probably all they could achieve with just his fiery brand.

'Powyss. Open your door. Us wants to speak with you! Unlawful imprisonment!'

A voice said: 'Get you gone, Abraham Price. The master will not speak to you!'

It was Jenkins behind the door still firmly closed.

'But him must speak. For us have weapons, isn't it.'

No answer. Jenkins was most like consulting with Powyss. Or else, Price sneered to himself, quaking just the other side of the door.

'It is our right to speak, men,' Price growled. '*Jenkins!* Us'll smash our way in! Tell your master that.'

'You'll be hanged first,' replied a barely perceptible voice. That other one, Samuel.

'Strung up, Price!' shouted Jenkins. 'We'll be watching when they turn you off!'

'Caleb, Jack, bang in a window. Go!' he said and stood aside to watch while the two shattered the nearest panes then thumped their sticks against the bolted shutters inside.

Price held up his hand and they stopped to listen. There was no sound, except the tinkle of a fragment of glass finally falling.

'Now, Powyss, will us speak with you?'

No reply.

They gathered together to consider their next move. Jack was for smashing all the windows one by one, Caleb for coming back later with a cart of straw and tar and firing the doors at back and front. They were entirely taken aback when a large figure loomed round the side of the house.

'Greetings, citizens,' Fox called out to them.

'It's a trick. Hold him, men!' Price ordered and they ran forward and each held on to some part of Fox's considerable bulk.

'Us wants Powyss,' Price scowled up at Fox, too short to meet him eye to eye.

'You should let me go. I am on your side,' Fox said.

'Another trick, isn't it.'

'No, Citizen Price – you *are* Abraham Price?' Price merely raised his chin. 'I am an old friend of Mr Powyss, but I am also a lover of liberty. I beheld the admirable Hardy at his trial.'

'If you be Powyss's friend you cannot be a friend to liberty. Him's unlawfully imprisoned two people in this house!'

'Mr Warlow agreed to live underground and will be well remunerated for it.'

'Him do fuck his wife, isn't it!' screeched Price. 'Stop, boy!' For Jack was scything frenziedly through every plant within reach as though Powyss had multiple legs.

'Ah. I know nothing of that. But even if it is true, adultery is quite another matter. It is not unlawful imprisonment. And the maid who opened Warlow's door did so without permission. She ought first to have asked Mr Powyss.'

Price snorted.

'She was wrong and has been held temporarily. There are far more important rights for which to fight.'

'What do you know of rights?' sneered Price, and the others sniggered uneasily.

'I speak of the rights of man. And of that great book the *Rights of Man* which you will find in my coat pocket, citizens.'

Price was disconcerted, suddenly felt cold as he sensed his plan crumbling away. Before he could stop him, Caleb thrust into Fox's pocket, produced the book and waved it at them all. Price ordered them to let go of the man. It was as if he'd eaten rotten meat: what he'd hoped to bite and chew was soft and foul.

He stirred himself. 'Tom Paine do say we must resist a despot.'

'Paine means monarchies and old governments, Citizen Price. It is for the *representative system of government* that we must strive.'

Price hit back: '*It is an age of Revolutions, in which everything may be looked for*, isn't it.'

'Well quoted, citizen! But hear this: 'It may be considered as an honour to the *animal faculties* of man to obtain redress by courage and danger, but it is far greater honour to the *rational faculties* to accomplish the same object by *reason, accommodation* and *general consent.*'

Price was punctured. At the very least he'd lost on a simple count of words. But he knew it was worse than that. He'd been skewered by his hero Paine himself.

With a rapid movement he turned and stalked off and the others, in sudden darkness without their leader's light, stumbled after him silently.

Fox knocked on the door of Moreham House, assured Jenkins he was alone, and was soon inside.

*

Gropes for the candle stump, flint, box. Easy in the dark; done it every day. Spark, flame. Shadows. Shadows shifting with the flame.

He's not dead. Not in hell. This is his bed. Devils haven't come back. He *frightened them off*. Cursed them three times. Said Our Father, save me from infernold divils three times. Jesus Save Me three times. Has to be three times or it don't work. Thinks he did it once before. Maybe that was a dream.

He's shivering. Door's shut against the devils. Needs a piss. Are they outside the door? Waitin for him. With the terrible bat from the book who'll clap him between his wings. Smother him. Gnaw him. He'll have to piss in the bed if they're still there.

Listens. Blood beats slowly in his head. Beat. Beat. Quiet. Been quiet a long time. Or is he dreaming quiet? Familiar scratching beneath the bed back and forth. Biters on the wall, too. Singes some with the candle flame.

He wants a fire. He's trembling. Needs heat. Shaking with cold and wanting to piss, he steps out, limps to the door. Opens it a crack, bit more, more, *nobody*, pisses himself.

He shuffles into the main room. Holds up the candle, looks about. *Nobody here.* Didn't he hear the key in the lock when the last devil left? Or did he?

Relief strikes a spark of energy. He hobbles over to the fire, scrapes out the ash. Fixes sticks, sea coal, small wood. It blazes and something in him warms even while he shakes.

Safe! No. Them'll try again, sure to! Suddenly stops. Cocks his head. I'm like a hare in thick mist, hearin a hound. Be that the key again? *Be* it? No. But I'll keep 'em out anyway. I'll stop 'em. Foot's not hurtin no more.

He drags the table first, pushes it hard up against the door. It leans because of the broken leg. He casts around. Wedges a doorless cupboard underneath. Then heaves toppled bookshelves, their glass stoved in, wooden lattice hanging. Chopped up chairs, smashed side tables, organ legs. Panting, smiling, he bends for more armfuls. Grabbles among hacked and splintered walnut, rosewood, mahogany. The pile nears the top of the door.

Safe! *Now* he's safe. Warmth creeps up his fingers from the grate. He draws forward the chair, stripped and slit. Stuffing drifts like old man's beard. He sits on springs, kicks off boots, rests his feet against the iron while it heats up. Toe-claws stick through ragged stockings like fingers.

After a while he stands to warm his legs and arse. Smell is strong. When it gets too hot he'll find new breeches. Them did send some once. Did they?

His stomach gripes. Will there be no food now the devils have taken the house? She-devils. Whore of Babylon. Scarlet. Purple. Breasts them do have and hooves. Hairy flanks like cows beneath their clothes. Tails like long cocks wavin out of their arses. Them've taken Powyss down to hell, sure to. And the other. Jenkins. Only she-devils left. Them'll starve im, shan't they?

Creaking! His heart stops. Something's coming down. Dare he look? He's so hungry. When did he eat? All days are one. He stopped eating before the devils came. Vomited. Did he? Dreamed he ate. Dreamed he couldn't eat.

Smell of hot meat. Will he open the hatch? Open it! She-devil crouchin inside, ready to spring. Open it a crack then. Crack. More. *No she-devil.* A tray, heavy silver covers.

There's no table; it's at the bottom of the heap against the door, his wood wall. He carries the tray to the fire. Gets down on the floor with it, on all fours. Cautiously lifts off the covers. Small she-devils might leap straight out, pull him into the flames. Rams his mouth with food.

*

The following day Fox tackled Powyss. He'd slept well after his confrontation with Price and perhaps Powyss had, too, as he looked a little less pale.

'My dear friend, I hope that today you will find yourself able to listen to my advice.'

He could hardly refuse, after Fox's successful quenching of the 'fiery gardener', as he named him. Indeed, when he'd come back indoors that night, having defeated the tiny revolutionary rabble, Powyss had made to shake his hand in thanks and burst into a flood of tears such that he was obliged to retire to bed without further speech. Fox decided that he'd become even odder with the years than he was when he'd known him as a boy.

Here was a house where subversion lurked in kitchen and pantry, where invasion threatened from without and where a madman was destroying the very fundament of the building, while its master sobbed, powerless, in his charming upper sitting room, simultaneously breaking the seventh commandment with the madman's wife! It was almost farcical.

Powyss agreed to everything Fox suggested. Warlow's door would be unlocked, opened up and Jenkins would make an announcement without going further than the threshold, to tell him he was free.

'In due course, you might consider some, should we call it "compensation" to keep Mr Warlow happy when, as is inevitable, he learns that Mrs Warlow, er, that you and Mrs Warlow, er ...'

'Yes, yes, I had already thought of that,' Powyss interrupted. 'I shall pay him the agreed £50 a year for the rest of his life even though he has not fulfilled the terms of the contract. I shall say that having survived four years is itself an achievement.' Here he began muttering to himself, something like 'how shall I ever prevent him', but it was not for Fox to hear. Clearly his thoughts troubled him, for he pressed his head with both hands as though to keep them from bursting forth.

'Excellent, Powyss! That's all very wise. Now, as to the maid, Catherine, do you feel able to be severe with her? And are you aware that a liaison exists between her and your firebrand gardener? My source has taken to releasing more cats from bags with the hot water each morning.'

'I am loath to lose Price. It is true he's surly and disagreeable, but ...'

'He's *much* worse than that, Powyss! He would have burned down Moreham House if he could!'

'He's a fine master gardener. I think it unlikely I could easily replace him. Oh yes, there are plenty of men who'll weed and dig and plant, but no one can graft like Price or hear a frost coming. No one can espalier a pear like him.'

'Surely he should be taken to the nearest lockup to await the magistrate?' Fox said this with probably unnoticeable temerity, aware of the awful possibility of an impending trial for himself.

'But you are on his side, Fox, surely? You told me that he quoted from the *Rights of Man*.'

'Yes, we threw collops of Tom Paine at each other! But Citizen Price is more than a radical, he's a revolutionary, a real Jacobin. And *without education*. A terrifying combination! I'll tell you what I think. I think you should question each of Catherine and Price. It will become clear what action should be taken when you've heard what they say. I will help you if you like. What do you say to that?'

After breakfast Catherine was sent up. Powyss and Fox sat behind the desk, their attempts to appear intimidating undermined by the charm of Powyss's pale-green sitting room, Fox thought, its walls papered with leaves he couldn't identify, though no doubt Powyss would name them if asked.

Catherine had not Annie's pretty face, Fox told himself. Indeed she looked as though she'd been given little opportunity to improve her appearance after much weeping in the dairy. She was in any case sallow-skinned, with too much nose, yet there was an undeniable spark of intelligence in her eyes.

Powyss began: 'Catherine, did you open the door to Mr Warlow's apartments?'

'Yes, sir.'

'How did you do that?'

'I took the key from Mr Jenkins's room. He left his door open; the key was hanging on a hook. I have put it back. It wasn't theft, it was borrowing.'

'And the planks nailed across the door?'

'I prised them off with a crowbar that I did find in Samuel's room.'

'The men must keep their doors locked against you!' Fox laughed, hoping to keep the mood light. He'd decided that Powyss should ask the questions, but at this point Powyss paused for so long that Fox felt a need to prompt. 'Why, Catherine ...'

'Yes, why,' Powyss pulled himself together. 'Why did you do this?'

'We did think it were time he were let out.'

'*We?*' Fox asked.

'*I myself* did think so,' she corrected herself.

'You said "we". Does that mean you and Abraham Price?'

Catherine looked down. 'Yes.'

'Was it his plan that you open Warlow's door? I am surprised at such cowardice to make a woman do it.' Fox had taken over the interview. Powyss shifted back in his chair.

'No! No, sir. It was my idea.' She looked at Fox with considerable annoyance. 'It was *my* plan. *I* got the key and the crowbar. I went down *on my own*. I went into John Warlow's place *on my own*.' She shuddered.

'What part did Price play in this plot then?'

'He did make me think.'

'A philosopher!' Fox said scornfully, hearing Powyss draw in his breath at this unnecessary unpleasantness.

'He did make me realise it was not luxury for John Warlow underground,' Catherine responded, showing her anger again. 'Abraham do know about rights.'

'So I learned last night! And what has he told you about them?' Fox was still disposed to be light-hearted.

'I have read the book *Rights of Man*.'

'He gave you that, did he?' he said, amused.

'It is *I* who helped him read it,' she said with pride, then dismay at having exposed her lover.

'Admirable! But Catherine, do you understand that your action has brought an end to Mr Powyss's important scientific experiment?'

She thought for a moment, then addressed herself to Powyss: 'Mr Powyss, sir, I am sorry for spoiling your experiment. But John Warlow is living worse than an animal. It is not right so to keep a human being.'

Powyss buried his face in his hands and Fox dismissed Catherine, telling her that Mr Powyss would call her again later when they'd decided how she might be punished.

'She shouldn't be punished at all,' Powyss said when she'd gone. 'She has brought me to my senses. Shamed me.'

'Well, let us see what Abraham Price has to say for himself, shall we?'

Fox found it hard not to like Price. Their confrontation the night before had stimulated him greatly. We bookish men do sometimes relish action, he said to himself. And Price was so wonderfully woody in appearance, so earth-brown and hard, standing firm as a thick-trunked tree, quite unashamed, if a little uncomfortable in such surroundings.

Fox began: 'Citizen Price. Last night I explained my position to you and, I hope, convinced you that I am myself a follower of Tom Paine. But can you deny that you tried to break into Moreham House and wanted to set it on fire: crimes for which you may hang, for which you might be lucky to be transported?'

'Powyss do employ me, isn't it. I answer *him*.'

'Mr Powyss is happy for me to ask questions for him. Do you deny trying to break in and set fire to the house?'

Price would not answer Fox, would not even look at him but turned pointedly towards Powyss. 'You imprisons two people unlawfully!'

Powyss stirred and Fox controlled himself.

'No, Price. No,' Powyss said quietly. He looked up at the man and Fox saw how well they knew each other. Years of whatever it was they did in greenhouses and new plantations had brought them closer together even than Powyss and him, for all their thousands of words penned.

'I did not imprison him, Price. Warlow agreed to the arrangement.'

'*Now* it's prison, isn't it.'

'I fear that it has become so. You are right. He is to be released anyway.'

Price was not so easily disarmed.

'You locked up Catherine!'

'She should have come to me first and asked. And she has been let out now.'

Price waved this away contemptuously.

'And Hannah Warlow, you do ...'

'Citizen!' Fox had to intervene. 'Neither Warlow nor Catherine was unlawfully imprisoned. Both are free or will be shortly. Mr Powyss will make all good with all parties involved. But meanwhile you have attacked property, broken windows, brought fire with you. You should be tried at the assizes.'

Price raised his chin and gazed over the heads of his inquisitors through the window at a dun sky. Fox could feel Powyss beside him sinking under the weight of accusation and doubted he knew what to do. He reached across for Powyss's pen, scribbled on some paper and pushed it to him. As Powyss read, Price continued to stare at the sky and meanwhile Fox couldn't help wondering if there would be any disagreeable mail for him today from London.

Powyss spoke: 'Price, if you will promise never to attack

the house again, to call off and calm down your men, I shall bring no charges. You shall none of you be tried, let alone hanged. I shall deduct the cost of repair from your pay and then we shall speak no more about any of this.'

There was a heavy silence. Neither Price nor Powyss moved. Suddenly Fox understood that they never would move while he was there, and he left the room.

Afterwards he chose not to ask Powyss what happened: what more was said, if Price had fully agreed to the terms, just what kind of promise he'd made. Powyss had become quite morose and was emptying a bottle of brandy, from which he offered Fox none.

In the afternoon Catherine was told that she was not to be punished. She had cleaned herself up, and Fox thought she looked altogether less unattractive when she received this news. How interesting are the effects of emotions on the body, he observed to himself.

Jenkins came to report that he'd unlocked Warlow's door, but upon trying to open it found an enormous pile of furniture immediately behind it, such that no one could either enter or leave. He'd shouted the announcement of freedom as loud as he could, he said.

The following morning there'd been no sign of Warlow. Instead, Jenkins appeared at breakfast to announce the arrival of a magistrate and two constables. Powyss and the magistrate, his neighbour Valentine Tharpe, greeted each other with familiarity if also detachment. Tharpe was embarrassed, the constables rather less so, and as for Jenkins, Fox caught sight of a smirk disappearing round the side of his face.

They brought a warrant for Fox on a charge of criminal conversation with Mrs Clarke; to appear at the King's Bench in two days' time. There was no choice. Fox left for London immediately.

Chapter 9

CATHERINE HATED THE COLD JANUARY mornings, rising when it was still night, splashing icy water on her face, shivering into her clothes. She tried to warm herself by rapid dressing, running downstairs. She hung over fires she lit, over the gradually heating water in the copper.

Annie had wished her a happy new year, but she saw little to look forward to in the year ahead. Annie had decided that marriage would make Samuel reasonable so *she* had something to be happy about. Except that she'd have to wait two more years until the new century when, Samuel said, he might be ready to propose. They seemed to think, absurdly, that marriage in 1800 would be more certain to guarantee happiness than in 1798.

There had been a cheerless Christmas. Cook's intransigence meant that certain food was still prepared and eaten and Jenkins, too, insisted on the traditional extra cleaning with threats should it be poorly done, yet everyone knew that Mr Powyss cared even less than ever about any of it, requiring only that supplies of brandy be obtained now that the cellars filled by his father were empty. They stuck to the old forms, knowing them to be cracked and hollow.

There was little spirit for the games and songs of previous years. Catherine refused to play the spinet. Jenkins grudgingly produced less primrose wine than usual while reminding them all that it was far superior to the bottles Boney was holding back. Samuel, more concerned about his master than anyone else was, tried to avoid Annie and bit his nails till they bled.

Abraham Price came merely to collect his food and drink, taking it back to his own place, from where, the day after Christmas, sounds of drunken bawling were heard. While there had been no more attacks on the house, it was known that 'meetings' were frequently held, and in the village and around the estate Price's surliness was generally found to be threatening.

Warlow still cowered. His door had been lifted off its hinges and placed to one side, but it was thought wise to leave his barricade untouched. Cook in particular said she would not stand to hear the shrieking again which might follow from its dismantling. At first, notes from Mr Powyss had been sent down, reiterating that the experiment was over, that Warlow was free to return to his home, that he would still be paid, but there had been no response. Mr Fox, who might have given good counsel, had gone back to London.

Catherine was haunted by what she'd seen in the underground apartments. There was nothing with which she could compare it. It was not like the meanness and disorder of her childhood home, nor yet the miserable dinginess of the blind pauper's hovel tacked on to one of their wattle and daub walls. This was wreck. Wreck and verminous squalor. Yet the man was *living* there. She was ashamed of her cowardice, should not have run away, should have stayed and talked to Warlow, persuaded him to come out. How foolish to have been scared like Annie! In fact she had made things worse, for it was then that Abraham had taken it into his head to make his stupid attack. And no doubt Cook's invasion had finally convinced Warlow to remain where he was.

Breaking with Abraham and her disgust at what she perceived as his pointless, thoughtless display of hatred, risking his neck and those of his followers, had left Catherine dismayed. Under his influence her sense of humour had gradually worn away; her tendency to laugh whenever she could had evaporated. The corners of her mouth drooped and she knew she was beginning to look sour.

As a further consequence, she lacked occupation. Teaching Abraham, being fucked by him in return, had been a novel and satisfying way of using what free time she had. That is until his revolutionary frustrations transformed it all and her tremulous anticipation turned into trembling dread. Now she must spend more time in Annie's company again, bored even more than before, but no longer inclined to shock her or make her giggle with embarrassment.

She rejected Abraham utterly. Refused to speak to him; made sure she was never out in the dark lest he waylay her. She tried not to think of the worst moments of the last months. Tried instead to dwell in that part of her mind that was newly charged with the ideas of Tom Paine, illuminated not by Abraham's explosions but by what she'd read.

One day she thought to push a plate of food under the leaning legs of the table that formed the base of Warlow's barricade.

'Mr Warlow, your food is here,' she shouted out to him. 'I'm going back upstairs and shall collect your plates later.'

It surprised them all when, hours afterwards, clumping loudly down the stone steps so that he would be warned of her approach, Catherine found not only empty plates for her to collect, but also his full pot and a bundle of clothes so foul they had to be burned directly.

*

180

Powyss woke and slept, woke and slept again. Samuel had been in, he knew, for the fire was lit, his clothes laid out. A line of pale light showed at the top of the shutters, but in January he wouldn't expect more. His mouth was dry, his head hurt between the eyes, compelling him to close them again. The bed was warm; why get out of it? He was alone, but then once, before that time with Hannah, he'd rarely not been alone in this bed. That time! When was it, that time?

He had no reason to get up. When he surveyed his grounds in his head, wandering through them in his mind, he knew that everything would either live or die without his presence. Most growth was static now in any case. Everything that needed to drop leaves had done so; stood waiting. Endured whatever came. Anything that could burst through frozen earth would do it with or without him: snowdrops, aconites. The wintersweet would smell without attention in its southern corner. The glasshouses had been cleaned in December; the labourers were employed elsewhere or not at all. Price would potter, stoke the hothouse boiler, sharpen his pruning knife. Fire up his followers. Powyss was certain he'd not heard the last of rebellion.

Fox was in London, so he wouldn't arise for *him*. He'd been relieved when he'd left, called to trial, quite downcast for a man so ebullient. He'd found him overpowering, though he was glad enough of his dealings with Price. What with the eruption in the underground apartments, the attack from outside and Fox's incursion into his private rooms, he'd felt cornered like an animal. Only his bed was his own. It was surprising there'd been no letters from Fox, he thought. Occasionally he wondered what had happened.

Sudden sunlight shone through the crack where the shutters met. He rose, kicked a bottle and three phials back under the bed, went to the window and opened the shutters to inspect the sky, slipping back into his matutinal habit of years: to assess the state of the weather, its threats and promises, then plan the day's horticulture accordingly. The cloud was high, driven by a south-westerly, patches of blue growing and shrinking rapidly, the sun appearing and disappearing. He felt its warmth through the glass, saw a frost melting. Looked down as he always did to check the *Magnolia virginiana* and thence out to the fields awaiting snow.

Someone was walking in the lane beyond the garden. Hannah with three of her children, two boys and Polly tugging at her hand, wanting them to turn into the garden. Hannah was looking straight ahead.

His heart surged.

'Come! Oh yes, come now! I'll get Samuel to call her in.'

As she neared then passed from his sight he perceived the slight change in her shape, an alteration in the way she moved. An explanation for her refusal to look towards the house, towards him, that sped him back to bed to drive his face into the pillow, bury himself entirely under the bedclothes.

*

A great coldness comes in from behind his wall of wood. At first he tries to close the door them'd opened. On his knees, half under the table. Poking with a broom through the narrow gap. Can't. Hayfork'd do it. But no door's there! Nothin!

Then it puts food there. The voice is the first she-devil, but he's so hungry. And it don't try to move his wall. Too heavy. A woman can't. Even a woman devil.

Once afore there was Jenkins's voice. They took *him*, sure to. After, papers come all written on. Three, four. Can't be from Powyss. They must have took *him*. It were divils writ them.

He doesn't read them; puts them on the fire. Won't read no more. Words are *bad*. Weaver's shuttle. Swift nor a weaver's shuttle. Won't read no more words.

The she-devil sometimes speaks. Kindly. Of course it's a trap. She's feedin him up to make a meal for other devils.

When them do try to drag him down to hell. Them'll try again sure to. *But them won't get in!*

He thinks he'll speak to it. So it knows he knows who it is. He sits behind the wall, out of sight. Waits in the cold. Hears it coming down the steps, opens his mouth and nothing comes out. Hears how it calls his name, piles up the plates. Just near him. Could jab it with a stick if he dared. Hears its breathing. Shapes his lips into a word, but he can make no sound.

It goes back up the steps, shuts the door at the top. He tries to groan. His throat squeaks. When did he last speak? He called out when the last devil came in. Big skirts it had. Covering the hairy flanks. Saw its hoof. It must've laid a spell on his voice when he shrieked at it.

He crawls back to the grate. Sups beer from the jug and tries again. Coughs his throat clear; spits a fizz into the fire.

Voice comes, growling, squeaking. He repeats his curses over and over. Starts the Our Father, goes as far as he can. Devils can't abide them words.

Church. Parson, he says. *Steeple. Bells. Christmastide. Eastertide.* Think hard! *Holy Book. Jesus.* Says them all again; counts off three for each on his claws. Gets rid of the spell.

He creeps back, sits and waits till it comes down the steps again. Practises beneath his breath. It comes. Puts plates down. He smells fish.

'She-devil. Listen!'

'*Oh!* What's that? Are you there, John Warlow? Are you just there, behind all this, all this furniture? Do you want to speak? Do you want me to listen?'

'She-devil!' he hisses.

'What's that? Did you say devil?'

'*She-devil!*'

'Don't be ridiculous! There's no such thing. I'm Catherine Croft. I work for Mr Powyss.'

Lie. Trap.

'*Devil!*'

'John, come out now! You have no need to stay there in the dark. In all that mess. I saw it myself. You surely cannot live in that.'

He growls.

'Shall I bring you scissors to cut your hair and nails?

Scissors! Could stab the next devil that comes in. Don't answer. Wait.

'If you won't speak to me then write what you want, John Warlow. Oh. Cook's calling me.'

He hears it go up the steps.

Is it a woman? No, no. Lies. Traps. Here he is safe. Nothin can get in.

Scissors. No. Tied up his hair years ago. And mirrors all gone. Nails. Well. Need more than scissors for them. To stab. Stab. Ah! That's it! They want him to *stab himself*. Kill yourself, you go straight to hell. He shudders. Shambles back to the fire.

*

She thinks: I should tell him but I cannot. He have sent no message to come so he must think I should not.

Samuel do bring the money now and fruit at Christmastide.

John still do live below. I fear always he will return. I think he be here when he is not. I see him come through the door. Think I hear him. Up the stairs when we be all in bed. Every night I do think he's coming, hear his tread. I fear so I do often shake. Polly ask me if I be sick. I say no.

The children all do know he will return. Margaret say she do wish he will not come back. Jack have left us.

Sometimes I think to go to the house. But he did say don't come until he send a message which he have not.

Shall it be disgrace to him? Yet it were love. A child of love if it survive.

What can I do? I cannot write to him for though I can read a little I did never learn writing.

People do see, I know they speak of it. It were better I tell him myself, but no I dare not go.

He will hear.

Surely he will take me in.

*

Whenever Powyss slept he dreamed. He was in a coach with his mother. Or was it a ship? They were travelling to some delightful unnamed town, at which they never arrived. She spoke happily to him, praised him for his wonderful experiment, patted his hand. He felt a great love for her, longed for her to hug him to herself, but she dismissed him and he slunk away. Another time he was lying on the brick path in the hothouse, his hands in piles of bone-dry leaves which he admired for their beautiful variations on the theme of red: dazzling variations from scarlet to a crimson that was black. He stood up and all about him the glass was smashed.

Or he'd wake in mortal terror, fleeing from a noxious beast he had no hope of repelling, that had begun as Fox accusing him of some misdeed and instantly transformed itself, as is the way of dreams, into Warlow, hideous, huge, entering through every door and window. In another, he destroyed houses and bridges made by his father; pulled them apart with his hands, trampled on them, triumphant, as they cracked and splintered, gashed his feet with cuts that shrieked. In yet another, he strode out across a weed-filled lake towards someone who waited for him on the other side, shadowy, longed-for. The weed held him until midway he began sinking slowly, hopelessly into the depths.

He dreamed *always*. Woke exhausted, needing to sleep.

Jenkins addressed him.

'Sir, I think to send for Mr Bywater.'

'I rang for Samuel, not for you, Jenkins.'

'I think to send for Mr Bywater.'

'It is true that I am unwell, Jenkins, but apart from the tincture which I administer to myself I do not need medical attention. Do *not* send for him and do not mention him again unless I ask you to.'

'They do speak of you in the village, Mr Powyss, sir. You have been abed for nigh a month.'

'They would not speak if you had not given them something to talk about! I have no care for what they say in the village.'

Nevertheless he got up and dressed. Samuel laid out his clothes each day whether he rose or not. He was aware of the young man's complete devotion. Since it was still cold he pulled on flannel drawers and buttoned a flannel under-waistcoat, thinking as he did so that at all costs he must prevent an intrusion from Bywater followed by gossip all round the county. Once, Jenkins would not have spoken to him thus. Now, Powyss's trust in him had thinned to almost nothing. Not that he was insubordinate like Price. Yet Powyss knew that Jenkins's authority increased proportionately with each demonstration of his own weakness.

He was sober, his thoughts unusually clear. He took tea in the sitting room, fidgeted a roll into crumbs, turned away from beckoning bottles on the table by the fireplace. Heard his mother's voice say, *Woe unto them that rise up early in the morning, that they may follow strong drink*. Recalled his boyhood dismay at seeing her stare out at the sky as if expecting salvation.

He *didn't* care what was said in the village. No doubt he had always been criticised there for lack of activity outside his house and grounds; for the oddity of his one generosity towards the villagers which took the form of baskets of strange and even undesirable vegetables and fruit. He hardly needed to begin worrying about them now.

Nor had he ever cared for the opinions of his landed neighbours. Yet there was Hannah to consider. How would they treat her, all those who came upon her?

For the last four weeks he had avoided thought completely. Although Warlow remained stubbornly below ground, he had not sent for Hannah for six months.

He dared not. Couldn't trust himself not to keep her and refuse to let her go, not to damage her with his ravening desire, causing Warlow to emerge finally with unstoppable violence. Money was delivered to her, fruit and wine at Christmas. He convinced himself it was enough; crowded out all questions with sleep, blinded himself with brandy and the other. Nothing needed him: the house ran itself; the gardens, well, it wasn't *quite* spring; Hannah was wise enough to look after herself. Think of all the children to whom she'd already given birth! She'd begun young, when Warlow rescued her from Kempton and took his reward. She was not old, perhaps thirty-five years, and strong despite her stature; he knew that well, though he tried not to think of her body. Tried not to think of her at all, and when he couldn't stop himself there were always bottles to blot out the light. In moments of extreme obfuscation he even congratulated himself on having removed Warlow from her life.

This morning he felt something like resolve. He'd walk. He'd not been outside the house for so long, but today there was a brightness that drew him, the wind had dropped and recent snow part-thawed. He put on his great coat and hat, ignoring unspoken comment from Jenkins, and set off.

Having made one sacrifice earlier in the form of no brandy he was able to make another in forgoing inspection of the gardens. Old habit turned him towards the glasshouses, yet he passed by them rather than going in. Recalling his dream he winced at the unbroken glass of the hothouse.

He caught sight of Price in the kitchen garden walking the paths, kicking snow viciously with his boots, retreated before he was seen and took the longer way round. In the new plantation dormant saplings stood moated by brown, pocked snow, patterns of bird footprints looping and whirling among them.

187

Finding himself breathless he stopped, listened to the continuous dripping, the harsh commands of crows and ravens somewhere near. He hadn't the energy to climb the hills and would walk instead through the fields on the lower slopes and circle back. At the thought of the house he became aware of mounting thirst and creeping cold. He'd not eaten at breakfast; rarely did these days. Hunger threw him back to boyhood, hours of wandering, vast helpings of cold meat and pies on returning straight to the kitchen. Now he would barely complete the walk and reach home and the bottle that cured cold, thirst and thought.

He passed along a bank against which snow had drifted into fantastic waves. Nearby new-dropped afterbirth adorned the snow like streaks of paint. Ewes lumbered away from him. Then he understood the calling of the carrion birds he'd heard before. A half-gutted ewe lay by a fallen hawthorn, her eyeless lambs here and there where the birds had cast them in the vigour of their eating.

The child was his. If a son and he acknowledged him, he'd be heir to Moreham House, to the Powyss estate and name. The idea confounded him. He pressed on home.

*

Day after day she brings food. Takes his plates. Pot. Speaks kindly. Says 'I'm no devil' so often he begins to wonder.

He wakes by the dead fire to soft sounds. It's here again! *Devil's got in!* He holds still. The sounds are different. Soft, small, sudden rushes. *Not* footsteps. Not rats neither. Reaches out for the lamp. Lights it easily since the glass chimney's smashed. And now?

A cat hurls a half-dead mouse about the floor. Runs after it. Crouches. Pounces. Shakes it about, hurls it again. Crouches. Pounces. Bites off its head. Crunches through fur, body, bones, tail.

He is calm. If it hisses at me it be a devil cat. If it be a devil cat then that be a devil woman that comes each day. Lying. If it don't hiss at me, it be no devil cat. And the woman be a woman.

He reaches for the poker. Struggles up from the chair. The cat looks at him, its pupils big in the gleaming dark. He shakes the poker at the cat, shouts:

'Devil cat! *Devil cat!*'

The cat lifts its tail, turns its back. Darts across the room at a movement it hears.

He makes up the fire. Sits again.

The cat comes out of dark corners, drops a frog at his feet.

He groans in sorrow. '*Rats not frogs!*'

The cat sits close to the fire but out of his reach. Cleans itself.

*

Annie was glad that it was Catherine who had taken charge of the task of winkling Warlow out of his horrid place. There'd been a time when she felt that only she had understood the poor man's plight. Cook was always heartless. Catherine, too, seemed not to comprehend at first. Samuel was completely without concern. But she had more than enough to think about now. For either she must use all of her meagre powers of argument to hold Samuel off or else her wiles to coax him out of a cold lack of interest in her. She couldn't understand *him* at all.

Catherine had certainly found a new purpose. Her introduction of the cat into Warlow's 'apartments' seemed to have been the turning point, though she couldn't say why. Her idea had been simply that the cat would keep down vermin. She had worried that he'd think it evil, a witch's cat, since he'd seemed determined to believe she was herself a devil. Why had he imagined that? There was an opinion in the village that he'd lost his wits.

Somehow she must encourage Warlow to dare to emerge. It was something that he'd finally ceased calling her a devil. She could hear his breathing on the other side of the barricade, was sure he was listening to her.

'John, it's Catherine once more,' she'd sing out. 'Here is your supper. I hope you do eat it all.'

It was strange to speak and receive no answer, until one day she heard him begin to clear his throat and stopped piling his plates to listen. There was something between a grunt and a growl, then: 'I hates fish.'

'I know you do. Cook forgets.' Or does it on purpose, more like. 'Give it to the cat.'

'Won't eat it.'

'She's too full of rats and mice then.'

He grunted in what she took to be agreement and she said no more.

There were three opportunities each day. He said little. Sometimes struggled to speak as if he'd forgotten how to even since that morning. She would bring food, wood, tobacco, kindling, and though he said no to clean clothes she left them all the same.

Then he agreed to pull out the small cupboard from beneath the table at the base of the barricade so she could pass through a bigger box of wood. She made sure not to look at him. Of course it was dark in any case, but she didn't want him to see the horrified expression she might not be able to prevent. She did catch sight of a claw-like hand, his left, and forced herself not to cry out.

She tried to talk on every occasion, however little time she had. After a meal of which he'd eaten every scrap, she smelled pipe smoke.

'Did you enjoy the mutton pie, John? With the currants.'

'Yes.'

'I made the pastry.'

'Very good.'

'Have you put on the clean breeches I did bring you last time?'

'You don't nag.'

'How is Puss? Cats are always called Puss in Moreham House, you know. They never have a name of their own.' She heard herself begin to chatter. 'Do you give her the milk in the jug?'

'Yes. Her likes it.'

'Has she caught plenty?'

'Her did find a nest of mice.'

'Oh dear. She must eat the parents then.'

'Out o' their shells.'

'Mice don't hatch from eggs!'

'I *know it*. It were to make you laugh.'

'Ah! Aha!' She laughed in amazement. He hadn't lost his wits then.

'John,' she said, regretting the question even as she spoke, 'who have you thought of most while you've lived down here?' His children perhaps. But oh, they did say he used to beat them.

'Oh. Oh I do think of Mary.'

'Mary?' She was relieved it wasn't Hannah.

'Mary were always good to me.'

'Do you mean your child Mary?'

'No! That be Polly.'

'Ah. So, Mary was . . .'

'Sister.'

'Your sister, Mary. She was good to you, was she?'

'She were always kind to me. She were there when I come from the scarin. Give me a nob of bread.'

'Oh.'

'Mary did keep me from beatin. When her could.'

She was taken aback to hear him sob and shamble away with a slow shuffling as if on all fours.

*

Catherine soon gathered that Warlow's sister Mary, whom he'd now mentioned on several occasions, had died some years ago. She'd seen the child Polly and an older girl, Margaret, in the garden, otherwise she knew of Warlow's children largely by repute. The more she talked to him the more she wondered about Hannah and about his children. She thought of her own childhood. Might Warlow have some affection for a daughter even if he had beaten his sons? Like her own father, who would weep at her with drunken, disappointed love then lash out at her brothers.

She decided that she might have something good to report to Warlow if she went to see for herself. And of course she was very curious. Hannah had not been to Moreham House for so long. People said she was near her time. She smiled shamefacedly, recalling her invasion of Powyss's library, how she'd enjoyed shocking Annie with her inspection of the carpet. How different she was now! She had changed because of Abraham. She felt much older, her younger self so frivolous.

She set off to Hannah Warlow's one afternoon. It was the end of April yet very cold. She held down her hat with one hand and trod along the muddy path, her nose streaming in the sharp wind, her sallow cheeks reddened. The cottage was in a clearing, its plaster worn to wattle in places, small window panes blocked with strips of wood where glass had blown out in gales.

The girl Margaret let her in. Awkward, sober with premature responsibility. Catherine felt for her. Hannah sat at the table sewing a garment, letting it out by the looks of it. Standing beside her was the little girl, Polly. Round-faced, she looked up at Catherine with serious intensity and suddenly smiled.

'I do go to Mr Powyss's garden,' she said proudly.

'I've seen you. Are you Polly?'

'Yes. Mother did go to Mr Powyss's house.'

'Ah. I brought you this lattice tart, Mrs Warlow. I made an extra one.'

'You are kind.'

'Cook won't know.'

'Oh, I hope not,' she said, indicating a chair for Catherine.

'Mrs Warlow, you look well.' It was true. Hannah's body had filled out of course, but so had her face. She was older than Catherine, almost too old to bear another child, yet Catherine envied skin that was not sallow, a small nose, eyes that startled with their strange colouring. A quiet certainty of being that she, Catherine, had never known. She suddenly understood completely why Mr Powyss had wanted her. Yet, *surely* she must be anxious.

'Your children, do they ... ?'

'They have heard somewhat. Margaret, Polly, leave me with Catherine.'

'May I call you Hannah?'

'You are come to spy on me.'

'No! That's not true. Of course I am curious to see how you are. I have not seen you for many months. You have not come to the house.'

'No. Mr Powyss have not called me. I did tell the children about John, he shall bring back a lot of money. I did tell them Mr Powyss helps us. But people talk so, say things.'

'Yes.'

'And Jack have left us. Gone with that Abraham Price. An evil man.'

'Yes.' She almost felt to blame. 'But listen, Hannah. I have begun to talk to John your husband.' She spoke cautiously; her listener tensed. 'I hope to persuade him to come out at last.'

'It were better he stay. Better he don't see me. Not yet awhile.'

'Yes. I understand.' She wanted to say, but couldn't, that surely it would be no better John seeing her *after* she had the baby than before. 'I'm certain it will take some time, though. Strange to say, the underground rooms have become his home, I think. When shall you be brought to bed?'

'In May.'

'I thought I could tell him how his children are faring,' Catherine said.

'He were fond of Polly before he left. She were the only one he did like I think. Childer were ever a trial to him.'

'Ah.'

'You must not tell him of me.'

'No. If he enquire I shall say you are well.' Then she had to ask: 'Does Mr Powyss know, Hannah?'

She saw her blench, look down at the garment. The pause was long. 'He do surely know.'

'You have not told him?'

'No.'

'Oh! You may need help when your time comes.'

'He do help us already. The children have clothes. We do eat a good meal each day. Mother did never have help with hers.'

Catherine was shocked. How lucky she'd been to have escaped this situation herself. She might have carried Abraham's child! Have lost her employment. Have had to live with him or flee and make her own way. Was Hannah simply terrified that John would get to hear, that she kept away from Moreham House? Or was it something else? It disgusted her that Mr Powyss's child was soon to be born and he, he did nothing but sit at home and dose himself with the contraband brandy which Jenkins was obtaining for him.

'He should *know*, Hannah!'

'*No.* And you must not tell him!' She rose awkwardly. 'Please do not tell him. Promise me!'

'I promise,' Catherine said too quickly.

Walking back, she admitted to herself that her curiosity

had got the better of her, that the visit had been fruitless. There was nothing more she could tell John Warlow.

And her feelings fought within her. For some time she had been sorry for *him*. The man had become like an animal; she wanted to help him retrieve his humanity if she could. But now she was more sorry for Hannah.

She felt a terrible dread. She wanted to storm into Powyss's room and shout at the man. Shake him into action before it was too late.

*

Each day he talks to the woman. He's sure she's not a devil: he's seen her feet. Catherine. She tells him to take down some pieces of wood. Calls it a barricade.

He shifts bits from the top. Wedges them under the table. Planks, boards, strips, slats. Legs, backs, seats, doors, drawers.

'Much better, John. Now I don't have to get down on my knees.'

Same for him. He stands, expectant.

'John, I have seen your daughters Margaret and Polly.'

'Oh, Polly!'

'They look very well.'

'Oh.'

There's nothing else she can say about them, hearing the vagueness cloud his voice.

'If only you could shift the, are they bookshelves?' So he does and they're face to face in the glimmering light.

She takes a step back. He sees it. *Don't go*, he thinks. Puts his hands to his face. Great beard all down his chest. Quick, hide away nails, claw hands! She's trying to smile. Dark woman. Not pretty.

If he could reach her he'd put his arms about her. Hold her close to him. Feel the warmth of her body. Hold her. Oh, hold her.

'I think Cook is calling me,' she says. *He* can't hear it.

She turns. Runs up the steps.

He's desolate when she's gone.

She won't come back now, will she. Won't talk to him. Kindly.

Is his face *so* bad? No glass, can't look. She saw his claw nails. He holds his body tight, embracing it. Torn with scabs, scars, pain; she can't see *that*, can she, where he's dug at the sores? But what she saw was enough.

He should never have removed the pile. The other one will come now. *She's* a devil. Or Powyss. Or Jenkins. She said they're in the house. Not gone down to hell.

He lifts up the bookshelves then heaves them back on the table. A finger jams in the door swinging off its hinge. He sucks it and it tastes of soot.

Behind the pile he's safe again.

Chapter 10

ABRAHAM PRICE HAD PROMISED POWYSS never to repeat his attack on Moreham House. He felt no obligation to keep the promise. Yet despite his tendency to act on impulse he had the sense not to want to lose his employment.

Fury would keep exploding in his head like wind in the gut. He raged at Catherine, that she refused to speak to him, turned round and walked the other way if they met outside. He despised Powyss. He was exasperated by Warlow, who'd begun so well with his destruction but now lurked in his dungeon like a dim mole and wouldn't come out.

He caught sight of Hannah Warlow one day with her great belly and that set him muttering and fuming. His hands trembled with a desire to grip and crush. He couldn't keep still, ran in the opposite direction from her and took a sledge-hammer to the quarry by the plantation to smash some stone to dust.

One May morning, early, as she unlocked the outer door to the kitchens, Catherine found herself pushed backwards by Price, who burst through, clasped one hand over her mouth and snatched the bunch of keys with the other. Muffling her face with her shawl, he forced her into the dairy, where he held her down on the damp flags and fucked her until he'd spent his violence.

No words were spoken. He pocketed the keys and left.

*

Days merged. Powyss knew no date though the light ticked somewhere in his mind. He existed in a mist, noticing nothing but what was immediately before him, his fingers, his knees, his glass. He sat at his desk, picked up his pen, put it down. Stood to look out of the window, at a scene too familiar to see. Walked to the other side of the room from the bottles of brandy, port. Checked there was laudanum in his pocket. Took up a book, flicked through the pages. James Hutton, *Theory of the Earth*. Why did he have that? Put it back on a shelf, any shelf. Sat down, stared at a newspaper flung at his feet. Threat of Invasion. Walked to the window again. Closed his eyes. Rubbed his throbbing temples. Half-filled a glass and drank.

Sometimes a previous self emerged. Told him that he should have met with Price weeks ago, run through this year's sowing plan, the tasks for the labourers; checked the condition of seeds collected last year; inspected the young trees in the orchard and plantation for signs of new growth. Had any not survived the winter?

There was always tomorrow.

Much later, when Jenkins said Catherine asked to speak to him he was not displeased at the diversion.

'Sir, I do believe Abraham Price is planning something.'

'Oh. What do you mean?' He looked at her and remembered Fox's comments about intelligence despite her looks.

'He has stolen some keys. I could not prevent him,' she added.

Here was a trial, another puzzle he could not solve. 'When?'

'This morning, sir.'

'Why did you not report it then?'

'I was not well.' He noticed that she was subdued, not like herself. He'd always thought her lively, even impertinent.

'Of course you know Price.'

'No! I have nothing to do with him no more!'

'And yet you say this?'

'Mr Powyss, sir, he has stolen the keys to the kitchen and cellars. I do think he has plans to get John Warlow out.'

'I see. Thank you for this information, Catherine. I shall endeavour to deal with it,' he heard himself say from a distance.

'And, sir. Mrs Warlow is brought to bed next month.'

He closed his eyes, dismissed her; she *was* impertinent.

He waited for her words to take effect. When he looked up, it was still light; he longed for darkness. He wished Price *would* remove Warlow, take him far away into Wales, from where he need never come back. Warlow was a sore. Powyss had freed himself from the shackles of the experiment itself, but beneath, the skin had rubbed away and bled without cease.

Yet if Warlow *were* to get out at last?

Powyss had become adept at forbidding memory, at disallowing speculation. His mental life was blank, drear, his calm alcohol- and opiate-induced. Then as dusk came on an image of Hannah, swollen with child, moved slowly through his mind; slowly, silently towards darkness. Her quiet perfection, her unaccusing look of goodness, her smiles when finally won, gladsome though quick to retreat. Her pleasure. Her magnanimity. Her offer: *I am yours.*

Why had he let her go? How could he have lost her? How had he carelessly let this ... Oh, it was love! It *was* love. Finally he knew what it was. That's what love was. And he had carelessly let it pour away into the ground! Irretrievable. *Why* had he done this? He had abandoned her, abandoned her just because he could not keep her.

And the child. What was that thought he'd had about the child?

He sought his glass, brandy, the consolation of cloves and laudanum: welcomed blurring, longed-for sleep, annihilation. Stayed his hand long enough to write four words on a sheet, fold it and instruct Samuel to deliver it in the morning.

*

Although several men attended Price's 'meetings' only two were swept into his plan of action. One was Caleb Hughes, young, idealistic, inspired by the knowledge that, like him, his hero Thomas Hardy was a cobbler. The other, Rhys – it was his only name – was a labourer like Warlow, long disgruntled with all employers and particularly Powyss, who once had dismissed him for theft. Neither was fired by the Irish rebellion as was Price, but both had taken part in the attack on Moreham House and were convinced by Price's assurances that this time all was simple. For a reason, obscure even to himself, Price kept Jack Warlow out of his plan. Forbade him with threats to leave his master gardener's cottage.

When the household was asleep they unlocked the door of the back kitchen and tiptoed in. Past Samuel sleeping fitfully, dreaming of brave deeds on a truckle bed in the narrow corridor between the back and main kitchens.

They were down the two flights of steps in moments and stood at Warlow's barrier, listening. There was no light, no sound.

'Get him down,' Price whispered, taking one corner of the bookshelves. 'Quietly, isn't it.'

With remarkable delicacy they removed each piece until the entrance was restored and, Price leading, stepped inside.

The room was completely dark. They held up their lamps; stood amazed. There was but one piece of whole furniture: a chair by the dead fire, its back stabbed, springs obtruding like mad manacles. A doorless cupboard leaned, a wooden chair sat legless on the ground. Fragments of wood, shattered glass and china covered the floor entirely except for two pathways and a space by the hearth where a cat lay in a tight ball up against the grate's last heat. One pathway led to the doorless cupboard. Price started along the other, his finger to his lips.

He had instructed the two not to frighten Warlow. Said that the stupid cow Rentfree had terrified him with her loud voice. Now he called out gently:

'Warlow. John Warlow. Your friends are come.' The pathway took them out of the room along the narrow corridor. They stopped to listen at a closed door, heard thumping and scuffling noises, a groan, then nothing.

Price knocked. 'John. Are you there? Your friends are here. Citizens, John. Will us come in?'

Nothing.

Price opened the door, held up his lamp as he stepped into the bedroom. It was not destroyed like the other room, yet there was no sign of Warlow.

'John, where are you? I am Abraham Price. I think you knows me? And here's Rhys. You remembers him? And young Caleb Hughes, cobbler's son. Us've come to take you home, isn't it.'

There was a terrible sob from under the bed.

'Ah John! *There* you are! Let's help you out.'

'Devils! Come for me! Don't take me, *don't!*'

'No, no, John. The devils are *women.*' Price was well prepared. 'Devils are women. Women are devils. Us is not devils, but working men like you, isn't it, men?'

Caleb and Rhys assented loudly.

'Show your feet! Show your hoofs to me!'

The men looked at each other, but Price had his boots off in a moment.

'Here, John. Him's no hoof, see?' Pulled off an earthy

stocking. 'Toes, isn't it.' The other two did the same and a row of naked feet stood by the bed.

'All men, see? Not a devil among us. Here, John, let me help you out,' said Price.

His hand was ignored. A knee appeared, a calf in shredded stocking, a foot in gape-mouthed boot. Another sob, smaller. The second leg was followed by the body squirming slowly to keep below the bed frame, heaving like a sick ram unsheared, a great shaggy head and, clear of the bed, Warlow rose onto all fours and turned his face to his rescuers.

He was at once terrifying and woeful, disgusting and pitiable. A choking stench came out with him from under the bed and Rhys turned from the room and fled, shoeless, his hand over his mouth.

'Come, John, let me help you up,' said Price, apparently unmoved by what he saw and smelled and unwilling to call Rhys back.

Warlow shook his head, gripped the bed frame, pushed himself up to standing with evident pain and peered with wet eyes at Price and Caleb.

'Us'll take you home, John. You needs not live here no more.'

Warlow didn't answer but lit a candle end with shaking hands and shuffled out. They followed him into the big room. He went over to the grate, got down onto his knees and began to scrape out the ashes with his claws and make small noises to the cat.

'You'll make a fire in your own house, John.'

Perhaps he didn't hear. He broke up twigs and laid the fire with small wood and coal, lit it with the candle, rubbed his hands together over the flames as they caught.

'Now, John, it be a good time to come home. You can tiptoe in all quiet like. Us'll help you. Up the stairs, out, along the path into the lane, through the wood. You remember?'

'Catherine'll bring me food.'

Price growled. 'You've a wife to bring you food, John. And childer.'

Warlow waved his hand, wishing them away. 'Catherine'll bring food. Her be no devil.'

'John, you have a home, isn't it!' Price's patience was ebbing rapidly.

'Fifty pound. Fifty pound a year.'

'Not any more. That's over, Warlow.'

'*Not over*. Fifty pound *for life!*'

'Oh, Powyss will give you your money. Powyss owes you a lot of money, Warlow, isn't it.'

'Devils took Powyss,' Warlow muttered. 'Or. Catherine said . . . '

'Her knows *nothing*,' Price said with disgust. 'The devils *should* take Powyss. Come now, John.'

'No. No. Not now. Another time.'

'Yes. You *must* come. You *must*. Powyss do fuck your wife, John Warlow!'

Warlow looked at him bemused. He wasn't really sure who this man was.

'Your wife. Your wife, Hannah. Remember her?'

'Yes,' he said slowly. 'I did have a wife. That were long afore. She did die, I think. I lives *here* now. I has my bed. My cat. Catherine bring my food. You go now.'

'Warlow, you *have* a wife. Even while you lives here.'

'I have a wife?'

'Yes, you have, yes. And while you've been down here, a prisoner, Powyss and she . . . '

'I be a *prisoner*?'

'Yes, Powyss have put you in this prison, John, and him's had Hannah in his bed. *Powyss do fuck your wife!*'

'*Ohh! Oh!*' His head jerked sideways as suddenly, finally, he began to understand.

'Think on your wife's mother, my friend. How she did fuck and fuck with Kempton, hatched all his brats. But *Powyss* be the devil himself, John. And now your wife do bear *the devil's* brat. You must come home and see for yourself. Come now.'

Price and Caleb helped Warlow to his feet, guided him gently by the elbows. Shuffling between them he became a docile child. He said nothing, but needed to rest often, panting with the physical effort greater than any he'd made for years. The stairs were the hardest; they must tell him which foot to raise and when to do it. Once out of the house he staggered at the slash of night air and shrank, oppressed by sudden space.

Caleb spoke to Price in a hushed voice: 'I'll see him to his house, but mother'll worry if her finds me gone.'

'Her'll not know.'

'If her gets up in the night.'

Price dismissed this, but Caleb was troubled.

'I don't think it right to tell him of his wife.'

'Sshh!' But Warlow, puffing and groaning with every step, neither listened nor heard.

'I fear it.'

'Then *don't*.'

'Not right to tell him. I wants no trouble.'

Price spat.

'You take him now, Abraham,' Caleb said, shivering. 'G'night.'

Price thought good riddance and stood with Warlow not far from his house whilst he rested and gasped for more breath.

'Women be devils, John. Devils and whores. Them'll lift their skirts to any man with a prick big or small. Them's itchy as hell.'

They went on.

*

Powyss held the first page of Fox's letter over the candle flame. As it blackened from the centre outwards he read:

trial   *against me entirely*
              seduced Fanny   ornament to her sex
conjugal fidelity and maternal   *in my own defence*
law of Greenland in respect to whales   let go
                    of the drogue
        implied slight   *too cruel*

Then the second page:

                        Thoroughly shamed!
      damages   immediately to sell my house
income, for the rest of my   lost all my London friends
        miserable self-induced

There came a third page:

                    Throw myself on your mercy
      live in M   help you in your diff
Few valuable books   bring the new Flora Londinensis

Curled. Blackened. All was ash.

*

No light. They find a rush on the table. The man Price lights it from his lamp. He remembers that smell of greasy scummings.

Price shakes his hand.

'Good luck, citizen,' he says in a low voice and goes.

Warlow's never been so tired. Legs ache up and down. Fire's out. He sits by its last warmth, covers his knees with a shawl hanging on the back of the chair. Falls deeply asleep.

Dreams he's in the field sowing. Kempton rides up. He's doing it wrong.

'You're no good, Warlow. Don't know how. I'll get someone

else.' He pushes Warlow and the ground is cold, hard with frost like rock.

'Powyss'll do it! I'll get *him*.'

Powyss rides up. Both men on horses. Kick him back down with their boots.

He half-wakes. Where *is* this? Not his bed, that's why it's cold. He shifts his position. Sleeps again.

Something creeps into his sleep, makes him open his eyes, listen. Stirring, voices overhead. Powyss! Listenin again! No, he can't think of it. Sleep. Sleep.

No Warlow boys scare crows any more so no one's up before dawn. Windows are small, blocked where broken. Light slips in around the shadowy room until a bar of brightness strikes him. Just as children's feet crash down the stairs straight to the hearth.

Gasps and shrieks wake him; he shields his eyes. Hears them back away.

'Mother!' Some run upstairs.

He turns from the one bright window. They stand in a huddle. It's where he lived once. Or is he dreaming? It's not where he lives now. Who are they? He doesn't know them.

Their faces show horror. Their eyes squeeze up. Like when the woman Catherine saw him. But they don't try to smile.

He opens his mouth to speak.

'What are you?' says one.

'Devil!' says a puny boy. 'Us'll *curse* you!'

'Get out, get out!'

'Damned devil, get out!'

'Devil, go away from here!' They scream these things together.

His throat is dry. He's hungry, thirsty.

'I'm ...' but nothing comes. He clears his throat and they back away further. It's not a dream.

'I'm John Warlow.'

The younger girl bursts into sobs.

'You're not! You're not our father! You're a devil man!'

He recognises her. She looks like Mary. But she recognises nothing. He sees her shrink from his animal claw. His head all over hair. Dirt and stink. His eyes begin to fill.

'Mary!' She runs from him, his outstretched hand.

Their mother appears. He had a wife before. But she were thin.

'You are returned, John.' He struggles to recall. There's something he needs to remember. It *is* his wife. Hannah, she's called.

He stands up and they run into corners or cling to their mother.

'It be not his fault him do look so,' she says to them. 'Get thy bread and cheese and go to school now. Little John make up the fire then go to Kempton's.'

The children disperse, then re-form in a knot and rush out. He is alone with the woman who is his wife. But not the wife he had before.

She mashes the tea, pours some for him. He sits. She hands him bread, a piece of cold bacon. Stands away from him.

'The childer have grown,' she says. She's looking at her hands.

This *is* where he lived long before. Mary's his, but the others are not; he doesn't remember them. Mary's sweet face. *But she did run away.*

'Mary . . .'

'Polly. Polly is a good girl.'

He stares at her. Something about Powyss he has to remember.

'*Powyss's* childer?'

She glances at him. Looks down quickly. '*Your* childer, John. Them's fed well since you left.'

The tea seeps in. Not a dream.

'Hannah.' She turns away, won't look at him. 'I live in the dark. You're growed fat.'

'It were five year ago you went.'

'Where I lives devils came. You're not like you were.'

'I know nothing of devils.'

'Women be devils.'

'What *is* it you *say*, John Warlow?'

'You're with child.'

She moves behind the table away from the talon pointing at her belly. Won't look at his face.

'Now I remembers. What him said. The man Price. Him said I were in prison. Where I live. When I were in prison, you. You. Where is Powyss? Where is he?'

He gets up out of his chair, swaying, looks about him. Lumbers towards the staircase. 'Where is he?'

'Mr Powyss is in the big house, John.'

'*I* do live in the big house!' She must wait. Cannot leave. Is glad she sent the children out.

'Powyss. Powyss.' He shuffles back on painful feet, round the table. His steps are small, feeling for shards and splinters. She pities him.

An enormous tiredness afflicts his limbs. He leans on the table, claws spread before him. He would lie down if he could and sleep. Sleep forever. *I'll put my head down on the table and she'll come and hold me. Like when I were a boy with fever. Mary did hold me to her.*

His head droops further. Tears pour onto his sleeves, his hands.

'You're tired,' he hears her say.

But the man's voice. The man's whining voice comes again.

'Powyss fucked …' He looks at her face all bleary now through his crying eyes.

'Powyss do fuck your wife, him say to me. Women be devil's whores. Them'll lift their skirt for any man!' He reaches out to grasp her. She backs away.

'That's not true, John.' Won't look at him.

'You do it with him when I be in the dark. Where I live.

You do it with him. Do it in hedges for a penny.' He's panting. So much talking. Remembering. 'Big or small.' Head is full.

He feels a surge of energy, like once before. In his arms, his shoulders. He stumbles round after her, grabs her upper arms, shakes her. Back and forth, back and forth. She cries out at the pain of his nails. She's as small as a cat in his grasp.

'Cry out, damn you! Cry out for damned Powyss now! Him's not comin. Kempton can't hire him. See, him's not here. *I'm* here. *I'll* do it, Kempton. *I'm* here.' His mind teems. He pushes her. '*Look* at me, devil, devil's whore.'

He shoves her again. She falls backwards, one arm trapped behind her back. Struggles to get up.

He drops down on all fours. Straddles her as best he can beneath her belly. Pinions her fist with his left claw.

'Devil! Devil! *Look at me!*' She turns her head away from his slaps, shuts her eyes at his spittle.

He hits her face to open her eyes, but she won't, won't look at him. Bangs her head against the ground again, again, again, again, again; his fingers slip and he presses – *make her look at me, make, make* – presses until he chokes the life out of her and when he removes his hands the blood from his claws is a string of beads about her neck.

*

Powyss woke because the shutters were still open. He groped for the bottle but it was empty, found useless phials in his pockets. Recalled fleetingly his note to Hannah.

She will come! He'll change his clothes, wash. The place must be tidied up, cleaned. He stooped to pick up bottles, shoes. Why hadn't Samuel done this?

There were several knocks at the door and Jenkins came in before he'd told him to. Too bad! Perhaps finally the man will have to go. He'll promote Samuel to butler. *He* can be trusted.

'Jenkins!'

'Sir, you must come. You must come now!'

'I *must*? Must come *now*? Jenkins, what is this?'

'Sir, Warlow. Mrs Warlow. You must come.'

A bolt. A bolt through the heart.

He ran straight out, with neither coat nor hat, through the garden, along lanes and through a wood to the wretched hovel. How long it took, how ridiculously long.

Samuel and Valentine Tharpe, the magistrate neighbour were there outside, waiting for him. At a distance, a group of young children stood silently, held back by village women.

'Powyss.' Tharpe shook his hand. 'Warlow is apprehended. I advise that you hear from your man here before you go in. I'll call him.'

He beckoned to Samuel who trembled at the sight of him, chewed his finger ends.

'I did bring your note for Mrs Warlow, sir. There were no answer so I did look through that window. At first I did think ...' He stopped and went red. 'I did see Warlow and Mrs Warlow on the floor, sir. But they did not move, you see, sir. And Mrs Warlow's face were looking towards the window. It were hard to see, sir. But I did think it were blue.'

'As I say, two constables have hold of Warlow, Powyss. Will you go in?'

Powyss shook, feverish though chill. His face was grey, his body thin, for in his recent condition he had not welcomed food.

Inside, Warlow was roped to a chair with a constable on either side. He was an extraordinary sight, for he seemed both man and beast: man because he sat upon a chair, his hands limp, almost lifeless as no animal ever held its limbs even in sleep; beast because his head was a mass of matted hair, his human features lost among it. On his feet were boots through which his nails protruded inches like an eagle's talons.

For a moment Powyss recalled a painted print he'd once seen of Nebuchadnezzar on all fours, mad, dwelling in darkness. The haunted face had hung in his imagination for days.

Warlow took no notice of them, his look locked within himself, yet at the same time somewhere far beyond.

Powyss barely glanced at him, having known all along that this was how the man would look. He couldn't think of him; wanted him expunged. He searched for Hannah.

'Take Warlow upstairs until I call you,' Valentine Tharpe instructed the constables, who until now, had stared at their feet, embarrassed. They unknotted the rope hesitatingly, but Warlow was entirely docile, and after they'd tied his hands behind him they made their slow way out of the room, as though leading an ox to market. Tharpe went and stood outside with the doctor, who had just arrived.

She lay on her back, clothes disordered over her swollen stomach, her head twisted, loose, her face a distortion.

He stood against the wall. A heavy silence from above, murmuring voices from outside oppressed him. He wanted to be sick, shifted his position and the plaster behind his back moved.

Oh, if he could tear the place down, this hellish hovel, this wreck of a habitation! Why was he here? What was this place to do with him, this wretched hellish place? This woman, her skirts raised, revealing her feet, her calves, a provocation. Oh, he had used her, *he* had used her. *He* had!

He must look; he couldn't. He must look, couldn't bear it. It was not her face! She was never like this. Yet he must look, must search her face, must find her again somewhere behind the expression of terror. There had to be something of her serenity, when at last she'd lost her suspicion, had ceased her resistance to him, it had to be still there, always there. Calm, containment, even pleasure behind the scream strangled in her pulled mouth.

He fell on his knees. If she opens her eyes, but oh they have closed them! Grey-blue even in this light, this darkness. If she opens her eyes she will smile and I'll tell her I never meant this to happen. Never. Oh, I'm sorry, I'm sorry, oh Hannah, Hannah. I abandoned you. Tried to forget you. Come home with me now! Come, oh come home!

He held back from touching her, for she was too precious and he unworthy. He began to shudder like a man in a palsy, clawed his head with his hands to rid himself of it. But he must touch her. Touch. It had been so long ago. He took her hand in his and despaired at its coldness, wanting to die too, longing to die.

He held her hand against his face, hearing only howling in his head. Why was she on the ground? Why was she here, on the ground, here, thrown down like this? He'd take her up, run back with her to the house, out of this hole, where she shouldn't be. She should never have lived here.

Her hand against his cheek, as it had been, sometimes in life. Still. Lifeless, her body yet suggested life. Might the child live? He placed his hand on her belly, but it was silent. The child will have moved, she will have felt it moving. Did it die at the same moment that she did? Did it die? *Could* it still be alive? Could it be merely quiescent? He must know, must find out, rose up to ask the doctor, but his legs shook so that he fell back down and throwing himself on her breast finally broke, wept, a child himself.

He would stay here with her. Why should he leave? He stroked her hand, talked to her, tried to explain, but how poor everything he said was, how feeble his excuses, what worthless declarations! He had not protected her, had not saved her. Had not saved himself.

There was a cough outside the door: the doctor needing to go about his business. Fury burst in him. No! You cannot come in. Get out! Get out! He wanted to scream at them. Leave me, me and her, she's mine, nothing to do with you. Get out! I *can* not, I *shall* not leave her.

A hand touched his shoulder.

'Mr Powyss, I must examine the body and write my notes. I can give you a powder for calming.'

Powyss laughed in scorn.

'I have plenty to calm me, plenty.' With help he stood, moved apart but would not leave the place, would not take his eyes from her. Again leaned up against the wall, plaster crumbling at his back.

The magistrate came in and went upstairs. There were heavy, shuffling steps as the constables guided Warlow down his own cramped staircase.

Powyss saw the creature and shut his eyes. He had no energy to kill him now. None. Man become animal. Man become animal by his own instructions. How could he kill his own creature?

As they took him to the door Warlow bawled out: 'No light! No light!'

'He's been living in the dark for years,' Powyss heard himself say. 'He will not be able to stand the daylight. You must cover his eyes and in due course he must wear spectacles with smoked glass in them.'

'He'll be hanged before then,' Samuel said.

'Was it you who raised the alarm, Samuel?' the doctor asked him.

'I ran straight to the constables and they did come with the magistrate here. They did think Warlow would fight, but he were still on the ground. He were asleep, sir.'

'Take me home,' Warlow said. 'The devil did die. It is safe. Catherine'll bring my food.'

'He'll go first to the Moreham lock-up, Powyss,' Tharpe said. 'Women from the village have taken the children away. Come now, man, I'll walk back as far as your house with you.'

They stood in the doorway until the procession was out of sight, Samuel, the constables, the hideous, hapless Warlow, blindfolded, stumbling along the rough path through bluebells.

There was a period of lucidity, like a perfect day when hills cut out of ice take each their place in the humming air.

Powyss rose soon after first light, resumed the old order of his life. He inspected the sky, made his rounds of flower garden, kitchen garden, glasshouses with notebook in hand, breakfasted and then went to the library to plan and read.

There was an immediate problem. Price had vanished. His clothes and few belongings had been cleared from his cottage and no one could find him anywhere. Enquiries in Moreham among his revolutionary friends and followers were fruitless. The boy Jack was missing too; thought to have run off with Price, who'd also taken Powyss's horse.

He drew up an advertisement for a replacement master gardener and meanwhile noted down instructions for the labourers.

In the library he sketched diagrams and made lists for the horticultural year, consulting Miller's *Gardeners Dictionary* as usual, checking previous gardening calendars he'd written.

The afternoon clouded. In the sweating heat of the hot-house he tripped on a chipped brick, fell against the door jamb and cut his forehead. Blood dripped through wooden slats onto the earth, smeared his hand and he went into the house to wash it off.

Leaning over the basin in his dressing room, watching the swirl of red in the water like smoke, he imagined it filling with blood from his slit throat. His razor lay nearby. Did he have the courage? Was it too good an end for him?

An opened bottle stood beneath the wash table, unopened phials in its drawers. The day had exhausted him; he blacked it out.

The following day he tore up the advertisement for the master gardener, summoned the garden labourers and sent them on their way with the order that they take what fruit and vegetables they could eat for a week. The diagrams and lists lay where he'd left them, the notebooks he'd taken around the grounds with him yesterday were in any case quite blank.

In came Jenkins, Cook, Samuel and Annie in turn, each to be relieved of his or her position, rewarded with a generous sum and a fair reference to be shown to future employers. Mrs Rentfree protested.

'I cannot think but that you do surely need a body to cook for you, Mr Powyss, for you certainly cannot do it yourself.'

'Thank you Mrs Rentfree, but I'd prefer it if you would now seek another position. This money should tide you over until you find an agreeable employer.'

'But who will employ a woman of my years, however good I am at the cooking? For writing I cannot.'

'Samuel and Annie will help you with your search.'

'Pah! Good-for-nothings. If you had only kept the Holy Book by your side, I always thought, Mr Powyss.'

Samuel pleaded, when it came to his turn. 'Let me stay with you, sir.'

'No. I'm sorry, Samuel.'

'I'm the only man who know how to handle your collection, sir.'

'Choose a piece, Samuel. Choose yourself a piece as a reward for your good work.'

'No! Oh no, sir. I couldn't never do that.'

'I am going away.'

'I'll go with you. Wherever you go, sir. Or let me stay and guard everything. I'm loyal, sir, more nor all the rest.'

'Thank you, Samuel. You have indeed been loyal.' But he waved him away and called for Catherine.

'Catherine Croft, I believe you have more intelligence and more sense than anyone in the house. Please sit here and listen with care to what I say.

'I am leaving and do not intend to return. I cannot live in

this house and shall close it up shortly when everyone has left. If it falls into ruin that will be a suitable memorial to my life.'

Catherine looked up at Powyss standing by his desk. He'd said that with a kind of pride that riled her.

'But it is your house, sir, where you were born and brought up. All your things, your beautiful things, your books!'

Powyss felt a ring of pain around the inside of his skull. Too much calm clear-sightedness. It had expanded like hot metal till he wished his head would split and cast its contents into oblivion.

'I cannot live here!' His voice was strangely high, contorted.

'It is right that you should be distressed, sir.'

'*Distressed!* I would die if I could. But I don't deserve such a reward. I must live. Live and repent each day that's left to me, each minute, each second.'

'I have ruined their lives! Hannah is dead because of me. No, don't object. Hear me. There can be no argument. There is only one side to the matter and it's this: I have ruined Warlow's life. Fox once asked me who it was all for. But the question is *what* was it all for. I'll tell you. For idle ambition, for a feeble desire to be acknowledged by those I admire. And I have killed Hannah and her child.'

'Your child, sir,' Catherine said quietly.

He looked away.

'John Warlow it was who did kill her.'

'*I* am to blame. He would not have done it otherwise.'

'He did beat her and the children. Did you know it, Mr Powyss, sir?'

'That is worthless talk. Now the children are motherless. Warlow was made mad by his existence underground. He has become a deranged creature, and it is I who have made him this!'

'Mr Powyss, I could . . .'

'Ah, you anticipate me. I *knew* you had more goodness in

you than the rest of them. Catherine, will you act as a mother to the Warlow children? The oldest, Margaret, will surely help. Will you do this?'

'It was my thought.'

'Price has gone, you can live in his cottage. Of course I understand there might be some unpleasantness for you in that, but I shall arrange for it to be painted, the furniture thrown out and sufficient pieces from this house to be moved in. I shall also arrange a monthly payment to you to cover all that you might need.'

'Sir, I . . .'

'Please do not hesitate! Do it please, for Hannah, if not for me.'

'I shall.'

'Thank you, Catherine. And I should like you to know of my other request, though it does not affect you directly.

'It would be quite wrong to hang or even imprison Warlow. Indeed he should not be tried at all, though no doubt that cannot be avoided. I have written a letter to the magistrate in full explanation, to Valentine Tharpe that is, and left money for a good defence lawyer. I am also leaving money for his care in some suitable refuge. Please will you support my case as far as you are able, to ensure that no harm comes to the man?'

'I shall. Oh sir, where will you go?'

'That I need not say.'

There was a pause. In anguish, barely audible, Powyss said: 'I might have saved her. See this. Samuel returned it to me.'

Catherine read: *Hannah, please come. Herbert*

'I wrote it, gave it to Samuel and asked him to deliver it *the following morning*! Why did I not send it *then*, immediately! But in any case it should have been written days before, *weeks, months* before. Finally, when pulled from my sickening lethargy by you, Catherine, I sent it *too late*. I have failed utterly, utterly. My endeavours were worse than worthless.

'There's a Latin phrase. You may not know it. *Ratio quique reddenda.* It means, each man must give an account of himself. Imagine mine! The very words would turn me to ash.'

'Oh, sir, you do torment yourself.'

'*There is only torment.*'

*

The house was in turmoil as Cook, Jenkins, Annie and Samuel rushed about, alternately packing their belongings and complaining. Jenkins was assured of a position, having sent off enquiries regularly for some time. He had to hire a carter to carry the enormous store of sherry which he intended to sell to a vintner in Hereford before arriving in his new post, financially superior to all the other servants there. Samuel sat on his packed box in the blacking room, staring into space, too shocked to chew. His own room. He had nowhere to go. Mrs Rentfree was unsure how angry to be while at the same time struggling in her mind to convert Mr Powyss's sizable parting purse into bottles of gin. Annie wept continuously, believing rescue could come only through marriage to Samuel, the offer of which was still not forthcoming.

Catherine found a quiet place and a pen and paper. She'd been moved by Powyss, honoured to take up his plan, though it wouldn't be easy. She thought she owed him more than just her spoken word and as soon as she could she handed him this note:

18 May 1798

Dear Mr Powyss,

I am honoured and grateful, sir, that you have asked me to look after the children of John and Hannah Warlow.

218

I shall do this as well as I can. I shall see they do go to school, too.

I will also tell the magistrate that you are right about John Warlow.

They do say that God is our only judge. May he protect you.

Please, Mr Powyss, do not despair.

Your faithful servant,
Catherine Croft

The other servants left, the house was locked up, and soon after, Powyss had gone.

Part III

Chapter 11

IT WERE THE WOMAN. *Catherine.*

He sits bolt up in his bed. Dawn buzzes at the shutters. Shan't light a candle. Never lights candles.

Her voice it were. Yes! *It were her did speak at the table.* Must have brought the food. Lot of food. Meat. Her did always bring his food when he lived, when he lived. When he lived in the dark. His place.

Them say it were years afore. But them do say things.

He strokes the cat nesting in the folds of his blanket. Sleeping to his warmth.

Her were kind. Not Mary, no. It were not Mary. Her did die, that he knows. He won't think of her end, no.

This one. *Catherine.* Them did get him out of his place (Light! hit him like an axe! Split his skull in half!). Did get him out. *It were his place.* Where her used to come. Never wanted to go out. Never wanted to. *Catherine'll bring me my food, I said.* He struggles to remember more, but it's all black. Sometimes figures rush through his mind, rush like bats, right close, nearly touch him, but he beats them away, waves his arms like flails, whack! whack! punches them out of his head.

Now he's *here*. This place. *Where I lives now.* With these people talkin and talkin. Can't understand them. And rules. Rules to get up in the mornin, go to bed. Can't sleep in my clothes. Wash! Have to wash. Rules when you eat. Not eat till others be served. Not eat food with my hands. Rules when you do use a hoe, when a rake, a spade. When you stop. Have to think of rules all the time.

And now her's here again. Come back. *That's good.*

He gets out of bed. The cat stirs, purrs, doesn't open an eye. No fire, not till night. He pours water from the jug into the basin, dips his face in it, rubs his hands over his shaven cheeks and chin, his close-cut hair. Rule. No breakfast unless you're clean and dressed.

Pulls off the night shirt, pulls on black breeches, white shirt, waistcoat, black coat. New boots. Used to wear clogs once. Morning light now, but he doesn't open the shutters. Never opens them.

No bread yet, he's up too early. Always wakes at dawn. When he feels it's come. House quiet, no one talking. He tiptoes out of his room. Breaking a rule. Hearing's so good he hears breathing through doors. He'll hear if someone hears him.

Puts on the spectacles while it's still dark in the house. Hooks them over his ears. Master in school did wear spectacles. He feels a bit grand.

Will he meet her in the garden? Later, maybe. Will he see her through the dark lenses? Will he know it's her? What's her look like? He's no picture in his head. Once he wanted to. Once he wanted to put his arms round her, once, afore, in the dark. *Did he?* Yes. Oh he did, yes. That's how he'll know it's her.

He takes a hoe and barrow from the building against the wall. Pushes down the path to the vegetable beds. Waves away birds with his hoe, small birds not crows.

Sometimes he longs for a field, not this garden. For a horse.

He can feel sacking at the tips of his fingers. Feel himself take it off the horse's back, reach down harness, leather straps in brass buckles, coaxing him into the ploughshafts. Breath warm on his hands and face. Smell of hide.

'Next year, Warlow,' the master says. Grew he's called. 'You've done well so far. We'll see how you do nearer to the house first. Wouldn't want to be shut in again, would you?'

He hoes among parsnips and leeks, carrots. Earth is dry, hard. Big empty onion bed waiting for barrows of muck from the stable. A few long beans remain. Pea plants are furred with mould.

I'll give her a handful of beans, he thinks. When I see her. Her'll like beans.

*

It will be a while yet till sunset. The climb is steep up Yarston bank, beyond the Cold Hill ridge, especially hauling hawthorn. Powyss piles branches onto others waiting to be cut, sits on the ground to rest, his back against the wall of the shack, which in any case he'd rather not look at, preferring hills fading into further hills, the enormity of sky diminishing him, diminishing everything.

His father's ludicrous rustic cottage. When he inherited the estate, he made it doorless and windowless, suitable for sheep. A low stone building with a thatched roof, a fantasy, elaborately curved, now grass-infested, rain-worn, where he sleeps, in a corner roughly cleared of mud and muck. On winter nights he heaves the door back into its frame, fills window gaps with their sentimentally decorative shutters, never intended for use.

He's been there two winters since fleeing Moreham House, understands now why people measure time in winters. From his childhood on, he always took to the hills when running away from some person, some situation. As he had after

225

Warlow destroyed his rooms, when he and Hannah walked in the garden and, Oh God, let him not remember!

But this is not the same as any of those times, for he'll never return.

At first he thought to go abroad, but even the briefest reflection told of absurd luxury, the Grand Tour all over again, money, trunks, arrangements, utterly inappropriate. Yet he had to get out, away, couldn't bear to be in the house. Hastily grabbing clothes, blankets and random scraps from the pantry, the servants having virtually emptied it, he climbed all day, well beyond his usual retreat to the further hill and the sheep shelter.

Soon after his arrival he thought he saw distant smoke rising from the direction of the house. Imagined sounds of riot, the air stirring with hostility. But having brought neither brandy nor the opiate, he'd already begun descent into the predictable horror he'd not troubled to anticipate. How long it lasted he didn't know, his fob watch not wound. Eventually emerging from hideous visions, he recalled his acknowledgement that the experiment had turned Warlow into an animal, so he, too, should live an animal's life. Warmed by May sun, mocked by the burgeoning life about him, he tried a little stale food, was sick, but sufficiently recovered to look about, think how to live.

He eked out the last supplies then lived off berries from the whins, plant leaves that didn't scorch his mouth, unripe cobnuts, spring water, was perpetually famished, weak. In late summer, severe rains, which elsewhere caused rivers to swell and burst, drowned countless animals, swept away bridges and roads, here, high above those disasters, nevertheless soaked him to the skin. He trod an unexpected marsh: foetid slime clothed his feet and legs. Wet sank into his bones. He caught a chill, sweated, shivered, moaned once more.

Suddenly a man appeared. Aaron, Bloor's shepherd, come to check the sheep after the storms. Stock still, aghast, his dog bounding and yelping until he silenced him with an inarticulate shout.

Both men were astonished.

'Aaron!'

The man was grievously shy, barely acquainted with speech. He opened his mouth and closed it. Must be Powyss.

'You must tell no one I'm here, Aaron. Please.'

The man stared, immobile.

'I'll pay you to say nothing. I've no money with me here, but one day . . . ' He tailed off. 'One day I shall. I promise you. Will *you* promise *me* to say nothing?'

The shepherd nodded.

'Tell *nobody!*'

Nodded, grunted.

'I shall not return to Moreham, you understand me? The elements will punish me, for I have done much harm. Much harm.'

Aaron considered this. Urgency flashed in his eyes.

'Winter. Cold.'

'Of course, yes. But I've a roof, look. There's plenty of wood lower down the hill.'

"Ow ye cut 'im?'

'It's true I've only my clasp knife, but I'll make do with branches I can break myself. And I don't mind the sheep being here. Do you understand? Only *don't tell Bloor.*'

Aaron nodded again. But was still troubled.

'Eat.'

'Oh well, maybe I'll snare a rabbit sometimes,' Powyss said vaguely, by now exhausted by this conversation.

A day later Aaron appeared again, this time with a sack. His dog ran up to Powyss, poked him with his nose as his master laid the sack at Powyss's feet, turned and walked away rapidly. The sack contained a saw, axe, rope, snaring wire, tinder box, large loaf and several pounds of windfall apples.

Powyss was touched, grateful, burdened by kindness from a man who owed him nothing. There could be no doubt these objects were all Aaron's, brought from his hovel which most certainly he rented from Bloor. With an apple tree in a perch of garden.

He wants nothing that he ever owned. Has left everything behind to rot, will think only of Hannah and his failure. His utter failure.

*

At night he sits by the fire. Like he did afore in his place. *This is not his place.* Them pictures on the walls, strange pots on the mantle. Curtains, candlesticks. He smashed it all once. *Did he?*

The master said: 'Here is *your room*, Warlow.' Not true. A lie. It's *his*, master's room, master's house. 'I shan't lock you in. It's not a prison.' What's he say that for? But him come in when him do feel like it. *In my place I were safe.*

But no! There were a devil. Devil did come in, *she*-devil. I did hide away under. Got under ... A weight bears down on him. *Squeezed under my bed!* Voices shouting at him *John John.*

Beats his head. *Look at the flames. Look at the flames and them'll go. Beat, beat. Beat out! There, them's gone.*

Fire's good. None o' them people in here. Them in the garden, talkin, talkin, them in the house. Talk. Talk. Not to him them don't. Them don't speak to *him*. Speak to their-selves. Mad. Them's mad people all o' them 'cept the master.

Madman said, 'murder murder murder murder murder murder' right up close in my ear wouldn't stop. Hit 'im with a spade. Master shut me in the cellar a day. 'We must punish you, John Warlow.'

Dark's nothin!

Madmen!

Something moves at his feet in the flames' light. Frog? I'll put it in... I'll catch it, put it... The cat jumps onto his knees. He scratches her under her ear, tries to remember when he caught frogs.

Them should've never took me out o' there. My place it were. *Get back*, I can get back. *Can I?* Not rules there. Not mad people. The woman Catherine, she be there. She were good. Were she his wife, were she? No. Wife? Did I have a? Where is *she*?

Nobody have a wife in this place. All men, one old woman. Master's no wife. No childer. Better no childer. Cooks, serving-men, no wife.

Young woman do come for vegetables in the morning. In the garden. I likes her. Plump she is. Round bubbies. I could. I'd. He feels a stirring. I'd fuck. 'John,' the man said, 'he do fuck your wife.' Who were that? Where's *she*? *Where's all o' them? Out! Out!*

He takes up the poker, jabs the coals hard, hard till sparks fly out onto the hearth and the lumps collapse. *What more can I?* Jab, smash, something what'd splinter nicely. Once afore I ... *Did I?* Looks around to see what there is but it's too dark and then he's dizzy. He knuckles his head, beats it, beats it to get it all out.

'Good night, John Warlow!' Master going about.

'Night.' Rule: always reply.

Rule: wash before you get into bed. Kicks off his boots. Drops the jacket on the floor. Wrestles off breeches and stockings, pulls nightshirt over his head. *Nightshirt!* Like a woman, he thinks.

The bed is warm, soft, the cat settles on the pillow. I'll look for her, find her. The woman Catherine.

*

Powyss survives two winters protected by a bucket of goose fat smeared in a layer under his vest, brought by Aaron, similarly clad. He is wholly occupied finding sustenance and fuel:

snared rabbits and moor birds, nuts cracked between stones, bitter sloes that gripe his gut, rowan berries, sorrel, and when snaring fails he pokes his fingers into his clothes, sucks fat from his fingers; in the scraped-out bucket he collects water or snow to melt; dead wood and gorse, dry enough to burn immediately, less dry to store. Sawing dense oak, hawthorn and holly warms him. Sisyphus-like he lugs logs to the pile at one end of the shack. His limbs ache, his hands are calloused, cut, wrapped in blood-staunching strips of shirt tail. Always thin, he becomes thinner. His eyes sink into their sockets, buried with grief and remorse; he loses teeth, his hair, what is left straggles over his shoulders, his beard is long and scanty. Washing is out of the question. Fastidiousness has gone, velvet and silk are filthy, muddied like sheep, his companions. He shits in holes he digs with his hands. Is driven by hunger to sleep for hours. He stinks.

He's dozing after eating the legs of a smoke-black, barely cooked rabbit. The wood store needs replenishing even if a third winter is not upon him yet, but he lets his eyelids drop, dreams that Hannah has returned, greets him, tells him she cannot stay, she must go back.

Opens his eyes to two children staring at him, fascinated. Watching him for some time, he suspects. The older child holds a thick stick. He stares back at them and for a while the looks lock as he wonders whose children they are, realising in dismay that unlike Aaron they cannot be trusted to stay silent. Which means he'll have to go away at last, far away and soon.

At this, he groans aloud, begins to stand, and the girl screams in terror while the boy yanks her by the hand, clutching his cudgel, and they run off screeching over and over so that he hears it for minutes after.

Now they'll come. They'll *all* come and gawp and interfere and advise, those neighbours he always disliked, can barely remember. Now he can never be on his own with his remorse. He must go back, prepare himself and leave forever.

But he ran away, isn't that what he did? *He ran away like a child.*

How complacent! To imagine that physical suffering would suffice! It comes to him that he must return. Return and face those very places where everything happened: library, bedroom, the Warlows' desperate cottage, Hannah's grave, for surely she was buried nearby.

He must face it all, face everything. Even Warlow, wherever he is.

It is an awakening.

*

In the cramped kitchen of the master gardener's cottage, Catherine is making bread. Her hands wrist-deep in dough, she tosses her still black hair out of her eyes. She's thirty-six, will never marry now, abandoned the idea of marriage when she took on the Warlow children and when she gave birth to Abraham Price's child, the fruit of his vicious triumph over her after he'd stolen the keys to the kitchens.

When she was carrying the child she dreaded giving birth to an infant with Abraham's face, flailing its limbs, arching its body, uncontrollable. That had been a recurrent nightmare. She longed, prayed, inconsistently, for a girl whose character would be like hers, not his, who'd surely look less like him, more like her. Not that that was anything to wish upon a child. She'd had a sister, though, better looking than herself. Perhaps a girl child would resemble her. In the last weeks of her pregnancy she often thought of Hannah, wishing she were still alive, to talk to her freely, absorb her quiet wisdom.

Although Price made a brief return, he vanished completely before the child was born, and Catherine suckled and cared for the baby as though he were hers alone. She hoped that Price would never hear of the birth. Was relieved to find the child looked like no one in particular. She called him Tom after Tom Paine. Of course she wanted to forget the violent months with Price, but she found she was able to disassociate him from the book that had cheered and inspired her back then. After all, it was she who'd completed the reading of the *Rights of Man* first, and, she believed, understood it far better than Price ever had.

There was a surge of disapproval and gossip in and around the village about her involvement with the dangerous gardener, and her pregnancy with his brat, but it was cancelled out by admiration for her taking on the unfortunate Warlow children, bringing them up with patience. With affection. It was an odd family. Six children of all ages, one woman, no man, but never short of money, living in a small cottage, charmingly papered and furnished, with pieces that were rather too good for it. The baby was frequently watched over by Margaret, the oldest Warlow child, and, as he grew, played with by his erratic, adopted siblings. That so many children claimed Catherine's attention was fortunate, enabling her to push little Tom's dreadful conception to the very back of her mind.

Now the house is quiet. Margaret has become a housemaid in Valentine Tharpe's nearby mansion and the two older boys are labourers in Hereford. Jack has never returned.

George and Polly, the two youngest, still live with Catherine. George is simple and Polly too good-natured to let go, Catherine feels, though they both find casual work on occasion. Tom, an unexpectedly contented child, is fussed over by the others, his days spent close to his mother. Her tasks are fewer, but there are still three children to care for, bread to make, hens to feed, washing, drying, mopping. In the evenings she reads with the children.

She makes a journey, leaving Tom in the care of the other two. For some time she's thought of taking Polly to see her father, for according to Warlow she was his favourite child. Well, the one and only child out of the lot he liked. Polly is just old enough to withstand whatever shock there might be, but Catherine decides it's wise to check on the conditions in which he lives first.

After his trial for Hannah's murder and on the advice of the magistrate, Valentine Tharpe, to whom Powyss wrote before he left, Warlow was placed in an asylum in Kinnersford, some twelve miles from Moreham.

Catherine sets off walking then takes the post-chaise: it's the longest journey she's made since she left home, a disenchanted yet hopeful girl.

Kinnersford Hall is new, an 'enlightened' asylum, she's been informed, a rather fine house among acres of woods and cultivated ground. The inhabitants are put to work in the fields, the flower and vegetable gardens and greenhouses. All eat three meals a day together and are expected to behave well and converse with each other in an orderly fashion.

Dr Josiah Grew greets her in his study. A small man, quite dwarfed by piles of books and busts on pedestals, he shakes her hand, his eyes darting impertinently over her face and body. He doesn't meet enough women who aren't mad, he reminds himself.

'Please be seated, Mrs Croft.' It's simpler for Catherine to be thought married. 'You have come to see John Warlow. May I ask in what way you are related to him?'

'I am no relation.'

'Ah. What is your interest then?'

'I have brought up his children these last two years.'

'I *see*.'

Catherine strongly dislikes the way Dr Grew's eyes flit about her, settling finally on her mouth. Now I know what it's like to be a bowl of cream put down for the cat, she thinks.

'It is not you who are paying his fees, Mrs Croft, and as he's here for the rest of his life I cannot quite see the purpose of your visit.'

'I thought I might bring his youngest daughter to visit her

father and wondered if that would be a suitable thing to do. I'd like to be able to see him if possible.'

'You will have passed Mr Warlow on your way to the house.'

'Oh! Where?'

'At present he works in the vegetable gardens.'

'But I walked past the vegetable gardens and saw no one that looked like him.'

'His appearance is vastly different from when he arrived. I take it you saw him when he was released from his underground apartments?'

'I saw him before that. It was not *release*, doctor. He would not come out, you know.' Dr Grew's inspection of Catherine becomes intense. He's pretty sure he's guessed who she is. Warlow's account of himself was incoherent; yet as always with the insane, there was a story to be found, its details forming their own logic.

'As to Mr Warlow's appearance we could not keep him in *that* condition of course. Upon arrival his hair and beard were shaved. The nails on both hands and feet were cut with great difficulty. You understand that we use no manacles here, but Mr Warlow was reluctant at first and we found it necessary to hold him down and cut his maculated clothes from him. His verminous and scabrous state required much bathing and the application of leeches.

'Throughout these procedures I addressed him with firmness but without harshness, in accordance with the latest practice, particularly as described by Drs Ferrier and Pargeter. For insane persons much resemble children, Mrs Croft. They respond to kindness.'

He notices Catherine becoming tearful during the course of his speech.

'And of course, all this was done in the first place in semi-darkness, since Mr Warlow had lived for so long without daylight.'

'But now he's out of doors!' Catherine protests.

'Yes. However, we have seen to it that he wears spectacles with darkened glass and will always do so. Moreover, he keeps his own room dark, very dark. I see you are much concerned about him, Mrs Croft.' She's coming, coming.

'In the last weeks of his life underground I took him his meals three times a day and we would often speak to each other.'

'Ah, Mrs Croft, then *you* are Catherine!' He knew it; oh, how he loves an emotional scene! 'At first we had much difficulty in making Mr Warlow eat, for he'd say always that *Catherine* would bring him his meal. We were obliged to, to …'

'Oh dear, oh dear.' Poor Catherine remembers it all so well and Dr Grew is obliged to shoot round his desk and comfort her, holding her against his expensive velvet jacket.

But it's not for this that Catherine has come. She wriggles out of his grasp.

'Please, can I see John Warlow and judge for myself whether Polly could stand to see him?'

'Or whether he could stand to see her.'

'Of course, that's so.'

'Indeed, Mrs Croft, and so you shall.' He rises, his hand resting on a pile of impressive new books. 'Join us for dinner and you will be able to observe Mr Warlow for yourself. You will also witness the orderly behaviour of all our patients as well as savour the excellent quality of the cooking here. It will be quickly apparent to you that after some early difficulties Mr Warlow has become calm, cooperative and content through the Kinnersford regime and by working with the soil as he was wont.'

*

The door in the wall lies on the verge. Powyss goes straight into the gardens, stepping through knee-high grass and tall nettles drying after springs and summers of rampant growth. Picks his way to flower beds just discernible beneath smothering weeds. Asters, *rudbeckia, coreopsis, phlox paniculata, penstemon*, all have lost the battle: things rank and gross possess it merely, he can't help but think. He passes skeletal glasshouses, glassless, the hothouse open to wind and rain, crouching cold frames, cold.

Most of the lower lights in the house have gone, too, smashed and roughly boarded over by someone, the main door streaked black where flames failed to catch. At the back he pushes open the door to the kitchens. Dank, denuded except where birds have nested. Abandoned by mice and rats.

Above, the main rooms are quite empty of furniture and carpets, and random wounds to doors and walls indicate violent attacks with implements of some sort. His collection has gone: Apulian vases, marble busts, engravings, fossils, Vesuvian lava. Stolen and sold or simply looted? Is there a trophy on every cottage mantlepiece: a Roman praefericulum, an erotic statuette? Do farmhands eat at elegant tables, bear the moral of Dutch fruit and flies?

Neither microscope nor telescope. His mother's ghostly portrait still hangs, though at a mad angle: he's not surprised it hasn't been taken, it's enough to scare a simple mind. Papers, pamphlets, torn pages cover the floor; yet many books remain on the shelves, some powdered with mould, their pages cockled. Books have no value for raiders who can't read, he thinks. He feels a muted joy: he's not seen a book since he left. Of course they're part of the life he discarded in despair, but sometimes, since then, trying to sleep in bitter cold or axing till his back ached, he caught himself longing for print in which to lose himself, listening to written voices that surfaced from his memory.

They've been upstairs, too, the invaders. He closes windows, opened presumably for the heaving out of desks and other large pieces, and through which snow and rain have blown and leaves gathered in drifts. The bedroom was stripped, the bed frame alone remains.

He clears a space by the fireplace, pushing aside leaves and broken glass. His mind is blank with hunger: he curls up on the floor and sleeps.

*

The dining room at Kinnersford Hall glows with late afternoon light. Eleven men and a woman are already seated at the long table when Dr Grew stands aside with exaggerated courtesy for the entry of Mrs Croft.

A polite nodding of heads takes place as he introduces his visitor and Catherine, seated on his left, soon identifies Warlow staring at his plate on the other side of the table. He's too far away for her to speak easily to him; on the other hand Grew's view of her face as she watches Warlow could not have been more perfectly angled by a billiard player.

Warlow certainly looks odd with his large features, squamous skin, close-cropped hair and eyes hidden behind small dark spectacles, the lenses smoke-coloured. Although his huge bulk seems awkward in his formal dress, he sits patiently waiting for his meal, perhaps willing it to appear upon his plate. He speaks to neither of his neighbours, nor to a fashionably dressed, florid woman sitting opposite him.

As in every superior house in England at four-thirty on this day, footmen and a butler bring in dish after dish and place them around the table. Covers are removed, Dr Grew carves and all help themselves from plates passed politely from one to another. Almond soup, mutton cutlets, ham, beef olives, jugged hare, celery and cardoons are succeeded by a fresh cloth and a second course of pigeon, roast duck, custards, stewed pears and jelly. The butler pours very small quantities of thin, dry port.

'Now you can see what a fine table we keep here, Mrs Croft,' says Grew in a loud voice.

'The jugged hare is delicious,' Catherine replies politely.

'Whoop, Jug, I love thee,' sings out a thin, tragic-faced man.

'Mr Stone has acted before His Majesty, you understand,' Grew says. 'He will quote you from any number of plays.'

'Tragedy, comedy, history, pastoral, pastoral-comical, historical-pastoral, tragical-historical, tragical-comical-historical-pastoral, scene individable or poem unlimited.'

'You *always* say that!' the florid woman protests. 'Tell us about your life in Drury Lane.'

'Drury Lane, Bury Lane, Fury Lane, Newry Lane,' a low voice intones, 'youry lane, myry lane, fiery lane, diary lane, hirey lane, spirey lane, LIARY LANE.'

'Thank you, thank you, Mr Furlong, that is enough.'

'The ear trieth words as the mouth tasteth meat.'

'Dr Hunter was a renowned preacher in his time, Mrs Croft,' says Grew, referring to this last speaker. 'He has a saying for every occasion. Isn't that so, Mr Warlow?'

Warlow looks up, unsure who has addressed him.

'I said Dr Hunter always has a saying for us, does he not?'

'Ah,' Warlow grunts, looking down at his plate again. But Grew is not to be put off. Mrs Croft must see how civilised he is.

'These are vegetables you have grown in the kitchen garden, eh, Mr Warlow? The celery, the cardoons.'

'Doons, spoons, moons, boons, loons, noons, runes, tunes, dunes, Junes . . .'

'Mr Warlow,' Catherine breaks into the incantation. 'Is there a cat in this house?'

'How prescient you are, Cath, er, Mrs Croft,' says Grew. 'I have heard that Mr Warlow does often take a cat upon his lap at rest times.'

Warlow looks up when Catherine first speaks. Ignoring Grew, she asks him: 'Does the cat like fish, John?'

Now Warlow stares towards the voice with his strange little black spectacles and all fall silent, forks poised, mouths agape. It must be a rare occurrence for him to speak. Although his eyes cannot be seen, his face begins to contort, his mouth to twist with the effort of remembering, of placing the voice, of summoning up an answer. Catherine suddenly regrets that she's spoken. The sound of her voice, which was more or less all that he knew of her, might provoke him in some unfortunate way.

Finally he gives a groan.

'I hates fish,' he says.

'Oh, I cannot *abide* fish,' says the florid woman. 'It does not agree with my constitution at all.'

'Madam,' says an earnest man with sandy hair, 'I shall correct you, for a fish is in no position either to agree or to disagree with you, it having neither speech nor learning, nor any command of logic. Moreover, it having been cooked, its brain or seat of learning, even if it possessed learning, which, as I said, it does not, would have been rendered inactive. And as to your having a constitution, with which the fish might agree or disagree, there I must correct you again, a constitution being rightly an ordinance or decree, the form of government used in any place or the law of a Kingdom and as to your being a Kingdom, Madam ... '

There's a prolonged growl from Warlow, to whom everyone turns. Is he ill? He clears his throat. They wait.

'*Words*,' he says with disgust. Then he stabs a piece of roast pigeon and chews it vigorously.

So the meal continues until everything has been eaten, all disperse to their rooms and Catherine walks off to collect the post-chaise. Warlow is well fed, clean, neatly dressed in his black coat and white waistcoat, she thinks to herself. He's not ill treated like people used to be in the old madhouses. However much she dislikes Dr Grew, Kinnersford is unquestionably calm, well run and, my goodness, full of grand furniture and paintings! She can't help but recall Moreham House as it once was. Bumping along in the coach, she wonders if they dine like that every day in Kinnersford. Grew is determined to impress, that's easy to see. Yet they all look healthy enough; it's apparent that no one is starving and all seem quite used to these occasions.

As to the state of Warlow's mind it's difficult to tell. He looked so very different from the 'deranged creature' about whom Mr Powyss had felt such guilt. The terrible figure with his great beard and claws she glimpsed behind the barricade.

She can hardly describe him as happy. But then, how *could* he be? Does he remember? What does he remember? What does he say to himself about Hannah? What is he thinking behind those dark spectacles? Who could ever know what dreadful thoughts live deep within.

She still wishes Hannah were there, more so since bringing up her children. But she can't hate John Warlow, can't condemn him. She can never forget the pathetic voice she used to hear when she took him his meals. The utterly wrecked conditions in which he lived.

It is long known that Abraham incited him. Caleb Hughes told everyone, if partly to absolve himself from any blame. Abraham Price had driven Warlow to do what he did.

Should she take Polly to see him? It is a thought left over from those strange underground conversations she had with him. She'll have to see the hateful Grew again if she does, and there's Polly's sweetness of character, which should not be bruised, her sunny disposition that should not be clouded.

She'll wait a while and think about it carefully.

*

The following day Polly and George are out earning pennies from Kempton, and Tom potters about in the yard, chasing hens.

Catherine opens the door to a beggar. After the recent dreadful harvests beggars call often, the word having got round that she is 'not without'. Emaciated, weather-bitten, his beard sparse, his borrowed clothes shabby, crumpled. This one really is in need of bread.

'Catherine Croft?' he asks, and immediately she knows it's Herbert Powyss.

'Mr Powyss! Oh, sir, you must come in.'

She puts food and drink before him without further question, seeing his condition and he, realising he needn't speak, doesn't.

He has cleaned himself, found clothes that must have been Samuel's stuffed in a cupboard: of no interest to the invaders, who preferred his own velvet and silk no doubt. Moth-holed, the garments hang on him. He's burned his stinking rags.

Eventually he says: 'I am grateful.'

'It has been a long time. Have you come to live, sir? But the house is in no fit state . . . '

'I shall live in it. It has a roof.' His breath comes in gasps and he speaks these words with effort, looking at her for a while as if expecting contradiction. 'Catherine, you have not changed.'

'Oh, I'm fat now, though my hair's not turned.' She regrets saying this, seeing how very changed he is. There's something about his mouth that's strange, obscured though it is by his ragged beard.

'You've been burdened with all the Warlow children. Are they well?'

'Not much of a burden, truly, Mr Powyss.' She tells him something of each one and then about her own child, Tom, who has sidled into the room and looks at him suspiciously from the other side of it. Not one of the children who saw him in the hills, too young.

'Oh my God, it never occurred to me! When you said Price had the key, that you were unwell. Catherine, I never thought of it.'

'Let me tell you about John Warlow, sir.' She'll lessen his suffering if she can, and indeed it is a relief to tell someone about her visit to Kinnersford, though without mention of Grew's impudence.

He listens closely and says: 'That is satisfactory. Dr Grew's fees are no doubt large. It is only right that his patients be well fed and clothed. Besides, he is using free labour!'

'I had not thought of that.'

'I have seen Hannah Warlow's grave. It has been cared for.'

'Yes, Polly and George keep it tidy. At first I tended it with all the children, but they are the only two left now.'

Polly, the little one, who'd looked like her mother, brushing the flowers for their scent.

'She likes to pick flowers to put there,' she continued, as if she'd heard his thoughts. 'She says she wants some flowers like stars, but I don't know which ones she means.'

'*Eucomis autumnalis.* Pineapple flower.'

'Ah!'

A great weariness overcomes him.

'You have had hard times, I can see, Mr Powyss.'

'You will hear things. Rumours no doubt, for I've not been far from here. Recently I came to my senses, realised I was wrong to flee. I wanted to suffer, you see, but physical hardship is not repentance.' He's spoken too much, struggles to find breath.

She says nothing until he becomes calm again.

'Mr Powyss, I shall tell you what happened to the house. But first, please will you come with me, for there is something I must show you.'

She leads him into the parlour where once she taught Price to read, coped with his crude embraces and finally fled his violence. She rarely thinks of that time now, though very occasionally a passing look on Tom's face reminds her of the man. It is inevitable, though she does everything she can to prevent him from becoming like Price.

The room is in any case transformed by signs of children, jugs of flowers, small piles of books and Powyss's two globes by the window. The one with its unknown lands and names like *Oceanus Occidentalis*, the other smaller, its tiny spider-like stars embedded in shapes of bear and plough and goddess.

'You will think I stole them, Mr Powyss. I hope you will understand that I wished to rescue them before they were broken or taken away and brought them here so that the children might learn from them. With this, sir, the *Star Catalogue*. Written by a woman astronomer, Caroline Herschel. I have learned a lot myself!'

'I am glad of it, Catherine. There are books in the house still. I'd be pleased if you would take whatever you want for yourself and the children who remain here.'

'If we could borrow a book or two occasionally . . .'

'Of course.'

The prospect is delightful for Catherine. To enter the library, even in the wrecked house, without first being rung for, or, and she remembers it with shame, creeping in furtively. To read the spines of all the books, to choose any one!

'Oh, but the house, sir, I must tell you about the house.' Another day. She sees he is borne down.

*

Kinnersford House, 2 September 1800

Dear Mrs Croft,

I enclose a letter to you from John Warlow. Today I granted him leave to exchange his gardening duties for writing, and his self-imposed task has lasted all day, he having torn up many unsatisfactory drafts (as he perceived them). He vehemently refused my offer of help, as you will no doubt discern as soon as you begin to read.

Trusting that you are in good health and looking forward to your next visit to Kinnersford,

I remain,
Your honoured servant,
Josiah Grew MD

Leter to CATH RIN

I did think   you liv heer. Thiss plas ware I liv now But you don't.   MR GRU did say. He did giv the long beens to the Kichin
*   I   am sory   you dont liv heer you wer kynd afor   I hav a cat she do sleep with me.*
I wil pic mor long beens for you   if you wil come heer.
Carits
ternap
leek
spinij   nex yer pease   sparra grass

J oh n   War low

*

'Sir, soon after you left, Abraham Price returned. He didn't show his face but I knew it was him from his handwriting, which was ever poor. He left a note you see. I kept it as evidence, though it was never used:

Keep Awa from th Big Hous tonit. Lock yr Doors.

'I took all the children with me to Mrs Lacey's and everyone locked their doors in the village, too. There was no time to warn the magistrate.
'He came with others, who knows who they were, and they

broke the windows and tried to set fire to the place. They smashed what they could and roared and yelled. We could hear even in the village. Everyone was terrified, I can tell you, Mr Powyss.

'I think they thought to find you there. They blamed you for Hannah's death and for John being arrested and tried.'

'They were right.'

'Sir, I do fear he may try once more when he hears you have returned. I fear it.'

Powyss says nothing to that.

'I think they grew tired of destruction. They say it wasn't Abraham who broke all the lights of the glasshouses.

'When some of the militia arrived the next day it was far too late: the men had gone. The militia locked the doors, boarded up the lower windows. But word got round that you could easily get into the house and that it was full of valuable things. Price and his men didn't take much. Their purpose wasn't theft.

'The children and I returned to this cottage, which they left untouched. But every so often shadows passed in the night. We'd hear loud whispers and wheels on the stones. People got in and stole what they fancied, sir.

'I told the magistrate, but he just wrung his hands. He stationed some of the militia to guard it for a while, but said he couldn't keep them there for ever, they were needed elsewhere. He didn't know for how long you'd gone away or if you'd ever come back.

'And then there were the Frenchmen, sir.'

'Really?'

'Prisoners of war. Escaped. They came at night, too, but, you know, nobody wanted to report them, they were that useful. Seven of them, there were. They'd help with the shearing and anything people needed. And they were cheerful and sang their songs and made toys for the children from wood and Bloor gave them straw for their bedding in the house, sir.'

245

'Bloor gave them straw?'

'They worked for him for almost no wages even when food was scarce. They cooked a treat.'

Though caught up in her narrative, especially this last bit, which caused her to blush, Catherine observes Powyss. It's hard to see his expression. His black eyes were always unfathomable. His shrunken face seems partially to smile, perhaps almost to sneer, though she's sure it is neither, just the way his flesh has fallen.

She sees how he holds himself still, stiff, dry and hard like a dead tree no insects or birds have wanted to eat or inhabit.

*

Her don't come. The master, Grew, gives him a letter from her, helps him read it. Her do thank him for his offer of beans. Her's glad he has a cat. Her be busy with the children. *Children?* What children? Hopes he is eating well. Hopes he do sleep soundly. Says her will come one day.

Words. You writ them, you read them. They do no good.

He picks fresh long beans. The last. Folds them up in his nightshirt with a bunch of small sweet parsnips. Takes a handful of tomatoes from the greenhouse, wraps them in a clean shirt. Puts it all in a sack and sets off. Just after dawn. Nobody about.

Straight down the drive and through the great gates with lions. Still nobody. Soon he's hot, stuffs his coat and waistcoat into the sack. Guesses the way, feels a strong urge to go left. Over that way.

He meets a boy.

'Moreham?' His voice growls, for he's dry.

The boy is frightened by the dark spectacles. Points him generally in the direction of the biggest hills. Speeds off like a hare. Too young to recognise the meaning of the good quality of Warlow's breeches, the respectable uniform.

He walks all morning. Nobody follows. Good. Sun behind him. He scuffs up stones. Doesn't know this road but it's like all other roads. He hears hoofs and wheels, hears before he sees, crouches behind a hedgerow. Better they don't see him yet.

Walks and walks. Is suddenly very hungry and thirsty. Brought no food nor drink! No money! But he never has money. Does he? Fifty pound! What was that? He had fifty pound once. That was it, he had fifty pound. Must have left it behind. Must've hid it.

He sits down at the edge of a cut field, pulls out his clothes from the sack: coat, waistcoat, earthy nightshirt, beans, parsnips still whole. Then shirt, yellow streaks. Them tomatoes, warm, squashed. No good. Can't give her *them*. He eats two, another two, pisses with joy in the stubble, lies down and sleeps in September heat. Dreams he's taking a horse to stable. Goes one way. Wrong. Goes another way. Wrong. No way's right.

When he wakes it's too bright even through darkened lenses. He turns into nearby woods, pushes his way through thickets until dense brambles drive him back onto the road.

Moreham, a carter says, gawping at him: five miles in *that* direction. Oh, he's tired. Too much walkin. Gettin old now. What is he? Forty somethin somebody did say. Did they? Or fifty was it? Fifty pound. Should've got a horse and cart with fifty pound. Never had a horse and cart.

It's late afternoon by the time he recognises the approach to the village. Damned Kempton's over there, church over there. Stop now. Rest a bit. Behind churchyard wall.

Hears cows come in to milk. Thwack. Thwack. Sticks on flanks. Cowman shouting. Sweet smell of soft dung slapping down.

Sun goes. Roofs, smoking chimneys, huge trees autumn-shadowed. Walls of the big house. Moreham House.

What's he come for? It were the fif ... No. What was it? *Who?*

A woman it were. That Catherine. That's it. *Her*'ll help him. Her'll come soon.

His feet begin to drag, want him to turn. Where'll he go? If he turn back where'll he go? Where he live now. Where *is* that? *This is your room, Warlow.* Where's that? He slows. Stomach clenches with hunger.

Her'll bring me . . . Her'll . . .

Pheasants suddenly clatter up, squawking. Heart lurches in terror. Feet won't move. *Won't.*

Dusk falls, drifts of smoke. His mouth is dry, dust in his throat. Darkling, shadows slash the road. A blackbird hurtles past, low, warning.

Cold runs over his shoulders like ants. He puts on the waistcoat and coat from his sack. Feels the beans and parsnips. *Can't eat them.* No. I'll give them. To the woman *when she come.*

Dusk deepens towards night. Too dark. Takes off the spectacles, still can't see. Air smoke-thick.

A bat skims past his head. He ducks, stumbles. Spectacles fall on the ground. *Where?* Crunch under his boot. Bends down to find them, kneeling, sweeping with his hands like he did afore. Like he did when he lived when he lived . . .

Bat. Bats! Them've come for him. Air full o' them. This place where he is. *Why is he here?* The woman'll . . . No! Them'll fly at him. At his head. Fly straight at his head, get in. Them'll *get in!* Crack their wings behind his eyes, crack! Crack! Fill his head up, flappin, flittin. Their teeth and claws are sharp, pins in his eyes, splinters, glass. He's got to beat them out!

Behind his eyes. Beat! Beat!

Black wings, devils, they wheeze, howl, thicken in his head so he tips right over and beats his forehead on the ground to get them out till there's only banging and him shouting, shouting, banging them out, dark becomes black blind blackness, banging, banging; then seeping, blood seeping under his fingernails.

Chapter 12

NEWS OF POWYSS TEARS ROUND the neighbourhood like a sparrow hawk. Tharpe comes to see him and, standing in the almost empty library, for there are no chairs, offers him accommodation in his mansion while Powyss begins to set about the considerable task of refurbishing Moreham House.

'It's the least I can do, Powyss. I'm aware of a certain degree of failed responsibility, but you left us no instructions for the house itself, only for the miserable Warlow and his children.' He looks at Powyss, hoping for a sign of gratitude, or at least understanding, but can perceive neither.

'I trust you have read my letter about the arrangements that were made for Warlow and are satisfied with them?'

'Yes. Thank you.'

'You are content to continue paying the huge fees to the Kinnersford Asylum?'

'Yes.'

'As for the house, it took a while to call up the militia, you see. So many demands for them nowadays. Since you were abroad, if indeed you were, though some say ... '

Powyss will not help him.

'Having been *away*, I don't suppose you are aware of the riotous tendencies erupting among the poor. Bad weather told against the harvests (frost in June, I tell you, sodden hay) and Pitt forced us all to eat brown bread, but the poor *refused*! Would you believe it? Disturbances throughout the country, not to mention war *outside* it.

'Please consider my offer, Powyss,' he finishes, when there's still no response.

For a time Powyss has a few other visitors and rushes out into the overgrown orchard to avoid them. Women are particularly keen to catch glimpses of his apparently cadaverous look, and cheap, ill-fitting clothing; they'd soak up the desolation of his house if they could. Their carriages stop at the gate, they peer through, some with opera glasses, then send their maids with pies, jellies, cakes, China tea; with instructions to draw out the true story of his disappearance from Catherine. Invariably they gather nothing except the maids' own imaginative descriptions. Elsewhere, gossip about his absence blooms from the exaggerated tale told by the two children.

The women always found the man unsociable, strange, with his obsession for plants and peculiar objects. The business with both Warlows, the mad experiment, the unseemly affair, the murder, remain awful, delicious subjects, still much talked about, especially, breathlessly, to strangers and visiting relations. But now, with neither garden nor antique oddities to occupy Powyss, for he appears to take no action to change the condition of either grounds or house, the windows being still boarded with him living *in* it, the gardens entirely overgrown, they are deeply puzzled at his existence.

They tell each other he's eccentric and keep their ears open for reports of delectably odd behaviour. Is it really true he's been living in a sheep shelter all this time? Those who do come across him find that smile of his odd. It takes time for someone to announce that it isn't a smile at all but a look of extreme pain. His silences are the worst, they say, with that terrible rasping breathing. Has he taken a vow, perhaps? Become religious? Does he want to be a hermit? It's hard to know how to treat him. Quite soon, to his great relief, they stop trying.

Catherine's first impulse is to give him food and drink, which he accepts. Her other impulse, strong in her nature, is to cheer, even to amuse, but this she suppresses. She sees that she can expect little from him yet. That he is, and again comes the same analogy, that he's like a tree. Struck by lightning, its core destroyed, a fragile, dried-out shell, its centre blackened. But alive. Such trees can live for years.

He comes to collect bread and milk from her, sometimes eggs, thanks her but rarely stops to talk. He's lived with no one but sheep for company for so long; words have sunk like silt. She knows there's a water pump in the kitchen of Moreham House and probably a plate or cup remains. Her child Tom peers round corners at the strange man. Hides.

The nights become cold. She longs to offer him bedding, of which she has plenty now that three Warlow children have left home, but doesn't press him, thinks he might ask in time. She sees him push a barrow through the orchard into the wood and return with branches of fallen trees.

*

Tied   tied   can't get   can't get my   arms
     Got in bats got in got in Couldn't get 'em out.   all them bats all them bats got in   got in my head   black in my head   black

Them did come. Them, some o' them. 'John Warlow what *you* doin here?' Locked me up.

Once afore I were locked in my place. *Were I?* Hammered nails in the door. That were *my place.*

John Warlow, what you doin here? Can't come here John Warlow. Go back, you lunatic!

Master said: *John Warlow we must punish you for running away.*

Runnin away? I niver. I were. I did take I did take beans
I were I were goin

Tied tied tied tied down tied down can't get can't
beat 'em can't can't

Master did tie me hisself. *John Warlow we must punish you.*
Can't get my arms John Warlow what *you* doin?

Them should niver have took me out

Get 'em out. Them's in my head can't can't get
my arms

Can't beat 'em off beat beat 'em out can't beat
'em out o' my head want to beat my head beat it
can't get my arms
   black black black

Arms tied them's tied my arms can't them's
tied tied them's tied

*

Catherine hears that Warlow was found on the edge of the village, bellowing and banging his head on the ground, was taken to the lock-up and the following day returned to Kinnersford. The village hums with the news, though it's unlikely to reach Powyss since he talks to no one except her. She decides not to tell him yet, but to find out for herself how it happened. So once more she journeys on foot and by chaise, once more meets the disagreeable Dr Grew.

Warlow was tied to a chair in the cellar, Grew says, and fed bread and water for a week.

'Like a child,' Grew tells her eagerly. 'He was punished as we punish a child. Gently, of course,' he says, noticing her alarm. 'We never use chains, but nevertheless the action was *emphatic*. I talked to him, Mrs Croft. I talked for a long time and reasoned with him. He has calmed.'

She supposes she must believe him, but she doesn't trust him, seeing that so much seems done for effect.

'I am delighted you have come,' he leers at her briefly. 'To prevent a further occurrence it could help if you talk to him yourself. Then he might be satisfied. For it was you he was coming to see, I gathered from his garbled words.

'Come this way. I shall be present in the background, should you need to call for help.'

It is a strange meeting. They sit on a bench near the house, the sun low in the sky. Catherine feels both annoyed and amused at the thought of Grew peeping out at them from behind a shutter. She'd rather be alone with John Warlow, who she's certain would never attack her. He seems bemused, perhaps listening to inner sounds. They hardly speak. What can they say to each other?

Catherine remembers the cat, so they talk about that.

Grew reappears after a very short time and she watches Warlow shamble away. Grew extracts a promise from her that she will return.

*

At night Powyss wakes every two hours. He gathers up straw left by the French prisoners and uses their blankets left behind when they were re-arrested. It isn't the cold that drives him to wake, nor is it moonlight, for the shutters have not been torn off. It's the habit of listening to the wind, sensing shifts in temperature, frost's claws, the bite of hail. Once, he reluctantly recalls, he would rise each morning to check the weather through his window from the warmth of the library.

He calls on Catherine.

'I shall arrange to raise the payment to you, Catherine, now that I am taking food from you. Do you have pen and paper?' He writes, sands and folds the letter with directions to Mr Streeter, Hereford. 'And please could you deliver this to Aaron, Bloor's shepherd?'

'Yes, sir.' She doesn't ask why. 'Should you like me to help in the house, Mr Powyss?'

'No. I have found what I need.'

'I saw you getting wood.'

'Yes, I'm making a store. Several trees have fallen in the storms. Some wood is already seasoned. It just needs to dry out.'

'At least you have books to read.'

Perhaps he doesn't hear her. 'I once told you I could not live in the house.'

'Yes, you did.'

'I was wrong. I *must* live there.'

She tries to understand. 'You have surely made amends by now.'

'Hannah is dead. I can never make amends to her.'

'But you have provided for the welfare of John Warlow and his children.'

'That was easy. I have money.'

'You have punished yourself for more than two years, Mr Powyss.'

'It is nothing. A shadow in time.'

'It's the whole life of my boy Tom.'

'Ah. Yes. Of course.'

'No one is punished forever, sir!'

'Catherine, please call me by my first name. You are kind and far too wise to be a servant.'

He seems tired out and leaves. She'll tell him about Warlow when the right moment comes.

*

Beds are covered in muck. Onions. Rhubarb crowns. Potatoes pulled for winter. He cleans cold frames, scrubs down greenhouse benches, scours flowerpots. Only ever digged, ploughed. In the time afore.

'Good work, Warlow,' Grew says. Not on a horse, Grew. Once he were. Were he? Tell him do this do that. Who were that? Master on a horse were some dream.

Says next year them'll show him how to prune grapes! If he don't run away again. I niver – I did *niver*.

Them'll show me to pinch out tomatoes. Good. I likes tomatoes. Work in the greenhouse never so hard like ploughin. Even like hoein in hot summer. Easier nor scythin down nettles. Easier nor writin down words.

Who were *that*? Made me writ words. Read books! W*ho*? I'll I'll . . .

The woman Catherine comes again. Sits on a bench with him in the flower garden. Asks him about his cat, what he gives her to eat. Brings him fruit tarts. Apple.

'Yes, John, I made these. Do you remember the tarts in Moreham House?'

'Moreham?'

'Yes.'

'Moreham. Hah! More ham. But we niver.'

'Never what, John?'

'Niver got more ham! Joke!'

'I expect your school teacher wanted you to learn how to spell it correctly. Anyway do you remember those little gooseberry tarts? Very delicate they were. I didn't make those.'

'Who did?'

'Annie.'

'Oh. Oh.' A bat flits through his mind. He eats the tarts quickly lest. Lest.

'Do you remember Polly, John?'

'Polly.'

'Your youngest child.'

'Polly. Be her kind like you?'

'Oh yes! She lives with us, John. She's growing up, but her face is still round, her smile like sunlight. A sweet girl. To be truthful, she is my favourite.'

'Oh!' Round face. Sweet. Smile.

Later, Grew says to him, 'She won't come often, but you must be satisfied with that. Not often must be enough, Warlow.'

'Her have children. Her be married. Catherine.'

'Hmm.' Grew had never believed she was married. 'There are women we cannot have, John.'

Her says one day her will bring Polly. But not yet.

*

She tells Powyss about Warlow walking all the way to Moreham, collapsing there.

'Catherine, why didn't you say so at the time?'

'I thought it would upset you. You were not fit to hear it, Herbert. And now I can tell you because it's over, he's back at Kinnersford and he's calm.'

'It's good of you to think of me. I shall go and see the place.'

'It were surely best you don't talk to John. There would be danger in that.'

'No, of course. But I'll speak to Dr Grew. You say they treat the people well, there.'

'They do, though I'm afraid Dr Grew punished him cruelly. Bound him to a chair in a cellar and fed him bread and water. I cannot see the necessity . . .'

He writes to Kinnersford and receives an immediate reply. Dr Grew will be pleased to see him, suggests a particular day and encloses some information that he hopes Mr Powyss will have time to read before his arrival.

The enclosure is a pamphlet, designed as an informative advertisement without mentioning fees, though Powyss now knows these to be considerable. The establishment is new, opened three years before the end of the century. Warlow must have been one of the first to be treated by Dr Grew's humane methods.

Perhaps there's an attempt to dazzle with names and terms, Powyss thinks, but he's struck by this section:

> We understand from the late, learned and celebrated Dr William Battie that 'Consequential madness', as opposed to 'original madness', is assuredly capable of remedy, since it involves what he calls the 'deluded imagination'. Put another way by the great philosopher John Locke in his famous Essay Concerning Human Understanding, 'madmen do not appear to have lost the faculty of reasoning but having joined together some ideas very wrongly, they mistake them for truths, and they err as men do that argue right from wrong principles'.

They err as men do that argue right from wrong principles. His own fatal decision on Cold Hill with the encouragement of Fox's letter: that the happiness of six children and one woman, and himself of course, far outweighed the misery of one man was surely a perfect example of arguing right from wrong principles. He'd seen it as the application of cool reason, of impartial, scientific calculation. Had deluded himself from the start of the experiment that his actions would produce something good, a significant contribution to science, when what they'd produced was hideous destruction. Light had brought forth darkness.

He skips to the paragraphs about treatment:

> The 'deluded' or 'errant' madman may be corrected, or, at least, helped from his delusions by the skill of the physician. Since the condition of each patient is unique there can be no general cures such as those used in treatment in former times and listed by Dr Battie as: bleeding, blisters, caustics,

rough cathartics, the gumms and foetid anti-hysterics, opium,
mineral waters, cold bathing and vomits.

   Moral Management in Place of Medicine can be the
only dictum for those who treat insane persons as we begin
a new and humane century. Gone are shackles and the
whip! Gone is terror! Instead, as Dr John Ferriar has written
most recently, 'a system of mildness and conciliation is now
generally adopted, which, if it does not always facilitate the
cure, at least tends to soften the destiny of the sufferer'.

Thus Grew promotes himself, Powyss thinks, though he
hopes the man believes it, too. If he really does practise in
the ways described, then Warlow is well off, though he'll ask
about tying the man up for a week. Even if cure were possible, Tharpe had told him that the trial judge had stipulated
Warlow never be released.

Powyss borrows a horse from a man in the village.

The journey to Kinnersford is not a long one, twelve or
so miles to the south-east of the county on rutted, unkempt
roads usable by wheel only in summer. The country is not
much different from that around Moreham, which Powyss
imagines is probably good for Warlow, who can never have
known anything different. He finds he's thinking quite easily
about the man, as if he were a boy he'd known at school.
Recalls, as in a bad dream, how he'd hated him uncontrollably.

Eventually, he passes through grand gates, the columns
of which are surmounted by stone lions, salient, and broken
chains.

Men stacking tree trunks in great piles by the road stop to
watch as he passes. Parkland turns into fields, which to all
appearances have had a good harvest despite what he's heard
about a poor spring.

Further along are vegetable gardens. Labourers wheel
barrows, weed neat rows of plants, roll gravel paths, scare
birds off late raspberries.

The men are all dressed the same, in black breeches and stockings, white waistcoats, black coats, unnervingly like the clothes he used to wear himself, once. Sober, decent, gentlemanly. You'd never guess these men are lunatics.

Flower gardens succeed vegetables and once more men in black and white stop to gaze. Yet another well-dressed patient helps him to dismount. Holding the reins, he bows and declares: 'The harvest is past, the summer is ended, and we are not saved.'

Powyss bows in answer. Suddenly recalls a phrase: 'We may yet find balm in Gilead.' The patient clears his throat, tuts, shakes his head and leads the horse away.

Powyss is ushered into Grew's book- and bust-filled study and they shake hands.

'Mrs Catherine Croft has been visiting, Mr Powyss. Are you aware of that?'

'Yes.'

'I see.' He opens a book on his desk and begins to scribble in it. 'I know the whole of Warlow's story.'

'Oh yes?'

'The experiment, the imprisonment.'

'Not imprisonment, Dr Grew.'

'I have read the report of the court proceedings and spoken many times to John Warlow.'

'Of course. Please tell me what you are doing to help his mental state. More immediately, why did he get out a few weeks ago?' Powyss shifts the attack back at Grew, but reddens, gasps with the effort. 'I pay large fees per annum for Warlow's keep … It is reasonable to expect … that he be prevented from running away.'

Grew clears his throat. Scratches at a particular place on his leg. How much more does he prefer discussion with a woman!

'Have you read my pamphlet, Mr Powyss? If so you will comprehend that for the physician to correct each patient's errant thoughts, or to relieve his deluded imagination, he must know everything possible about the patient's life before the onset of what we are pleased to call "consequential madness".'

'Indeed. Have you begun the correction?'

'I'm sure you will understand the full extent of the humanity and gentleness we employ in our treatment of those who live here. Moral Management, Mr Powyss. No one is *imprisoned*.'

Infuriating, this Grew! Powyss rushes to his own defence.

'Warlow was the *willing subject* of my experiment, he was *not* imprisoned. When the experiment broke down and he was allowed to leave, he wouldn't do so.' He coughs heavily, forces himself on.

'And I hear that *you* imprisoned him yourself in a cellar on his return from Moreham, putting him on something worse than a prison diet.'

'Oh, merely a light punishment as one might punish a child. Have you children, Mr Powyss?'

'No.'

'You will have experienced it yourself as a child, most surely.'

'I did not.' Dislike of this complacent, well-dressed doctor brings on a fit of coughing. Grew fiddles noisily with objects on his desk as he waits for Powyss to pull himself together.

'Dr Grew. It seems there are times when your practice contradicts your theory. Perhaps at other times you are *too* humane, for who knows what Warlow might have done in Moreham the other day had he not been discovered.

'I've come to assure myself that he lives comfortably but also that he will not escape again. I trust you'll show me your establishment.'

Grew grinds his teeth, controls his impatience. He sees that Powyss, for all his coughing and wheezing, is determined; yet while he feels strongly resistant to the dominance of this man who can afford to pay but is dressed like a beggar, it is, after all, Powyss who is paying. He decides it's time to raise the fees.

'As far as Warlow's escape, as you put it, is concerned, it will not happen again. We use neither locks nor chains here, rather wise counsel and kindness. Only occasionally is a patient bound. When the need is pressing, we may, perhaps, resort to the use of laudanum. Just as you might do yourself.

'I pride myself on the enlightened nature of the asylum. Indeed, Mr Powyss, we have that love of reason and scientific investigation in common, do we not? We are both men of the enlightenment.'

Books, busts, shadowy portraits. Learned papers, impressive titles: *Moral Management*. Powyss recognises it all. The man sits before him, a smaller, unshakeable version of the self he once was.

'Of course I shall show you round the house and gardens, though it would not be wise for you and Warlow to meet, so I shall not ask you to dine with us as, on a previous occasion, I asked Mrs Croft. She had a most enjoyable meal with us. Has she told you about it?'

'A little.' If only he were sitting in her kitchen with her now rather than here!

'I see. However, I should like you to observe how Warlow behaves with others in a formal situation, so I suggest that you *watch* him during a meal. I have an excellent device, at present in our dining room: a screen in which I have had small eyeholes made, completely concealed by the intricate pattern painted on the outward side. It can be moved anywhere in the house, according to whom I wish to observe. I am extremely proud of this invention and intend to patent it.

'Now, when you stand behind the screen you may be able to spy on Warlow and at the same time hear everything that is said with ease and without causing the least suspicion.'

*

261

He finds himself oddly unmoved by what he sees in Kinnersford House. Dr Grew secretes him into the dining room by the door through which the butler and footmen bring the dishes. Grew's screen is a dramatic object, a piece of chinoiserie, painted with elaborate scenes of ladies with sunshades walking over bridges, past pagodas and waterfalls, of fishermen in pleasant boats. Birds and insects fly over these watery episodes and two perfectly placed holes have been drilled into the heads of a pair of storks, flying like spears through the sky. A second set of holes has been drilled lower down through a weeping tree. This is for Grew, who is short, when he himself wants to observe behaviour on other occasions, unseen, prior to writing up the results in a learned paper.

Powyss watches Warlow, whose eating is rapid and voracious, and listens to the conversations that teeter on the edge of chaos. The food smells good and he shifts from foot to foot, hungry, bored, his back aching, exhausted by his interview with Grew. Forces himself not to cough. Warlow is quite transformed from the matted beast Powyss had last seen, and stares down at his plate the whole time, ceaselessly forking his food. Except once when he seems to lock eyes with Powyss during a pause in the mad talk. He looks up, stares at the screen for several seconds, grunts and then resumes eating. He can't possibly have seen me, Powyss thinks, especially with those dark lenses.

*

It were! A thing did move. I did hear a sound. Breathin. I did hear breathin. Hear it. It were. It were. Yes, it were! Somebody!

He stands in his room not moving. Thinking.

I did hear. When nobody did talk. Behind the painted trees. Them panels all painted. Trees and birds and that. Gold and red, gold birds flyin in a black sky.

It were him. *Him.* Listenin! *Listenin.* Weren't that . . . ? That were *listenin* afore. Where I did live in that place afore. Years afore. I did hear him listen. Did I? Then. *Did I?* Dark it were dark there. This place where I live's not dark. But him's listenin, *him's still listenin to me!*

Now? Be him listenin *now? Here?* He holds the oil lamp along the walls of his room, as once he did years ago. Feels the surface. All smooth, no holes. Up on a chair to the ceiling and down. Takes chair to the next bit. Up, down. Drags chair. Up. Down. Walls not like. Not like walls . . . He lies on his bed with his clothes on. Dreams he's in a pit in the ground, *him's* there leanin over the pit. Pokin him with a spade. A fork, a hoe.

'I can hear everythin. I know everythin. You cannot get out, Warlow!'

He grabs the end of the hoe, pulls, to pull him into the pit, *I'll kill him, kill him, I'll kill him*, but he wakes up. All a sweat. Cat jumps off the bed.

Him!

He were called . . . Called P . . . P . . . What's he called? I can go there. I did go there. *Did I?* I did. I can. I knows the way.

'Good night, John!' Grew on his rounds.

'Night, Mr Grew!'

*

'The Warlows' cottage has been razed,' Powyss says to Catherine.

'The villagers pulled it down because of the murder. Kempton was angry at losing rent; he said someone else could have lived there.'

'Maybe I should pull down Moreham House, too.'

'I think you should not be hasty!'

'I have watched you with George, Catherine. A strange, absent boy. You're not his mother, yet you are kind. Patient.'

'That's easy. I borrowed Bewick's *Fables* from your shelves.

When I was a girl my teacher lent it to me. I love reading it with him.'

'If I don't pull down the house I'll sell it and give the money away. To whom shall I give it, Catherine? What do you think?' He is adrift. He might say anything.

'I dare say there are good people who would use your money well. The house could become an orphanage maybe. But don't be hasty. Let me help you think what's best, Herbert.'

He looks at her but doesn't speak.

Oh, he'll try her patience quite as much as George does! But she'll help him, for he is a poor, wrecked creature. Yet pity is not enough. It is a dead end, she thinks, does nothing but warm the pitier. If she could make that lopsided face smile at her!

That there's talk about them in the village only encourages her the more. Let them prattle about the mad Powyss who once took a labourer's wife into his bed, and is now consoled by his housemaid. Let them prattle!

They don't know that the consolation is all in the form of words, kind gestures, of neatly hemmed shirts, eggs carefully collected, bread baked with fondness. Don't know how often her thoughts turn to the man.

*

Catherine is right. It would be pointless to destroy Moreham House. Thinking of her, remembering how she exclaimed: 'No one is punished forever, sir!' he is cheered, his spirits lift. In a moment he knows that he no longer wants to live in the house, perhaps not in Moreham at all.

He rides to Hereford. Puts the task to Streeter, his lawyer, to arrange the sale of the house and find somewhere else for him to live.

'You will wish to reside in London, I don't doubt, Mr Powyss?'

'Certainly not. Somewhere the other side of Hereford. A much smaller place than Moreham.'

'Moreham will sell eventually because of its timber, even if you have neglected to maintain coppicing, Mr Powyss, and despite the poor condition of the house. However, bankruptcies are rife. You have only to read the lists in the newspapers.'

He stops at Picard's, the instrument-maker, and buys a pocket telescope. He'll give it to Catherine before he leaves, to help her with the Herschel *Star Catalogue*. It's the first time he's entered a shop, the first time he's assessed an object for its mechanical and aesthetic qualities for years. The first time he's ever bought a beautiful thing for someone other than himself.

*

She is surprised, delighted by his smile as he hands her the telescope.

'What is this that covers it?' she asks, stroking the green and white.

'It's rayfish skin. Let me show you what to do.' She fetches the *Star Catalogue*.

'It is small enough for the children to use,' she says.

'Yes, I thought of that.'

'Thank you, Herbert.' She holds his glance, but he has other things on his mind.

'I saw Streeter, you know, the lawyer who supplied you with money while I was away. He has always handled the estate affairs. I have decided to sell Moreham House and have instructed him.'

'But this is *hasty*, Herbert.'

'No, not really. Talking to you has made my mind clear.'

She'd wanted to help him, not send him away!

'Where will you go?' She dreads to hear.

'I have asked Streeter to find a smaller house somewhere outside Hereford.'

'Oh Herbert, I shall miss you.'

He looks at her. Is suddenly aware.

Embarrassed, she adds: 'I mean I shall miss your company. Even Tom will be puzzled.'

'Yes. Ah yes.'

She has wondered whether to warn him of the local gossip, to protect him. It would be better he hear it through her than through indirect hostility or direct impertinence.

Yet if she does, it might propel him away more quickly, and the idea of a deeper friendship, if it has not occurred to him, might straightaway die. She has begun to yearn.

'It may take months to sell the house, Catherine. Remember, the country has been at war for seven years. Streeter tells me it may not be easy.

'In any case I am not yet ready to leave. There is one final thing I must do. The other day I remembered the afternoon the experiment began. I was ebullient. Just before he was locked in, I said to Warlow with a terrible cheerfulness: "Good luck Warlow! We meet again in 1800." Oh, I can hear my voice! And it is 1800 now.'

'I'm sure it's better that you do not meet him, Herbert. Why do so just because you said that, then? John Warlow is comfortable, reasonably well looked after. Leave him, Herbert.'

'Yes, you're right, quite right about that. However, I want to know what he went through down there.'

'Oh why? What is the need? Was it not enough to endure two winters on Yarston Hill?'

'Not the same! On Yarston Hill there was daylight, I had the company of sheep and birds, and once in a while, Aaron and his dog. I was free to go home even though I did not do so. Warlow was locked in the dark and had nobody.'

'But why do it yourself?'

'I need to know.'

266

'For how long will you stay there? Surely not for *years*? Shall I send you down delicious meals and wind up your chamber pot?' She tries to joke him out of it.

'Of course not for years, and you need do nothing, Catherine.'

'How long, then?'

'Give me a fortnight or so.'

'Will you promise me that once it's over, you will put everything behind you? Will think less and less about the past?'

'You always speak good sense.'

'Then promise me.'

'I promise.'

*

Powyss's memory of the apartments is of how they were when he arranged them in 1793, when he enjoyed a week there himself, charmed by the organ and amused by the dumb waiter lift, pleased by the large number of books and papers he'd read without distraction. He knows nothing was done to the apartments after Warlow was lured out. Their condition will be bad.

At first he can't understand why so much broken wood lies at the bottom of the steps outside the door, imagines the invaders of the house destroyed the furniture when they found there were no racks of bottles.

But of course: the barricade. Warlow had shut himself in. And Price, in order to get in and coax the man out, had dismantled it.

In the main room, table and chairs have gone, mirror and paintings are shattered pools of glass. Two pieces of furniture remain. The wing chair by the fireplace extrudes stuffing, its frame, arms, bones. The chamber organ stands tall against the wall, one door off, the other askew, empty of pipes, its keyboard hanging down, for all like a dying man he'd once seen in a London street, brutally stabbed, his guts exposed. The terrible look of dismay on his face.

The door to the lift has gone but the pulley seems intact: he could wind down some wood and kindling. He takes his lamp to the bedroom where nothing is broken, but the bedding smells as foul as anything he's encountered. Sheep muck is sweet by comparison. Warlow must have lived in the bed for days at a time, succeeded since then by vermin, and now all is overlaid with the stench of mould, of rot.

Upstairs he loads fuel, his own bedding into the shelves of the lift and for a second load, bread, milk and cold bacon to last some days. Catherine has made him a small plum cake. There are candles in his pockets and he takes down a blank journal and pencils.

He makes up a fire. Tongs and poker are still there, unbroken, unbreakable. One large candlestick, one small one. He props up a two-legged table on a pile of rubble, places his blankets on the chair by the fire upon which he can both sit and sleep.

What on earth went through Warlow's mind when he lived amid destruction? Hatred: he must have hated me as I hated him. Regret, self-accusation, that he'd been foolish enough to take this on? Surely at first he may even have enjoyed the place? He was warm – warmer than *he* is now – had good food, clean bedding, clothes, books, organ. Oh, what point is there in listing it? The man was stuck, confined in this low space with no light: day and night merged into perpetual darkness.

The clock is a heap of splinters. He's left his watch upstairs. There is no possibility of measuring the time.

He lays out his writing materials on the small, madly leaning table. When he first called on Catherine she'd given him letters that had arrived during his absence. He destroyed them all except one, from Fox, which he now finds among his things, unread.

Dated months earlier, Fox, hearing something of Powyss's troubles, had written that he understood why he'd not received a reply to his request to join Powyss in Moreham. After his own disaster, the trial, loss of house, money and friends, he was just at the point of despair, Powyss reads, when an old engraver offered him a room in his house in Walthamstow, where, well away from anyone he knew, Fox was earning his keep helping with the printing of trade cards and advertisements, theatre and lottery tickets.

I frequently turn the star wheel of the printing press and amuse myself thinking of it as Fortune's Wheel.

Might they resume their correspondence, he asks. Promises Powyss that he's not sold the new *Flora Londinensis* and hopes to give it to him before long.

Powyss puts the letter to one side. He'll deal with it later.

He picks up his journal, should begin writing but is struck by the pointlessness of doing so. This is not an experiment. No one will read what he writes.

He casts around for a book. Didn't he once hear Warlow laughing at Voltaire? Oh, surely not! He must have been mistaken. And there aren't any books now. Among heaps of broken glass and splintered wood on hacked boards are rips of pages from that terrible frenzy, shreds of paper as though for the nests of huge mice.

But no, here's something squeezed beneath the burst springs of the wing chair. One of Warlow's journals, 1795, its binding scored by the springs and something else, Warlow's talon-like nails.

The pages are mostly blank or almost so:

I   *did eat*

and

The man was not keeping up his diary, so important for the investigation. So, the experiment had already failed two years after it had begun.

In the centre pages he finds wavering letters copied from *Robinson Crusoe*:

THE

LIFE

AND STRANG   SUR PRIZIN ADVENT   URES

OF

JOHN

WARLOW   OF   MOR HAM PLOWMAN

Beneath this a stick man crossed out, but on the opposite page a face. A circle with eyes and nose and hair scrawled down both sides and over the whole of the lower half.

The eyes look out at Powyss from the page. A disproportionate body holds a candle with a tiny flame.

Except for the face, the body, the candle, every bit of the page is scribbled over with black pencil. It must have taken time to create all that darkness. So much darkness.

*

Eats a good breakfast. Sets out to the timber cutting along the avenue, to lop branches. Axed timber for Pulverbatch, didn't he? After Christmas when them'd always drunk up them's wages.

Them shan't see him go off. Him's furthest away, down the road. Them's gatherin or stackin, doin it all wrong, don't know how. Thinks them'll cut knots and knurls! Mad, them in this place.

Strikes his short axe into a stump. 'I do trust you with it,

John Warlow,' Grew did say. That place where he did live afore, no axe there. No knife. Were that so? No *knife*? Yes. No knife, no scissors. That's it! He pats his pockets: bread, cheese, scissors. Changes his mind: tucks the axe into his belt beneath his coat.

Wind is cold. Move on. Two coats, waistcoat, shirt, undershirt. Big gloves, hat, boots. Likes these clothes them gives him in this place.

Now he's goin to the other place. Where he was afore. Lived. *His place* it were. Going because of *him*. Him listenin. That's it! Listenin and he never said.

And fifty pound. *Him never did give it me!*

Frost clings in cold hollows. Ground is hard. He wants to stop and eat, but the sky's no longer clear, there's no sun, no warmth. He bites as he walks, swallows down lumps, soon has hiccups which don't stop.

Two carts pass. Noise of wheels on frozen mud, carters shouting to each other hides the belching from within a clump of holly bushes.

He's a pain in his chest. Stone in his boot. He cheers himself, reminds himself. Him listenin, listenin, him, him, fifty pound, fifty pound. What did the other man say? What were it? 'John,' he did say, 'Powyss ...' Ah! That were it! *Powyss.* Powyss were listenin! *It were Powyss behind them panels. Damned Powyss. Spyin.*

He looks round; that him behind, spyin? Or in the wood? 'John,' he did say. 'Powyss, he do ...? Powyss, he do fuck ...' He hastens.

Still light when he gets to Moreham. Keep away from others. Them got him afore, didn't they   John Warlow, what *you* doin here? Go back, you lunatic! Dodges, ducks, waits behind buildings, crouches. Oh, he's tired! But them's going home now, shutting doors.

No gate in the wall. Wall of the big house.

He's in the garden, walks through dry stalks of dead dock,

between great umbels of frosted hogweed. Which way? Dusk has come. Folds up the spectacles. House looms at him. No lights. Its doors, windows, eyes all closed. Where to go? He shudders. Can't turn, too late.

Powyss do . . . Big prick or small . . .

Creeps up to the house. Doors shut, windows nailed with boards. Nobody there. Get in somehow. He's tired, tired. Get in. Sleep.

Stumbles round it, feeling for a way in.

Door to the kitchen opens at his push.

*

The fire goes out and Powyss has no idea how long he was asleep, no notion if it's night or late afternoon, though he suspects it's not morning. His bladder's not full, he's not hungry, the journal remains blank; the imperative is heat. He lights a new fire in the warm grate, packing it with more wood to last longer. A few birch logs burn with a fury, hot, brief.

That must have been Warlow's imperative, too, before and after he destroyed the place. And then, with a fire blazing, what? What next? For Warlow the next meal, that's what punctuated time for him. That was something. But what about in between?

He recalls that Warlow rarely changed his clothes or washed, a cause of much disgust on the part of Cook and Jenkins. But he himself has lived for two years unwashed, in the same clothes. When warmth and food occupy the whole attention, who cares for clean linen and soap?

Books, organ he dismisses. Folly! And he asked him to *write!*

Before the experiment, the man's life had been an unchanging round. Why should he read? What could he possibly write? Perhaps he missed his children. Surely he missed Hannah, but possibly he didn't. He lacked the company of fellow workers with whom he drank, though he'd said it wouldn't matter to him.

Once, the unchanging round had kept him alive. Provided an ordered year, an occupied day, the regular spectacle of life and death of animals, crops and trees. Irregular weather of course, but the absolute certainty of light following dark. Day never failed him.

He thinks of his own time living in the shack. Two years of exhaustion, cold, pain, hunger, squalor. But day always succeeded night. There was always light, even in the worst weather. He had space, when he wanted it, occupation, relentless occupation. The beauty of hills and sky.

He had deprived Warlow of all of this. Underground, Warlow's world became a shrunken mental pulse. And then to have to *leave* the place in which, in the end, he had encased himself, a protective shell of destruction: of course he felt terror! My God, the poor man. *The poor man!*

*

Moonlight splashes through the kitchen window. Sky's clear again, that's more frost comin. There's the stairs. Recognises them. Soon he'll sleep!

Down and down. Becomes dark, has to feel his way. Sleep there. Sleep. All I wants now, in my place where I did live. *Where I lives.* My bed. In it. Under it, safe from devils.

Reaches bottom of the stairs. Oh! Smells wood smoke. Light flickers through the doorway. Someone's lit me a fire! That Samuel lit it afore. Hammered nails in the door. Flickers onto the heaps of wood, planks, doors, chair legs, drawers. Remember? What the woman Catherine said. What she say? Barrier were it? Some word like that. I'll build it up again. Be safe. I were safe there. Were I? *Catherine'll bring me my food.* First I'll sleep. Then Catherine'll . . .

Somebody in there. In my place. Where I lives. *Somebody's got in. Where I lives!* He sidles to the opening.

Man sittin by the fire. Not movin. Be it that man who said John, Powyss do ...?

He pats his pocket. Still there. Remember? No scissors, no knives. She-devil did want me to stab myself. *Cut your hair and nails.* Stab yourself means go to hell straight down.

The fire draws him.

No, not *that* man. Can't see the face, head's behind chair back. Shuffles closer. Asleep. Don't wake 'im.

Sees small feet. Hears rasping breath. *Him! Him!*

Waitin for me. Listenin to me now.

Takes out scissors. *John, Powyss, he do ...*

'Powyss!' he screams out, 'you do ...', hurls himself at the prone man, who jerks round at the sound and Warlow drives the scissors hard into his side.

'Aah! Aah! Warlow! Warlow, I was thinking about you. Ohh!' Pain magnifies in his side as Warlow pulls out the thick blades and stands, struck.

Is it Powyss? He stares at the man who's hurriedly raised himself up and is pressing his hand over the bleeding wound. Beard, patched clothes, strange face. *Is* it?

'Warlow, you've ...' Powyss vomits. Registers the whole reversal: Warlow, well fed, dressed in neatly cut clothes.

'Warlow! What the ... You've ...'

His voice. It is him. Powyss do fuck ... Warlow plunges forward with the scissors again to drive them into the devil, but Powyss gets behind the chair that oozes its stuffing like old man's beard. How appropriate! His mind runs on. Two old men.

Warlow cannot get near enough, fire's on one side, dark the other. He throws the scissors at the head behind the chair. The head ducks. He bellows with fury. Pulls out the axe. Takes the dark side.

Powyss feels blood pour through his fingers, stanches the wound hastily with his coat. Sees Warlow's weak eyes, the man panting in exhausted, blind rage, moves away from the chair and with a sudden, new strength lunges at Warlow's arm, grabs his wrist, forces him to drop the axe, then throws himself on the man.

Finally to kill him! Finally to kill the foul creature he created! The energy he so often used to feel explodes in him. Oh Hannah! How always to fuck her was to destroy Warlow.

'Yes. I *did*. I *did*!' His hands are at Warlow's throat, thumbs press the windpipe. 'I'll kill you, Warlow, you murderer. *You killed her!*' He cries out in pain at that memory, in lust to kill, in passionate desire for Hannah: exhilaration surges through his body.

Warlow, choking, pulls away out of his grasp, stumbles backwards. Tired. So so tired. In the firelight Powyss sees the large candlestick, reaches out for it, its heavy, weighted base uppermost, sharp-edged, fatal, and with both hands raises it high over the shaven head, the blinking eyes.

Brings it down, straight onto the flagstones, merely brushing Warlow's shoulder on its way.

And he rushes up the stairs, dying flames lighting his path. Into clear moonlight and frost.

Out of the depths, out, out. He coughs painfully, holds his side. Words come back that he, godless, has neither thought nor read since childhood.

Out of the depths have I cried.

He staggers through the gardens, retching, out into the field. I'll go up the hill. Cold Hill. Look on my life.

He's losing blood. It's soaked down his breeches and stockings into his shoe, his hands thick, sticky with it. The energy's gone. He's faint. Thinks he hears horses' hoofs on the road, carriage wheels, shouts. Grew, surely. He starts up the gradient but it's rough. His feet catch in brambles, he falls, rises up and stumbles on again.

Now the death will come that once he'd longed for but no longer wants.

275

Warlow will live.

His attention is caught by coruscations of lightning in the east. A meteor like a brilliantly blazing ball passes from north-west to south-east very high in the sky. Will Catherine see it? He feels a savage spasm of regret. Will she point it out to the children? Of course she will.

He sees its lone journey, disordering the pattern of the night, makes out a shower of red sparks that fall as it becomes extinct.

Author's Note

I have volumes of the *Annual Register* from 1789 to 1814 and found this in the 'Chronicle' of the volume for 1797:

> Some time ago, a Mr Powyfs, of Moreham, near Prefton, offered by public advertifement, a reward of fifty pounds for life, to any man who would undertake to live for feven years under ground, without feeing a human face; and to let his toe and finger nails grow during the whole of his confinement, together with his beard. Commodious apartments were provided under ground, with a cold bath, a chamber-organ, as many books as the occupier fhould defire, and provifions were to be ferved from Mr P's table; on ringing a bell the reclufe was alfo to be provided with every convenience defired. It appears that an occupier offered himfelf for this fingular refidence, who is now in the fourth year of his probation, a labouring man, who has a large family, all of whom are maintained by Mr P.

I was fascinated by this account, though unable to find out anything more, especially how it ended. I wrote a short story in an attempt to understand Mr P., another from the point of view of the man underground, then realised that both deserved fuller consideration. The novel is entirely my reimagining of the episode.